ONLY WATCHING YOU

Utterly thrilling psychological suspense fiction

MARK WEST

THE
BOOK
FOLKS

Published by The Book Folks

London, 2022

© Mark West

ISBN 978-1-80462-000-7

www.thebookfolks.com

For Alison and Matthew

Prologue

It was twilight when they came for her.

She moved cautiously through the growing darkness, keeping to the shadows and treading quietly. The boats around her, beached and canted to one side, creaked and groaned. An old bell attached to one of them pealed mournfully as the breeze caught it.

She heard them coming, hunting her down. The realisation they'd come as a group was scary but also somehow exhilarating. Adrenaline ran through her veins and tingled in her fingertips. They talked quietly, as if unaware their voices carried on the air, although she couldn't make out the words. Their closeness brought fresh panic and she suddenly felt nauseous.

There was no time for that, she had to keep moving. Holding out her left hand, she found the hull of the nearest boat and worked her way towards the stern. Beyond it was another vessel, then another. A narrow channel between the boats led her to a pallet walkway running alongside the chain-link fence down to the water. An owl screeched from somewhere, its hoot startling her.

Ahead she saw light reflecting off windscreens through the trees. Her pursuers were quiet now and she couldn't tell if they had split up or not. She felt, rather than saw, movement to her side and whirled around. The float hung on the side of the boat and it made her shiver, bad memories threatening to overwhelm her. She shook her head to dislodge them.

She stepped onto the walkway and moved towards the gentle lapping of the water at the quayside. Three boats along, something rattled and, pausing, she looked into the darkness.

"I see you." She recognised the voice immediately and felt the same nervous charge as before. It was him, the hateful bastard.

"You," she said, her voice steadier than she'd expected it to be. She lifted the can in her hand.

"This has to end." The man sneered and came towards her, stepping through the shadows.

Chapter 1

Claire Heeley saw the mystery man on three separate days before he tried to run her over.

On the fourth day, she heard his car a moment or two before she saw it and by then it was too late, the collision inevitable.

Bracing herself, she waited for the impact.

* * *

She always warmed up on the patio before her morning run, then jogged to the end of the street before turning down the hill. Her muscles had relaxed by then and all she had to worry about was regulating her breathing, the playlist on her iPod helping her keep pace.

She ran past the Co-op where the staff were busy sorting the milk and bread. Sometimes, if they spotted her, they'd wave and she always waved back. Beyond the Co-op, she ran towards the main road.

Hadlington at 6 a.m. was a sight to behold, especially on fine summer mornings with a slight chill in the air and the low sun casting long shadows. There weren't many pedestrians and only a handful of hardy commuters were making for the first London train. She could focus on the run, trying to run to the beat of the music without having to walk and catch her breath. She'd run before Scott, her son, was born and returned to it after her husband Greg left. Desperate for a stress-busting exercise, running helped her embrace the concept of being in control again. Greg was also a reason for the timing – her route took her towards the hospital and his shift started at 7 a.m. so the chances of seeing him were remote.

She saw a familiar face outside the butcher's. The old man always wore a heavy coat whatever the weather and dark-blue jeans with the hems rolled up several inches. One day, he'd introduced himself as Stan while they queued in the Co-op and she now called him Old Man Stan, though never to his face. He was often out early, trudging up the main road with a shopping bag and would wave and call "good morning".

Today, he stared into the window seemingly lost to the world. She waved but he didn't turn around.

Her route, a three-mile run around town, was part of her morning routine. Out of the house by six, home by six thirty and straight into the shower, breakfast at seven and off to work by eight.

The market square dominated this older part of Hadlington. The big parish church occupied most of the west side while eighteenth-century buildings flanked the other two. A lot of the cars at that time of the morning belonged to people who carpooled to the train station and they tended to park in the centre of the square.

That Monday, as Claire ran past the library and across the road, she noticed a black Astra. It was parked nose in at the very edge of the square, well away from any others. The man behind the wheel, wearing mirrored sunglasses, was looking at his phone. He looked up as Claire went by, though she couldn't tell if he was looking at her or beyond. Then she was past and went on with her run. By the time she'd looped back to the market square, having pushed herself hard up the final hill, the Astra had gone and she was aware of its absence only vaguely.

The next day, the car was parked on the other side of the square, backed into a space against the church wall. She stared at the number plate, trying to commit the HKP suffix to memory. It took her a moment to notice the driver, almost hidden behind a copy of the *Daily Mirror*. Again, he was gone by the time she got back to the square.

He'd moved back across the square the day after and this time he blatantly watched her cross the road. She felt self-conscious and uncomfortable, watching her feet for a while before looking back as he dropped his phone into his lap. They regarded each other until she was past and, again, he'd gone by the time she got back.

She found herself thinking about him during the day and the creepy idea he was checking her out made her feel uneasy. She didn't recognise him – hardly a surprise, bearing in mind the ever-present sunglasses and the gloomy interior of the car – and why hadn't he acknowledged her if they knew one another? There had to be a perfectly reasonable explanation for his being there, but she couldn't think what that might be.

Annoyed she was worrying about him, Claire started her run fifteen minutes later on Thursday. The mystery man wasn't on the square and the sense of relief she felt betrayed how much he'd been playing on her mind. She ran her secondary route, across town through the new estate and back, the exercise buoying her mood. She took the corner into Church Walk on the road and heard the car before she saw it but by then it was too late.

Pulse racing, Claire pushed herself up and forwards onto the bonnet to avoid the bumper. Her forearms slapped on the cool metal as she kicked her legs back to get them away from the car. Claire felt herself slide back. She grabbed for the windscreen wipers blindly, desperate to hold on.

The car shuddered to a halt, the engine stuttering and dying.

"Shit," she said, heart hammering. Her fingers and toes filled with painful pins and needles. She took a deep breath and slowly looked up into the windscreen.

The driver sat open-mouthed; his eyes still hidden behind mirrored lenses, but she recognised him as the man who'd been watching her for the past few days. This close, she could see acne scarring on his jowly cheeks.

"Fuck," he mouthed.

Claire pushed herself off the bonnet and her legs felt like jelly as she stepped towards the kerb. She was relieved to see Old Man Stan rushing towards them and waving his arm as his shopping bag fluttering in the breeze.

The engine turned over and caught, grabbing her attention.

"You," she said, pointing at the driver.

He checked the mirror, slammed the car into gear and pulled away. Claire slapped the bonnet as hard as she could.

"Who are you?" she called.

He looked at her but didn't say anything. The heat of anger rushed through her and, just below it, a sense of terror.

The man drove the few yards to the top of the road and Old Man Stan shook his fist at him. The car turned down the hill towards the railway bridge and was out of sight in seconds. Only then did Claire allow herself to drop. She sat on the kerb with her knees to her chin, her head dipped between them to stave off the nausea. She breathed deeply and ran her hands up her shins but didn't register any pain.

"Hey, Claire, are you okay?" Old Man Stan knelt beside her, his knees popping and making him grimace.

"Did you see that?"

"I did. He was going way too fast."

"I know."

"But you were running in the road."

"I didn't hear him."

"Nobody ever does, love." Old Man Stan patted her knee. "He was stupid, but it was probably six of one, half a dozen of the other."

She looked at Old Man Stan with a scowl then leaned her head back and closed her eyes.

"It was close though," he said, as if vaguely aware he'd offended her. "He was going too fast."

Her thumping heart was a reminder of just how close it had been.

Chapter 2

I slipped up.

I've been watching you for weeks, keeping my distance, biding my time, trying to suppress the rage that rushes through me whenever we pass by too closely, but it's always been on my terms until today.

I can't believe I was so stupid, but I keep telling myself you didn't recognise me or, at least, you certainly didn't seem to.

After all this time, it would kill me to have everything fall apart before I got the chance to make you feel the pain I've had to live with this past year.

Because I want to see you suffer, I want to see you agonise, I want to hear you crying yourself to sleep, your throat raw and your eyes dry because there are simply no tears left.

I have such plans for you.

Chapter 3

Claire watched the display of her clock. The alarm went off when the digits flicked to 5:45 and she reached over to switch it off then rolled onto her back.

Normally she'd be dragging herself out of bed to go for a run but not this morning. She'd spent most of yesterday replaying the scene in her mind – turning the corner, the car coming towards her too fast – and could still feel the impact and the cold hardness of the bonnet. His staring face was a vivid memory.

If it hadn't been for Old Man Stan, she'd have been convinced the man meant to run her over, even if that didn't make any sense. She didn't recognise him and hadn't done anything to antagonise him, other than run by three times in as many days.

Her mind turned it over and the thoughts churned her stomach and made her queasy. If Stan was right – she was in the road, after all – it didn't explain why the man had been watching her. She couldn't figure it out and didn't want to burden Scott with it either. So the thoughts ran unbidden and gathered credence with every moment she didn't counter them with logical argument. She was scared of what might happen next and the very fact she was frightened annoyed her. Not enough to put herself at risk, certainly, but her annoyance was a hot and festering ball in the pit of her stomach.

The simplest way to deal with it for the moment was to change her routine. She'd run tonight instead, even though the extra traffic and pedestrians would annoy her.

Claire sat up and ran a hand through her hair. The clock now read 5:50 and as much as she didn't like the idea of her routine being dictated by someone else, she knew this was safer. She picked up her book and tried to lose herself in the words.

* * *

The message from Amy Brown had come out of the blue a week ago. Although Claire had known her since they started working at the same bank the best part of twenty-five years ago, they'd only kept in touch sporadically.

> *Hi Claire*
> *Long time no speak, eh, where does the time go? I thought I'd drop you a note because I heard through the grapevine that things weren't good between you and Greg, which I'm really sorry about — you two were so good together. I'm writing because Gayle and I split up last year and it hit me really hard so if you wanted a sympathetic ear, I'm here for you.*

Touched, Claire had messaged back, and they agreed to meet. Amy still worked at the bank and suggested a little cafe she liked.

Frank's was tucked away in a little side road off the high street and had three large windows with his name stretched across them.

Claire pushed open the door. Half a dozen tables stood between her and the counter, behind which a large man in a baggy yellow T-shirt was writing on a pad. Under a rack of hanging pots and pans, a woman had her back to the seating area as she worked at the hob. A thin haze hung over the counter as if something had overheated. The air smelled of bacon and onions, and made Claire's stomach rumble, her bowl of cornflakes a distant memory.

The man looked up as Claire pushed the door shut behind her. "Don't worry, love," he said. "It never shuts

8

right. Take a seat wherever you fancy." His salt-and-pepper hair was greased into a quiff.

Amy was sitting by the far window and waved Claire over.

"It's so good to see you," she said and stood up so they could hug.

"And you."

Amy had always been the outgoing one who started conversations in the pub, and always had good ideas for something to do. Today she was dressed in a well-cut trouser suit that fitted where it should and her tightly curled hair was a richer shade of brown than Claire remembered it being. When Amy smiled, her cheeks dimpled.

"Let me get you a drink," Amy said. "This place might not look great, but the coffee is superb and the toast is wonderful."

"I'll just have a black coffee, thanks."

"Okay," Amy said and gestured at the empty seat across from her. "Sit down, I'll be back in a minute."

Claire sat and watched her friend go to the counter where she called the man Frank and chatted as he poured the coffee. After Amy handed her a filled-to-the-brim cup, she sat down. They talked for a while about mutual friends and how long it had been since they'd properly had a chat, but Claire could see she was holding something back. Eventually, it clearly became too much.

"So," Amy said and raised her cup to her lips, holding it with both hands. "How are you?"

Claire shrugged as she stirred her coffee. "I'm, you know…"

Amy sipped then put her cup down. "Just tell me to shut up."

"No, it's fine."

"I'm nosey, you know that, and I'll keep asking questions until you either storm out or pop me one." She smiled. "Remember?"

"I remember."

"So how serious is it?"

"Very. We'll be divorced by the end of the year."

Amy nodded, pursing her lips. "How's Scott taking it?"

"As well as you'd expect. He's fifteen, with everything that entails, and seems to change all the time. One day he'd do or say something and whisk me back in time to when he needed me and that's lovely. Other days he might say three things to me and two of those will be coded grunts."

Amy smiled. "And how are you dealing with it?"

Claire sipped her coffee. "Getting there, though I was blindsided at the time."

"It's often the way. I was gutted when Gayle and I split up because I just didn't see it coming. We'd been on holiday and I thought things were good but apparently they weren't."

"Was anyone else involved?"

"I think so – at least she moved in with her new girlfriend very soon afterwards. It seems the importance of our ten years together weighed more heavily on me than it did her."

"I'm sorry to hear that."

"Yeah, that stung." Amy's eyes glistened and she bit her lip.

"Greg had an affair," Claire said, her voice low. "I only knew it because he broke down and told me, I wouldn't have guessed otherwise. He'd started drinking again which he hadn't done heavily since we first met and when I confronted him about it, everything seemed to spill out."

"Maybe he wanted to be honest."

"Or maybe he just wanted to unburden himself."

Amy let out a surprised laugh.

"I know," said Claire. "Harsh, eh?"

"Not necessarily harsh, just more than I was expecting."

"Greg called it harsh when I said it to him," Claire said, and Amy laughed. "Do you see much of Gayle now?"

"No," Amy said with a rueful smile. "No kids, so no need for contact. Life moves on, which is the delight of it, I suppose."

Claire nodded. "The hardest thing I found is how lonely I feel. I mean, I still have friends and Scott's in the house apart from the weekends but there's this emptiness."

"I lost some mutual friends and that hurt."

"I did too and wasn't expecting it. That really hit me."

Amy steepled her fingers and rested her chin on them. She looked like she wanted to say something and Claire raised her eyebrows.

"Sorry," Amy said. "I was just thinking how losing those friends really affected me. I didn't want to get back into the dating game or pick someone up – well let's not be coy, I wanted a shag, but it wasn't that…"

"It's the company."

"Precisely. So I joined a group."

"A dating group?"

Amy sighed, her "no" lasting a theatrically long time.

"A lesbian no-strings-attached shagging club?"

Another theatrical "no" and then Amy held up her right index finger. "Actually, that's an idea."

They both laughed.

"No, it's a friendship group for people who find themselves at a crossroads in terms of location and lifestyle." Amy laughed at Claire's frown. "That sounds like I'm just regurgitating the pamphlet, doesn't it? It's for people like me who are suddenly adrift at an age when nipping out with mates to the nightclub isn't really an option. Or people who move to a new area with work. That kind of thing."

Claire smiled. "And it helped?"

"I loved it so much that I became the group secretary at Christmas." She rooted in her handbag for a flyer she handed to Claire.

"The Hadlington Friends," Claire read, "a friendly group of sociable adults looking to meet new people, make new friends and take part in social events around the local area."

"The idea is to not put anyone off," said Amy. "Someone who's terribly shy isn't going to want to come along to a group if they think it's full of cliques, are they?"

"You don't have cliques in your group?"

Amy pulled a face. "Some, but it's generally friendly. We meet twice a week and you go when you want to, with no pressure."

"Sounds interesting."

Amy leaned forward. "I know I sound like some kind of zealot, but it really made a difference for me. Why not come along and see how you feel?"

"When do you meet?"

"Nights out on Saturdays – this week we're going for a meal and then on to the cinema – then a club night on Wednesdays at The Rising Sun."

"I can't make this Saturday."

"So come next week then. You can sit with me. I host the new members' table and we've had some newbies come along over the past few weeks." She paused. "What have you got to lose, Claire? We don't bite."

"I know, it's just…"

Amy finished her sentence for her. "You're in your early forties and starting all over again wasn't something you'd banked on doing, right?"

"Yes. I feel like I did something wrong and got pushed back to being a shy and unconfident teenager."

Amy put her hand over Claire's. "I've been there, okay? It wears off. It perhaps doesn't feel like that now, but it will."

"I'll give it a try." Claire glanced at the clock above the counter and stood up. "I've got to make a move." She looked around. "Is there a loo?"

"Over at the back by the specials board."

In the toilet, Claire decided the idea of company sounded good. She wasn't interested in finding Mr Right, but new friends would help set up a new life for herself.

"Thank you for this, Amy," she said when she got back to the table.

"You're welcome." Amy pulled Claire into a hug. Her hair smelled of blossom. "It was good to see you."

"And you."

When Amy let go, Claire looked for the flyer. "Did you put it back in your bag?"

"No. A bloke saw it and seemed interested in the group so I gave it to him."

"Blimey, you're racking up the new members, aren't you?"

They left together and Amy gave Claire two air kisses.

"I'll see you next Wednesday," she said and walked away.

* * *

The phone rang late on Friday night and startled Claire.

She'd had dinner with Scott and decided to tell him about the incident by the church but made light of it and suggested she'd tripped and fallen on the car. He was concerned initially then began telling her something that had happened during a maths lesson and she contentedly let the conversation drift. She went for her run leaving him to load the dishwasher and grumble about the amount of work he had to do.

Running through the early-evening streets with the sky a haze of blue and orange made her feel better. The roads were busy and the pavements outside pubs and restaurants were cluttered. She had to run in the road around some of the larger groups where people shouted and laughed at each other, too wrapped up in their own lives to notice her.

She did her regular route and enjoyed the burn in her chest and thighs. Scott was in his room when she got

13

home – "thrashing Jez on FIFA," he told her when she poked her head around his door – so she peeled off her running gear and treated herself to a long, luxurious bath. She curled up on the sofa afterwards, nursing a half-bottle of wine and catching up on some programmes she'd recorded.

Now she pressed the pause button and Graham Norton froze as he pulled a face. Nobody rang a landline at 10:45 unless there was a problem. She jumped off the sofa but the phone stopped ringing.

She heard movement from above and then Scott's heavy footsteps on the landing.

"Mum? Phone!" He'd got to the upstairs extension before her.

"Is it Gran or Grampy?"

"No, it's Dad!"

"Okay," she said warily and picked up the phone. What the bloody hell could he want at this hour? "Yes?"

"Hey, love."

Claire listened until the line clicked as Scott put down his receiver. "Greg, do you realise what time it is?"

"It's Friday." His voice had a softness she recognised, which suggested a few shots of JD and maybe some wine.

"What time it is," she repeated. "Unless you're ringing to tell me some family member is in hospital, I'm not going to be happy."

"Hey, love, chill out. I didn't mean to ring this late."

Claire focused on Graham Norton as she took a couple of deep breaths. "There's no need for you to ring, if you remember, unless you want to speak to Scott."

Greg paused as if trying to process what she said. "I wanted to speak to you. Scott texted me earlier about your accident."

She was annoyed he knew and was showing concern because he had no right to. "It was an incident, not an accident."

"He said you'd been run over."

For Christ's sake, Scott, she thought. "I got clipped by a car but I'm okay."

"Right." He sounded almost disappointed. "I was going to suggest..."

"Greg, I'm okay. There's no need for you to ring me or offer to help or anything else."

"But..." He paused and she listened to him breathing. "I..."

Her patience gave out. "If that's it, I'm going to hang up now."

"Please don't."

"Why? Are you at work?"

"No, I'm at home but I thought it'd be nice to chat..."

"Goodnight, Greg," she said and put the phone down.

Chapter 4

They had moved into the house just before getting engaged.

Greg was still training to be a nurse and working for an agency with any spare time he had while Claire attended night school to get her professional banking qualifications. On the advice of her dad to buy as much as they could afford, they'd gone for a three-bed semi-detached, even though it wasn't in the best shape. For a couple of years they were very poor but Claire loved the independence. She enjoyed the making of a home and those long weekends spent with paint flecks on her face and in her hair. The street was pleasant and relatively quiet, an ideal place to love and grow and they did both happily for a long time.

And then Greg and Matilda happened.

He left, after too many arguments and angry sleepless nights. Claire redecorated – finding the sensation of paint in her hair an unpleasant nostalgic lie – and decluttered, taking a while to reclaim the house as her own place of sanctuary and peace.

* * *

By the following Wednesday, the car incident felt more like a nonsensical bad dream and Claire was annoyed she'd let herself be frightened enough that she was still running in the evenings. She hadn't seen him or the Astra since.

She parked outside the house and grabbed her handbag and briefcase and got out.

There was a flurry of noise and she felt something at her ankles, accompanied by high-pitched barks. A white Labrador puppy looked up at her then ran to the back of the car and skidded on the pavement. Regaining its feet, the dog barked and ran back towards her.

"Hello, dog, where did you come from?"

"Sorry about that, Claire."

She turned to see her neighbour Roger coming out of his front door. "Annie opened the door without checking where Lightning was."

Claire smiled. "You called your dog Lightning?"

"No," said Annie, coming out of the house behind her dad and kneeling beside Claire to fuss the dog. "He's called Harry, after the singer. Dad calls him Lightning because he thinks he's funny."

Claire raised her eyebrows at Roger. "You actually think you're being funny?"

Roger shrugged. "According to teenaged daughters, dads can't be funny."

"Strangely enough, the same applies to the mothers of teenaged sons."

Annie held out her hands and the dog jumped up at her. Holding it tightly, she stood up. "Is Scott about, Claire? I was going to show him Harry."

"He texted me an hour or so ago to say he was meeting his friends at the skatepark so I doubt he'll have come home early."

"Right."

Annie looked down, her smile fragile, and Claire recognised the look because she'd seen Scott wear it recently too. He'd known Annie since Roger and Lou moved in two years ago and they'd got on well since their first meeting but the atmosphere between them had changed recently. Annie was almost nine months older, though still in Scott's year and she'd blossomed in that time from a cute young girl into a pretty teenager. Scott seemed to have grown too quickly as well, with gangly limbs sometimes beyond his apparent control.

"How about I get him to call round when he's back?" asked Claire, in an effort to cheer her up.

"That'd be nice," said Roger. "Maybe he could take Lightning out for a walk."

"He's not called Lightning," Annie said quietly through gritted teeth.

"She assured us she was really looking forward to dog walking, but it seems to pale against sitting in the garden and playing on her phone and throwing the ball for the dog to chase."

"Dad." The word gained more letters and syllables than it could surely sustain. "You're embarrassing me."

"I do apologise, princess," Roger said with mock solemnity.

"Good grief," Annie said and turned to Claire. "If you could say to Scott about Harry, I'd really appreciate it."

"Of course I will."

Annie went through the front door.

Roger smiled sheepishly at Claire and rubbed the back of his head briskly. "Sorry about that, I can't seem to do right at the moment."

"It happens."

"Yeah." He looked over her shoulder. "Ah, looks like you've been targeted."

"Eh?"

He pointed towards the house and she turned, not seeing for a moment what he meant.

"Must be a new kids' game or something," he said.

A hangman – gallows, noose, stickman – had been chalked over the house number by the front door.

"That's weird."

"No more than anything else kids do," he said. "Anyway, how are you? It's been ages since I last saw you."

"Lou said you've been in Barcelona a lot recently."

"They set up an office there and I have to go over every now and again. You've travelled with work, it's never as glamorous as it appears."

"True but it's Barcelona."

"Oh, lovely country, but I see more of the airport, taxis and office interiors than the city itself."

"But the food's good."

"It is." He looked at her, as if weighing up whether to say something. "I know Lou's here more than me but, you know, with everything going on if there's anything you need..."

I just need you to stop talking about it, she thought. The business with Greg was the last thing she wanted to discuss, especially since she was nervous about her first friends group meeting this evening. "I know, Roger, thank you."

He touched her forearm gently. "Just give me a shout."

"I will."

"Anyway, I've held you up enough but I'm glad you got to meet Lightning. If he ever gets on your nerves barking, knock on the wall and I'll muzzle him."

* * *

The house was quiet.

18

Dumping her bags and heels by the front door, she called "Scott?" up the stairs in case he was cocooned in his bedroom wearing headphones. There was no response. She went through to the kitchen, switched on the kettle and washed her hands while it boiled. She took her cup of coffee upstairs to the spare room – which had long since been pressed into service as a study – and sat at her desk under the window overlooking the back garden.

She opened her laptop and connected with her workplace server. A client's spreadsheet had been glitching and she'd figured out why on the commute, but it took longer than she'd expected to fix. It was almost half an hour later when she finished.

Claire saved the file and went downstairs to the kitchen. Scott would eat with his friends, so she microwaved a jacket potato and added some tuna, eating in peace on the sofa.

By now it was almost six thirty and even with the food her stomach still felt fluttery. She'd suffered more nerves since the split than ever before and the thought of going into a pub and meeting a group of new people – even with Amy there – was a scary concept.

She shook her head. Now wasn't the time to suffer with doubt. After a shower she'd get dressed smartly then go out and wow them.

* * *

Wrapped in her dressing gown with a towel wound around her hair, Claire checked the laptop. The screen showed a warning box: 'Contact broken with remote server'.

"Dammit."

She tried saving again but got the same warning. They'd been having server issues at work for a few days and the IT bods didn't seem to have any idea what the problem was or how to fix it.

Claire got her flash drive – shaped like a Pokémon and bought for her by Scott a few years ago – out of her handbag. She plugged it in and saved the file.

The front door opened and banged shut.

"Hi Mum!"

"I'm up here."

"I'm down here. Did you make me any tea?"

Claire slumped. "No, you didn't say you wanted any."

"Good, I didn't want any, I was just checking."

He came bounding up the stairs two at a time and poked his head around the door. She smiled at him and he grinned back. His thick dark hair, so unlike hers, was gelled and styled so it flopped over his right eye. He wore joggers and a North Face T-shirt and Nike trainers. His face was red and moisture glistened in his hairline.

"Good time at the ramp?"

"The best. We've spent the last half hour dropping 360s on the six foot."

She didn't understand but nodded enthusiastically all the same. "Sounds good. Done your homework?"

"I'll do it now."

"Make sure you do."

"Uh-huh," he said, edging out of the doorway.

"And take off your trainers."

"Mum!"

"I'm walking around barefoot here," she said. "You know the rules."

"Okay."

He leaned against the door frame and took each trainer off by standing on the back of the opposite one. Then he kicked them downstairs.

"That's not what I meant," she said, but he'd already gone.

Re-saving the file, just to make sure, Claire shut the laptop and went into her bedroom. She blow-dried her hair, put on underwear and then applied some make-up. Standing in front of her wardrobe, she scanned the hangers and tried to figure out what best to wear to make a good impression. Jeans and a T-shirt were comfortable but didn't really suggest she was making an effort.

She selected a pair of grey trousers and a short-sleeved blouse and dressed quickly. She dithered for a while about whether to have two or three buttons undone before letting her lapels go with an exasperated sigh. It'll do as it is. She brushed her hair then padded along the landing barefoot.

Scott's door was partly closed and she smiled at his handwritten sign – 'Parents Keep Out' – before knocking lightly on one of the panels.

"Can I come in?"

"Uh-huh."

She pushed the door and her nose wrinkled at the combined scent assault of deodorant, hair products and old socks. His room looked like a bomb had gone off, but she'd long since given up trying to get him to keep it tidy and nowadays only made him return old cups and plates and put his dirty clothes in the laundry basket. She didn't have to sleep in there and he was welcome to the mess.

He sat on the bed with a beanbag over his pillow. Posters covered the walls and computer magazines were stacked on his bedside table. His TV sat on a bookcase and played a music video with the sound so low she could barely hear it.

His desk, as ever, was a clutter of electrical bits and pieces. Scott loved to build gadgets and take apart devices to figure out how they worked. His Raspberry Pi computer seemed to be growing across the shelf above the desk with wires connecting it to various black boxes. Last summer, they'd spent an evening on the patio as he explained it all and she'd enjoyed listening to his enthusiasm.

"Hey," he said and favoured her with a brief glance. "I'm working on an app. How're you?"

"Not bad. I saw Annie with her new dog earlier and she asked me to tell you to call her."

"I will," he said with a small, almost embarrassed smile. "You look nice."

"Thank you."

"Are you going out?"

"Yes, it's my..." What should she call it? She suddenly felt foolish, as if their roles were reversed. "My thing," she said, trying to calm her fingers which had started to dance. "You know, we talked about it."

"Your meet-up thing?" He smiled. "Dad calls it the Sad Bastards Society."

Affronted, she frowned. "Well that's not nice. And how does he even know?"

"Because I told him."

"Of course." She looked at her fingers. "It's still not a nice thing to say though."

He nodded in agreement. "Are you nervous or something?"

"I am." She laughed but there was no humour in the sound.

"Why?"

"Because I'm going to meet a group of people I don't know."

"You always tell me that I should just walk in and be confident, then people will want to talk to me."

"And you've now revealed one of the great parental cover-ups."

Scott inhaled sharply. "You mean you told me a lie?"

"Not a lie, so much, as a blatant untruth."

He laughed. "You'll be fine, lots of people go to singles clubs these days. It's that or Tinder."

"It's not a singles club, Scott."

"Are you sure? Dad said..."

"I don't want to know what your dad said. It's not a singles club."

"Okay then." He smirked and looked back at his tablet. "You look good, Mum, you'll be fine."

She smoothed her trousers over her thighs. "Thank you."

"You're welcome."

Claire turned to go.

"And, Mum?"

She stopped in the doorway. "Yes?"

"If you do pick someone up, do I have to call him Uncle when we meet over breakfast?"

She walked downstairs. "Goodnight, Scott."

"Goodnight, Mum. Have a good time."

* * *

Although she intended to have some Dutch courage as soon as she got in the pub, Claire decided to drive so she'd be limited to the one glass. The temptation otherwise might have been to imbibe more than would be sensible.

The Rising Sun had a large car park to the rear. She parked under a street light and followed the road around to Gold Street. Her nerves bubbled up with every step – what if nobody spoke to her? What if she didn't like anyone or fell over when she went through the door? She shook her head at all the what-ifs she'd have told Scott not to worry about. This negativity was pointless, and it was perfectly natural to be nervous. She wouldn't fall and people would talk to her and if they didn't she could head straight home.

She stood by the front door of the pub. Half a dozen people were standing at the bar. A note on the window to one side read: 'Hadlington Friends meets here tonight.'

Here goes nothing, she thought, and pushed open the door.

Chapter 5

A modern song with enough 80s pop elements that it could have been from the era competed with the rattle of cutlery on crockery from a small dining area by the window. Conversation drifted towards her from the men at the horseshoe-shaped bar on the right. Off to one side, a handful of older women sat around a table playing Scrabble.

There was no one else in the pub. Disappointed, Claire went to the bar and waited for the barmaid. "White wine, please."

The woman poured her a glass and Claire paid as she looked around in case she'd missing someone coming in.

"Are you okay, love?" asked the barmaid.

"Yes thanks, I was just looking for..."

"The friends group?" The barmaid smiled at Claire's surprise. "No worries, love, they're upstairs." She leaned over the bar and pointed to a door in the far wall. "Go through there towards the toilets then, just before you reach the gents, there's a staircase. Go up and you're there."

"Thank you, you're a lifesaver."

"Oh I wouldn't go that far," said the barmaid with a wink and went back to pulling a pint.

Claire went out the bar into a corridor and found a steep narrow staircase. Through an open door at the top, she could hear people talking.

"Here we go," she said and started up the stairs. Her nerves fluttered but she knew everything would be fine as soon as she saw Amy.

She paused on the landing then took a deep breath and went in.

* * *

The room stretched the width of the pub and tables were dotted around the space. Perhaps twenty people were in the room and some turned to look at her, smiling as they did so. That made her feel better and she smiled back as she looked for Amy. She spotted her at a table near the door with two men and a woman.

Amy jumped when Claire put a hand gently on her shoulder and she looked around quickly.

"Claire, you came!" Her face lit up.

"Of course."

Amy jumped up and gave Claire a quick, tight hug before stepping to one side and facing the table. "Another recruit to the newbies table," she told the others.

The two men nodded at her. The woman frowned quickly then smiled.

Amy indicated the chair next to hers and Claire sat down. "This is my old friend Claire. We've known each other for, what...?"

"Far too many years."

Amy laughed. "It must be getting on for twenty-five now?"

"It must."

"So this is the newbie table which everyone'll graduate from at some point – people here are lovely and friendly but we all know it can be nerve-wracking to try and make conversation in a room where you don't know anybody."

"That's a fact," said one of the men who looked to be somewhere in his forties. He had a nice face with blue eyes behind black-rimmed glasses, thick brown hair and a ready smile. "I was terrified."

He stood up and held out his hand. Claire shook it automatically.

"Mike Templeton," he said.

"Claire Heeley."

The woman, slim and thin-faced with very dark hair, held out her hand and Claire shook it. "Eva Pelham."

"And this is Ben over here," said Amy.

He stood up and shook Claire's hand. "Ben Montgomery," he said. He had a chubby face with kind eyes and thinning sandy-coloured hair. He looked very nervous. "How are you?"

"All the better for having come in here and spoken to people."

"It makes a difference," said Mike.

"And the fact none of you ignored me is a plus too."

Amy tapped her arm lightly and shushed her. "You're too self-deprecating for your own good."

"It's sometimes easier," said Ben, not looking at Claire.

"Sometimes." Mike nodded.

"Okay," said Amy, a little too brightly. "Eva was our previous newest member and joined last week in time for the cinema trip I told you about. Mike joined the week before and Ben came along a couple of weeks before that."

"All fairly new, you see," said Mike warmly.

Claire smiled at his friendliness and he returned it.

"I'll show you around," said Amy. She surveyed the room then led Claire to the far side where a tall woman with short hair and a hard face was leaning on a table talking to two women.

"This is Jane Peck, she's the group leader."

Jane turned and Amy introduced Claire and they shook hands.

"Glad to see you, Claire. Amy has told me a lot about you."

"She's told me a lot about your group too."

"A lot of the organisation is down to her, let me tell you." Jane leaned forward as if she wanted to impart a confidence. "I need to tell you, before we start, that this isn't some dating scam even though some people do get

26

together. It's also not full of those people you might try to avoid on the bus."

One of the women sitting at the table laughed. "That's what my son said it would be."

Jane nodded. "It's really not." She was a good few inches taller than Claire, perhaps edging on six foot. "I came out of a relationship and, if you'll pardon the melodrama, felt cast adrift. Being unexpectedly single in your forties is not the same as it is in your early twenties."

"No."

There was an eruption of laughter from the doorway, and they all turned to see what was happening.

"Ah, Pete and Elizabeth. You'll have to excuse me Claire, they met here a few months back and got engaged at the weekend."

"How nice," said Claire.

Jane patted Claire's arm. "I do hope you like it here," she said and crossed the room to pull a short, dark-haired woman into a tight embrace.

"She seems nice," Claire said to Amy.

"She's lovely," said Amy. "Come on, I'll show you the balcony. Our smokers have adopted it but it's nice out there on pleasant evenings."

A door across the room had been propped open with a small weight. Claire followed Amy through to a balcony that overlooked the car park. A waist-high wooden rail closed it off. The pub kitchen must have been below because Claire could smell steak and garlic and curry spices. Three people stood in the far corner and chatted as they smoked.

Amy leaned on the rail. "Not too overwhelming then, I hope?"

"Not at all," Claire said and realised her nerves had almost gone.

"It's a good newbie table even though I don't know Eva all that well. Ben and Mike are decent blokes but Ben's painfully shy. We do have a laugh though."

"Thank you for suggesting it."

"No problem. You'd do the same for me."

They went back into the room. Ben and Eva were still at the newbie table – him fiddling with a beer mat as she checked her phone – but Mike wasn't.

"Shall we mingle?" Amy asked.

"I will but I need to nip to the loo."

"I'll see you in a mo then."

After Claire finished in the toilet, she stood at the sink and washed her hands then quickly sent Scott a text.

SBS is going well, not so sad after all. Will see you later, love you xx

She was on her way back up the stairs when a man wearing blue jeans and a white dress shirt came out of the room. Rather than wait for her, he started down and she wondered if there'd be enough space for them to pass comfortably.

"Hi," he said, when he was four steps above her.

"Hi."

"And who're you?"

"Claire Heeley."

"Ah yes, the cute blonde friend."

Had she heard him right? "I beg your pardon?"

"You're a newcomer, aren't you? I was talking with Amy at the weekend, and she said we might be getting a fresh member, if you'll pardon the pun."

He had a nasal voice and his tone suggested he was trying to be amusing but it wasn't really working.

"Yes," she said, after a pause that lasted perhaps a bit too long, "of course."

"I'm Keith Hasslett," he said and took a step closer. "Pleased to meet you."

He held out his hand and Claire looked at it then at him. He smiled and nodded towards his hand. She shook it. His palm felt soft and clammy.

"It's a pleasure to meet you," he said and took another step towards her. "So what brings you here?"

He was confusing her because his attitude and tone were at odds with his friendly words.

"Well I was at a loose end and…"

"I know what you mean," he said.

Another step and he stood over her. She could smell his aftershave and felt her hackles rise.

"Sometimes," he said, "we can't see the wood" – he paused for the briefest of moments – "for the trees."

He shifted slightly to the centre of the step and blocked her way.

Chapter 6

Claire took a deep breath, trying to shake off the feeling of intimidation and claustrophobia. "I'm sorry, you've lost me."

He smiled as if appraising her. "Wood for the trees. We're looking for something to cling onto and yet they're around us all the time."

Her discomfort grew but she didn't want to step back and give him that satisfaction, although without asking him to give her the space, she wouldn't be able to get up to the room.

He tilted his head to one side. "And what's your story?"

"Well, it's kind of personal."

"I understand that."

"And I'd rather not…"

"…discuss it in open forum? No, that makes perfect sense."

Claire looked over his shoulder towards the doorway and willed someone to come through. "Thank you. I don't mean to be rude."

He made a non-committal noise and she looked at him. He wasn't looking at her face, his eyes were locked to her chest.

"Excuse me," she said with annoyance. When he looked up at her she pointed at her face. "I'm up here."

A momentary flash of panic crossed his face. "I hope you don't think I was looking at your chest."

Claire's annoyance grew. "That's exactly what you were doing."

"How rude," he said. "If you must know, I have a mild form of strabismus."

"What?" How had she somehow caused him offence? "I don't…"

"A squint," he said with the tone of someone explaining a simple concept to an idiot. "I sometimes can't help where my eyes appear to be looking."

"I didn't realise," she said. "I'm sorry."

"I assure you I wasn't looking at your chest," he said and puffed out his own.

Hearing him say the word made a ripple of tension roll over her shoulders. The staircase felt like it was shrinking around her. "Please stop saying that." Did he have a squint? She wanted to check – if he did then she'd feel terrible, if he didn't she'd be repelled.

Someone came up the stairs behind her. Keith looked over her shoulder and took a step back to give the newcomer space. Claire watched him.

"Everything okay, folks?"

She turned to see Mike standing three steps behind her. He smiled at her and then at Keith. "How's it going?"

"Okay," said Keith. "I didn't catch your name, chap."

"Mike. And yours?"

"Keith."

Mike nodded, as if the name meant something to him. He looked at Claire and smiled brightly. "So, Claire, how're you enjoying your first evening?"

"It's going okay, thanks."

He looked at her, at Keith, then back at her. "Since you and I are moving up the stairs and Keith here is clearly heading down, why don't we let him past and we can carry on."

"Of course," she said and pressed herself into the wall at her right.

Keith edged past, careful not to touch her, and nodded at Mike as he passed him. Claire went up the stairs quickly and into the room where she waited for Mike.

"Thank you," she said.

"Are you okay?"

"Yeah, I'm fine."

"Good. I know you could have dealt with the situation; I wasn't trying to rescue you or anything."

She waited for a smile that didn't come. "No, I know."

He nodded and walked behind Eva who watched them both.

"What happened?" she asked as Claire sat next to her.

"Claire met one of the other members," said Mike as he sat down.

"That doesn't sound as positive as it should."

"It was nothing," Claire said. "I probably got the wrong end of the stick or something."

Mike raised his eyebrows but didn't say anything.

"Who was it?" asked Eva.

"Keith?" Mike said. "Shortish bloke, grey curly hair and chubby cheeks. I didn't hear what he said but Claire didn't seem pleased."

They all looked at her and she felt on the spot. "I thought he was being off with me – a bit lechy if I'm honest – but then said he had 'strabi-something' and I was being off with him. It was uncomfortable."

"Wandering eyes?" asked Mike.

31

"Something along those lines."

"Yuck," said Eva. "I hate that."

"So," said Mike, "our chubby-cheeked chum aside, is tonight what you expected?"

There was something about him she liked. He leaned forward, elbows on the table, but it seemed more like he wanted to make sure he heard her properly than eagerness. And the more she thought about it, the more she liked him saying he wasn't rescuing her. If he was using this as a dating agency, she supposed, he'd have made his move when he could have presented himself as a knight in shining armour.

"I didn't know what to expect," she said. "My son had his worries."

"How many kids do you have?" he asked.

"Just the one."

"How old is he?"

"Fifteen. But giving me enough grief that he could be two or three years older. What about you?"

"Giving you grief?"

She laughed. "No, not really. Do you have any kids?"

"A daughter. She's twelve but in Instagram years that puts her somewhere in her mid-teens." Mike leaned back in his chair and looked at Ben. "What about you, mate?"

"No, no kids for me."

"What about you?" Claire asked Eva.

"No. We talked about it but, well, you know, the way things went it's perhaps a good thing we never did."

"I'm going to nip down for a drink," said Mike, "anybody else want one? My shout."

They all started to protest but he held up his hand. "No, I insist. Ben, mate, what's your pint? Eva? Claire?"

The drinks order taken, Mike went downstairs and Ben followed to give him a hand. Claire turned to Eva.

"Amy said you started at the group on Saturday."

They talked about the cinema and Eva admitted she hadn't had much fun and hadn't enjoyed the film.

"Which is terrible," she said, "because now I sound like a real grump."

"Of course not."

"Oh I know I do. I often find new people overwhelming and everyone here" – she gestured vaguely towards the centre of the room – "are either better at faking it than I am, or they've known one another for ages."

"I'm not good around new people either," said Claire. "In fact, if I didn't know Amy, I wouldn't have come along, so you're braver than me."

Eva offered her a smile. "So you'd think."

"Did you only find out about the club recently?"

"Sort of. I've been away for a while and only came back a couple of weeks ago."

"Away somewhere nice?"

Eva pulled a face. "Not really. I was in the Fens looking after family." She took a deep breath and let it out slowly. "When that got sorted, I found a job here and moved back but then decided I needed something a bit more." She forced a smile. "So why did you join?"

"Because I…" Claire wasn't sure how much to say. "My marriage collapsed and I wanted some company other than work colleagues, my yoga buddies and my son."

"People don't understand, do they? When mine collapsed I…" Eva took a deep breath. She looked very pale.

"Are you okay?"

"I'm…" She paused. "No, I don't think I am."

"Do you feel sick?"

"No, it's…"

"Light-headed?"

"Close enough."

"Let's get some air, we'll go out on the balcony."

Claire helped Eva to her feet and they made their way across the room slowly.

"Sorry," Eva muttered.

Claire followed her through the door and they stood across from the smokers. Eva leaned her elbows on the rail and tipped her head forwards.

"I'm sorry about this, I feel such a fool."

"Don't worry," said Claire. "Just breathe deeply."

"Thanks for helping me."

"No problem."

After a few moments, Eva straightened up. "Do you think you could get me some water?"

"Mike should be back with the drinks by now."

"I asked for a spritzer, but I'd love some tap water."

"Yes," said Claire, "of course."

"Thank you, you're wonderful."

Claire put her handbag down and went back into the main room. Amy was standing by a window with Jane and shrugged her shoulders as if to ask whether anything was up. Claire stuck her thumb up and walked to the main door. Mike and Ben were coming up the stairs, so she waited for them.

"Everything okay?" asked Mike.

"Eva felt a bit off, so I took her out onto the balcony for some fresh air. She wants some water."

"Okay, I'll put the drinks on the table."

Claire went down to the bar. The Scrabble ladies had given up on the game and were now sitting in a large circle, drinking and laughing.

"What'll it be, love?" asked the barmaid.

"Just a glass of water please."

"Sure." She went through a doorway and Claire heard a tap run. "How's it going up there?"

"Alright, I think."

"Glad to hear it," the barmaid said as she came back and handed over a glass, "here you go."

"Thanks," said Claire and went back upstairs.

Mike and Ben were chatting at the table and she noticed Keith in a group at the back of the room. He saw her looking and his eye flickered – was it a twitch, as part

34

of his squint, or had he winked at her? She felt a chill across her shoulders for the briefest of moments and then it was gone. Shaking the image from her mind – it was a twitch, it had to be a twitch – she went through to the balcony. Eva was still leaning on the railing but standing straighter now, looking at the setting sun. A breeze blew her fringe off her face.

"Here you are," Claire said, handing over the glass.

Eva held it carefully, whispered "thank you" and took three big gulps. "I think I'm okay now."

"Glad to hear it."

"Thank you for helping me, you don't know me from Adam."

"You're welcome."

Eva smiled. "Shall we go back inside now?"

* * *

People began drifting away at the end of the evening and Amy gathered her "little gang of newbies" around her.

"So, is everyone coming back next week?"

Everyone said they would.

"This Saturday, if you're interested, we're meeting at the Rock N Bowl in town. We'll have a couple of games then retire to the bar for a drink and a natter, plus there's a burger place if you fancy something to eat and don't have any functioning taste buds."

The last comment took Mike by surprise and he choked a laugh.

"It'd be great to see you," she continued, "but I understand if people have plans. Give me a buzz beforehand if you're interested so we have an idea of who'll need a lane. Does everyone have my number?"

Everyone took the opportunity to swap numbers and Claire found herself growing to like the idea of being part of the newbie gang.

Chapter 7

I was in the park today.

I like the park. I like being surrounded by nature, I like the open space and I love the sound of kids laughing and playing. Do you ever go? I really hope you do and I really hope you enjoy it so when it's taken away from you, as it should already have been, it's another thing for you to desperately miss.

Desperately missing something, or someone, is pain beyond words and I look forward to the day you can share that misery with me.

I saw your son at the park. He's grown up into a striking young man, hasn't he? What is he now, fourteen or fifteen maybe? It's amazing how quickly time flies.

He's very good on that scooter. I stood and watched him and his friends for a while. I didn't say anything, even though I really wanted to.

He wouldn't know who I was though, would he?

I'll bet you haven't told him.

I expect that'll be up to me.

Chapter 8

Claire got up with the alarm

After pottering around the quiet house, she made coffee and sat on the patio to drink it as the early haze dissipated. She missed her early morning runs and decided she shouldn't let herself be frightened out of her routine.

If she was careful – no music for the first few runs – and kept her eyes open and finally got round to buying a rape alarm, why should she allow this man to force change upon her?

The more she thought about it, the more annoyed she got.

* * *

Claire used her lunchtime to walk through the town centre and found an electrical shop almost across the road from The Rising Sun.

One window of Ray's Electrics was filled with televisions, vacuum cleaners and Blu-ray players, the other covered with a sheet of hardboard. A little bell tinkled lightly as she went in, and the other three customers ignored her as they perused the shelves.

"Can I help you?" asked the man with a friendly smile behind the counter. He was in his late sixties and the few wisps of hair that clung to his head were long and white.

"I hope so, I'm looking for an alarm."

"We have plenty but Halfords down the road is better for cars."

"No, it's for me."

"Ah, a personal alarm?" He took a blister pack down from the shelf behind him and handed it to her. "This'll do the job, it's the one I gave my wife." He pointed to what looked like a wrist strap. "You pull that and it sounds 120 decibels of alarm. It's bloody deafening, take my word for it."

The alarm would easily fit into the palm of her hand so she could run holding it. "That'll fine, thank you."

"You're welcome, love. It always pays to be careful."

* * *

Claire texted Scott before she left work and told him to put the dinner on. She got home just before six and the smell of lasagne burning greeted her.

"Scott?"

"Up here."

"Can you smell anything weird?"

"No."

"Fine," she said and kicked off her shoes and went through to the kitchen. She turned off the pinging oven alarm, opened the door and stepped back as a thick wave of heat brushed her face. Her homemade lasagne was bubbling madly and the edges had crisped black.

"Dinner's ready," she called. "Come and set the table."

She heard the thud as he rolled off his bed and then his breakneck pace down the stairs before he ambled into the dining room. "Hey."

"Hey yourself. Didn't you hear the buzzer?"

"I had my earphones in."

"And you didn't notice the time?"

"No," he said, with the conviction of someone who absolutely shouldn't have been keeping his eye on the clock. "Didn't I put it on right?"

Shaking her head – some battles were easier not to get into – she took the lasagne out of the oven with gloves and left it on the hob as she got the plates. When she'd divided their portions, she handed the plates to Scott and poured herself a glass of wine.

"So how was your day?" she asked after they'd started eating.

"Not bad. Chopper was a twat in design and got sent out. Then some Year 8 fell over by the sixth form block and started crying and all he'd done was bang his knee. Such a noob."

"Absolutely, never cry in front of anyone is today's top tip."

"Word."

Claire smiled and ate some more lasagne. "Have you heard anything of Harry?"

"I saw him earlier on. Annie was playing with him in the back garden."

"Roger said she liked to."

"He's cute."

"I haven't heard you use the word cute since you got rid of your Moshi Monsters."

"Moshi Monsters?" He grimaced as though she'd told the most dreadful joke ever. "That was years ago."

"I know," she said, pulling a face. "So did you play with him?"

"No, I was sitting on the patio."

"You never sit on the patio."

"I do."

"Do you?"

"Yeah, when you're not about."

Scott looked at his plate, but Claire watched his face and saw the slight smile playing at the corners of his mouth. Maybe Annie wasn't the only one with a slight crush.

"Did you speak to Annie?"

He looked up cautiously. "A bit."

She didn't want to put him on the spot because he was at the age when getting him to talk about anything was difficult enough without putting extra barriers in the way. "Good, I wouldn't want you to ignore her for the dog."

His face relaxed slightly. "I wouldn't do that. We had a little chat and she showed me some of the tricks she's teaching Harry."

"Sounds lovely. Are you seeing her or Harry later?"

"No, I'm back down the skatepark." He rubbed his lip. "But we might meet up later on and perhaps go to Starbucks."

* * *

After her shower, Claire took advantage of the pleasant evening and sat on the patio in her dressing gown waiting for the kettle to boil. She looked into a cloudless sky slowly turning indigo and felt perfectly peaceful. The kettle clicked and she went into the kitchen and found there was only a thimbleful of milk left in the bottle.

"Bloody hell, Scott."

The wine had gone down particularly well earlier but she'd set her heart on the coffee as she checked her phone messages and enjoyed the last light of the evening. Plus, Scott would need milk for his cornflakes tomorrow.

She went upstairs and quickly got dressed in a T-shirt and jeans and went out.

The gloom of evening was settling across the sky. There was no one else on the street and Claire walked with a quick pace, taking the opportunity for a bit more cardio.

She turned down the hill and four cars passed by in quick succession. None were Astras. A few moments later a horn blared and she turned. Someone in a grey hoodie crossed the road as a car bore down on them, ignorant as they studied their phone. The horn blared again but the hoodie walked calmly to the pavement and stopped under a lamp post.

The car went by, and Claire saw the driver shaking his head angrily. She continued walking. A dozen or so yards on, she crossed the road and glanced back towards the hoodie. The person was still looking at their phone but with the hood up she couldn't see their face and felt like she was being watched.

The hoodie looked up at her as she reached the pavement.

Claire walked into Shelley Street and towards the bright lights of the Co-op store. A man came out of a house a few doors down struggling with a Border collie cross pulling hard on its lead.

"Someone's eager for a walk," she said.

"You wouldn't think I take her out twice a day, would you?"

Claire watched them go and saw the hoodie had come into Shelley Street too. They stood in the shadow of a wall and Claire suddenly felt paranoid and silly, panicking about some kid probably on his way to meet friends.

She gripped her purse tightly and kept walking. She heard a scuffing sound and, without breaking her pace, glanced back. The hoodie was walking towards her with shoulders squared and head down.

Could it be her stalker in disguise? He'd seemed bigger but then she couldn't tell if the person in the hoodie was male or female, old or young, and that alarmed her.

She picked up her pace and focussed on the front doors of the Co-op as her heart raced. She didn't want to look behind in case the person was closer. She thought of the rape alarm in its packaging on the mantelpiece, as useless as if it was still in the shop.

She went into the Co-op doorway and the hoodie walked by, apparently not in a hurry as they headed towards the market square.

"Shit." Her stalker had really wound her up. He'd sown seeds of paranoia that had blossomed by themselves and made her get anxious over someone heading into town.

As she thought about the hoodie, she realised the person didn't have the gait of a teenager and anyone older surely wouldn't wear their hood up on an evening as humid as this. Wearing the hood suggested hiding their identity and why would they do that?

Could she have made a mistake? Maybe it was her stalker?

No. She shook her head to dislodge that train of thought. Her stalker was taller and heavier, the person in the hoodie was average height and nowhere near as heavy.

Claire bought her milk and, after checking cautiously to make sure the hoodie had gone, briskly walked home.

* * *

Claire awoke with a start. Her bedroom was dark and it took a moment for the clock digits to swim into focus.

Her mobile screen was lit and showed Greg's face. She picked up the phone and saw he'd sent her a text.

Hi, pulled a late shift, hope this doesn't wake you.
We need to talk.

Angrily, she dialled his number and he answered immediately.

"Hey, I didn't expect a reply." He sounded surprised. "I only wanted to leave a message."

"It's quarter past three in the fucking morning, why send it now?"

He stuttered in response, but Claire couldn't make out any of the words.

"Greg, I swear to God this is the last time you do this to me."

"Sorry, babe, really, but we need to talk."

"Is it about Scott?"

"No." He sounded confused. "It's something else. I need to speak about…"

"I've told you this Greg; if it's not about Scott then we have nothing to talk about."

"But…"

"No more," she said and ended the call.

She put the phone on silent. This was the last straw. She wasn't going to be held hostage anymore – not by bloody Greg and certainly not her stalker. She'd run tomorrow morning and take the rape alarm and if she saw the bastard, she'd deal with him there and then.

Enough was enough.

Chapter 9

The nerves kicked in as Claire warmed up on the patio, but she wasn't going to give up. With the rape alarm gripped tightly in her right hand, she started her run.

It took longer than usual to get into the rhythm because she wasn't following a drumbeat, but by the end of her street she'd found a good pace and her breathing was steady. She listened to the birds and the sound of her trainers hitting the pavement.

Her heart rate rose as she passed the Co-op but she kept going and gripped the alarm tighter. Her breathing got heavier as she passed the library and the fish and chip shop. A few more paces and she'd be at the corner of the square.

What if he was there?

What if he wasn't?

Three more paces.

If she gripped the alarm any tighter she'd break it. Keep moving, she thought, try to regulate your breathing.

Claire ran onto the market square. The normal group of commuter cars were parked in the centre and a quick glance proved her stalker wasn't anywhere to be seen. There were no Astras, black or otherwise.

She felt elated and wanted to shout but kept it inside. She couldn't relax completely because he might be somewhere else on her run, but she'd overcome something this morning and was proud of herself.

Her muscles felt good as she ran down the hill towards the railway bridge. A storm drain was just to the left of it and someone had painted a gallows on the blank concrete face, as if starting the biggest game of hangman they could. Two dashes were under it.

Claire ran under the bridge and up the hill towards the shopping centre, turned off at the hospital main entrance and ran along the high street back towards the church where the accident had happened. She took the corner carefully, but the road was empty and she ran down it towards the market square.

Old Man Stan came out of the Tesco Express store as she ran by.

"Hullo, missy," he said and raised a hand in greeting. "Haven't seen you for a bit."

"No," she panted. "Perhaps see you tomorrow though."

"I look forward to it," he called and then she was gone, heading home for a welcome shower.

* * *

When her desk phone rang at work it broke Claire's concentration on the payroll she was checking.

"It's James," her boss said when she picked up. "I've got Steve in from Moore Associates and we're just reviewing the spreadsheet, but it doesn't seem to have changed from the other day. I thought you were going to fix the glitches?"

"I did," she said and opened the relevant directory to click on the file. She opted to 'read only' as James Harris was listed as using it and it only took a moment to see he was right. She remembered the server issues. "Shit, I did it at home and saved it onto my flash drive. I'll upload it now."

"Marvellous," James said with thick sarcasm. "We can't do anything until we've looked at it so the quicker the better, yeah?"

"Yeah, okay. Give me two minutes."

Annoyed with herself, she put the phone down and reached under the desk for her handbag but couldn't find the Pokémon flash drive anywhere.

"Shit." Her cheeks felt hot with embarrassment at the mess-up. She checked her bag again and thought back to Wednesday night and what she'd done with the flash drive after Scott came home. Nothing came to her except that it had to be in her bag and she was just about to tip the contents out onto her desk when the phone rang again.

"It's been five minutes," James said and she could hear the steel in his voice. They'd worked together for several years and got on well, but his temper was notoriously short when people let him down – especially if they'd left him unprepared in a meeting.

"Sorry, I can't find my flash drive." He made a sound that might have been a word or might not. "I'll make the changes now."

"How long will that take?"

How long had it taken on Wednesday? "Half an hour, at most," she said.

"Oh come on, Claire," he hissed. "What the hell are we supposed to do for half an hour?"

"I'm sorry, James." She felt more of that shameful heat on her cheeks. "I'll sort it."

"Do it quickly, we need to see that spreadsheet."

"Okay," she said to a dead line.

* * *

It took fifteen minutes to revise the spreadsheet and email it to James. He didn't reply, which concerned her – he'd normally ping back a thanks at the very least but this time, clearly, he wasn't happy.

Claire worked until her colleagues began leaving for lunch. Rich smells wafted through from the microwave in the common area. She grabbed her phone and handbag and went into the corridor. James's office was near the entrance and she hoped he was either out with Steve or so buried in work he wouldn't notice her.

She was wrong on both counts and hadn't even passed the door when he called, "Claire, have you got a minute?"

"Yes." She leaned against the door frame. "I'm so sorry about earlier."

He nodded. "Bit of a fuck-up."

Through the blinds behind his desk she could see the lunchtime activity of Hadlington.

"I don't know what to say. I revised it at home, saved it onto my flash drive but that's gone."

"Gone?"

"It's normally in my handbag but now it's not."

"You do realise I had to sit with Steve Moore – one of the most boring men I know – and make conversation for fifteen minutes?" His tone was light, but Claire caught the edge to it.

"I'm so sorry."

"Is everything alright?"

"Yes, of course." She frowned. "What do you mean?"

He shrugged. "I don't know. Stuff at home, that kind of thing. You haven't mentioned the Greg situation for a while, but I assumed it was all resolved."

"It is resolved." She'd discussed Greg and Matilda with James because they were in Sheffield overnight at a conference and he understood the situation because his wife had run off with one of their mutual friends. James had been sympathetic and positive then but now it felt like a dig. "This isn't about Greg."

"Is Scott okay?"

"Yes, everything at home is okay." Annoyed at his suggestion her home life was intruding on work, she managed to keep her tone neutral. "I just lost my flash drive."

He gave her a smile that looked forced. "Just checking. We go back a long way and I didn't expect you to let me down."

46

What else could she do other than apologise? "I'm sorry," she said through gritted teeth.

He nodded and the forced smile stayed in place. "We'll draw a line under it, yeah? Are you off for lunch?"

"I am. Did you want anything?"

"No," he said and turned to look at his monitor as if silently dismissing her. "But thanks."

Claire left.

* * *

The queue at the deli she liked came out the door which didn't ease the annoyance Claire felt. How could she have lost that flash drive? It lived in her bag and there was so much on it, not just work but personal stuff too including photos.

"Claire? What a coincidence."

She turned, not recognising the voice and it took a moment or two to place the face.

"Eva, nice to see you."

"And you." Eva gestured at the queue. "Busy place, eh?"

"It's not usually this bad," said Claire. "So do you work in town?"

Eva looked down at herself. "You think I'd dress myself like this if I had a choice?" She wore black trousers and a red polo shirt with 'Abbey Recruitment' embroidered over her left breast. "Do you work in town?"

"May & Sons," said Claire. "A couple of streets over."

"We should arrange to meet for a bite to eat one lunchtime."

"I'd like that," said Claire and meant it.

"Good. I can't stop but when I saw you, I didn't want to go by without saying hello – I joined the group to make new friends, not to ignore people."

"I'm glad you did."

"Are you going bowling tomorrow?"

"I'm looking forward to it."

"Great," said Eva and walked away. "I'll see you there."

* * *

At home, Claire got a bottle of wine and a glass and carried them out to the patio. She slipped off her shoes and sat with her feet on the tabletop. The sun had moved to the right of the south-facing garden, leaving most of the table in the shade. She poured herself a generous glass and leaned back with her eyes closed.

She heard snuffling and it took a moment to connect the sound with Harry. She assumed he was in his own garden, but the sounds got louder and when she opened her eyes she saw him standing on the lawn, watching her.

"Hey, Harry." He cocked his head to one side, tongue lolling. "Where's Annie?" Harry moved his head. "Does she know you're in here?"

Harry flicked his tail and his head darted around to see what the movement was. As if anticipating the start of a great new game, he did several complete spins and then took off for the end of the garden before racing back to where he started.

"I don't have a ball," she lied, and his ears perked up with the last word. There were a lot of old footballs in the shed, but she didn't think Scott would appreciate any of them getting bitten by a dog.

Harry raced to the fence and back again then stared at her with his head tilted. He wasn't going to give up. Claire stood up with a groan.

The two houses shared the yard which was divided by a five-foot fence that ran to the end of the garden. At the base of the entry were two gates and she went through hers, opened Roger and Lou's and knocked on their back door. Someone called from inside. The door opened and released a waft of home cooking.

"Claire!" said Lou. Her wild black hair was all over the place and a blue-and-white-striped apron protected her blouse. "How are you?"

"Okay thanks, just reporting an escapee."

"An escapee?" Lou frowned then the penny dropped. "Oh, the little bugger's out again?"

"It's not a problem but he's doing circuits in my garden."

"I'm so sorry. Hang on, I'll come and get him."

Lou wiped her hands on the apron and took it off as she stepped into the yard. "There must be a hole in the fence somewhere. I'll get Roger to have a look over the weekend."

Claire led Lou into her garden. Seeing his mistress sent Harry into another excited round of fence-and-back and he added a few barks in for good measure.

"Come on, Harry," Lou said. She squatted at the edge of the patio and held out her hand. Harry ignored her. "Come on, dog."

When he ignored her again, she stood up and rubbed the back of her thighs. "Dogs aren't really my cup of tea," she said. "Annie promised she'd walk him, but Roger's taken him out the last few nights."

"Is Annie about?"

Lou frowned. "She's out with Scott." The surprise clearly showed enough in Claire's face for Lou to smile. "Didn't you know?"

"Teenaged boys tell their mums very little."

"Teenaged girls too. They've gone for a Starbucks."

"He did mention something about going for a drink."

Lou smiled. "I think it's sweet. Back in my day I was lucky to get asked to the local Wimpy."

Claire laughed. "Me too. So is it a date?"

Lou took a step closer, making their chat seem more clandestine. "Not as much, though I think she'd like that."

"I think Scott would too."

"They're good kids."

"Lou?" Roger called from inside the house. "Are you out here?"

"Just rescuing Claire from Harry," she called back.

"Something's burning and something's pinging."

"I'll be right there." Lou touched Claire's arm. "Sorry about Harry," she said.

"No problem."

"Harry!" Lou hissed and the dog looked at her as if aware he was out of line. "Get here."

Harry walked meekly to Lou and, after sniffing her fingers, raced up the yard at full speed and disappeared through the gate.

"Hello, Lightning," said Roger.

"I'd better go," said Lou, "before I burn the house down. I'll see you later."

* * *

Scott came home at a little before seven. Claire was still on the patio, trying to decide what to have for dinner. She'd made a coffee to help her think.

She heard Annie giggle then Scott laugh before he opened the entry door. His heavy tread echoed in the enclosed space.

"Out here," she called as he closed the gate and she listened to his progress down the yard.

"Hey," he said.

"Hey yourself. Shouldn't you be at your dad's now?"

"Nah, I texted him to say I was going to be a bit late."

"I can run you round there if you want, I've only had a glass."

"No, it's cool, Mum. I'll take my scooter."

"And your rucksack?"

"Yes, Mother," he said and sat heavily on the chair opposite her.

"Fun evening?" she asked.

He shrugged. "S'alright."

"Do anything nice?"

He looked at her, squinting. "What do you mean?"

"Did you go anywhere nice?"

"Just to Starbucks."

"Was it fun?" Sometimes the level of interrogation required to find anything out – her mum likened it to "getting blood out of a stone" – wearied her enough to give in quickly but she was willing to push a bit more now.

He looked wary. "Yeah."

"Good." She smiled, nodding.

He looked at her as if waiting for her to say something else. She kept quiet.

"What?" he asked.

"Nothing."

"You're spesh," he said and pushed out of his seat.

"I try," she said and held out her hand. He gave her a low-five as he passed and stopped before he stepped into the kitchen.

"I took Annie," he said, "if you must know." She nodded. "It was nice." She looked at him. "She's not my girlfriend."

"That's okay. So long as you had a good time, the rest can come later."

"Mum," he said disparagingly but, as he walked away, she saw him smile.

Chapter 10

Claire hadn't been bowling with adults for years – all her recent trips had been for birthday parties where she'd sat and watched rather than play. She walked into the noise of twelve lanes packed with players and went to the bar as she tried to spot someone she knew.

Amy saw her first and gave Claire a quick hug. "Hi! I've been looking for you. We've got four lanes for the night and I've commandeered this one for the newbie group."

She led Claire to the last lane. Mike was sat at the computer talking to Ben. Eva listened in on the conversation and pulled at strands of her hair.

"Should be decent games with the five of us," said Amy.

"I don't know about decent," Claire said. "I haven't bowled in ages."

"I hadn't before I joined the group."

"We're going to storm it then."

The others greeted Claire warmly when she got to the lane. Mike offered her a lopsided smile and she felt something twinge in her belly for the briefest moment. She hadn't felt anything like that for a long time.

"How are you?" he asked.

"I'm doing alright." She wanted him to give her that smile again.

He glanced over her shoulder. "Glad you decided to come back to the Triple H."

"What's the Triple H?"

"Please don't start that again," Jane said from behind her.

Mike smiled that wonderful smile again. "The Hadlington Happy Honchos."

Jane stood between them. "It's not called that," she said, affecting the tone of an older sister dealing with a pesky little brother. "He's just doing it to wind me up."

Mike winked at Claire. "I think it fits perfectly."

"Hadlington Happy Honchos," said Claire and Jane looked at her with wide eyes.

"It doesn't even make sense," Jane complained. "How does Honcho even fit into that context?"

"According to Google," Ben said looking at his phone, "you're the honcho."

"And you're happy," said Mike quickly.

Jane smiled thinly. "I still don't think it's funny."

Mike squinted and smiled. "I know," he said.

Jane sighed and turned her attention to Claire and Amy. "I'm glad you could all make it. I hope you have a lovely evening."

"We will," said Mike.

Jane shook her head slowly and rolled her eyes at Claire. "Have a good time."

The newbies got their bowling shoes and balls while arguing good-naturedly about whether to put up the lane bumpers or not. They decided to. Claire sat next to Ben, and everyone seemed to be talking at once. None of them had bowled recently so the conversation turned to bragging and Mike and Ben set up a bet as to who would score the most. The winner got a drink and Claire found herself getting dragged into it too.

Mike sat at the computer to put in the running order and Claire was first up. She stepped onto the lane and looked at the pins.

"I don't know if I should tell you this," Mike said. "But I can see through your blouse."

For a moment she believed him and felt the lightest tinges of embarrassment colour her cheeks then she turned to him with a smile. "If you can see through this cardigan then the blouse would be no match for your X-ray vision, would it?"

Mike smiled and Ben laughed.

"Sledger gets sledged," Ben said.

Claire lined up her shot and knocked down four pins. Her next shot left one pin standing doggedly upright.

"Unlucky," said Mike.

"Ignore him," said Ben. He took his shots and left three pins standing.

"Unluckier," said Mike, with a grin.

Eva glared at him as she walked onto the lane.

"Wouldn't dare say a word," he said and held up his hands.

She held up her index finger until he was quiet then took her shots. Three pins stayed up and she glared at him again.

Mike got up for his turn and glanced over his shoulder. "Are we ready?"

"You've got a bloody great big hole right in the arse of your trousers, mate," said Ben.

"Your thong is showing," said Claire.

Mike gave an exaggerated "ha-ha" and wiggled his bum. He lined up his shot and got a strike. When he turned to them a big grin creased his face. "I am your master."

"Only a master of evil, Darth," said Claire.

Mike laughed. He gave her a high five and sat next to Eva. Between shots, Claire watched Mike and Eva talking but it seemed like he was asking her questions rather than having a conversation. Claire sat with Ben in an uncomfortable silence she couldn't seem to break until a song she hadn't heard in ages came through the sound system. She began to sing along and realised Ben was singing quietly too.

"You know this song?"

"Of course," he said. "I love it."

"I thought I was the only person in the world who'd ever heard it."

They sang along until the instrumental break.

"I saw it on *The Chart Show* one Saturday morning," he said.

"Me too." She touched his arm briefly and it made him jump. "I went into town that afternoon and bought the single. You are the first person I've ever met who not only knew it existed but could sing along to it as well."

"Good taste, you see."

And as they talked about music and favourite albums, Claire found herself relaxing into the conversation.

* * *

54

Mike won the game and celebrated with an elaborate bit of hand waving that amused Claire enough to applaud him. He bowed for her.

"Right," he said. "Let's get some drinks."

"Sounds good to me," said Ben.

"I'll set up the next game," said Amy. "I want to see if he has any other victory dances."

Claire's mobile rang and showed Scott on the screen. She had to press the handset to her ear over the general hubbub. "You okay?"

He said something she barely heard. Mouthing "I'll take it outside" to Amy, Claire walked out to the car park. The warm night was almost cloudless, punctuated by a smattering of stars.

"Mum? Are you there? Did you hear what I said?"

"No, it was too noisy. I'm at the bowling alley."

"You're bowling?" he asked, his tone incredulous.

"Don't sound so surprised."

Someone shrieked with laughter from inside and she walked away from the doors.

"Who've you gone there with?"

"My friends group," Claire said.

"Are you winning?"

"No."

"Is everything okay?"

"Everything's fine, you rang me, what's up?"

"Not much."

Claire looked around as she waited. The bowling alley was sandwiched between residential houses – shielded by a line of tall trees – and the derelict Hadlington Town football stadium. No one else was in the car park and the night seemed very quiet.

"I've been talking to Dad," he said finally. "He said he needs to speak with you."

"No," she said and felt a familiar flare of anger in her belly. "Come on, mate, you know that's not how we do this. Things don't go through you."

"But he said he's tried speaking to you."

"He's got in touch twice this week and was drunk both times – including the call in the middle of the night."

"He said he's sorry."

"Has he told you what he wants to talk about?"

"No."

The doors opened and let out a quick stream of laughter and music. Claire glanced behind her, aware of someone walking towards the cars parked by the trees. The door closed and cut off the noise.

"I can't talk to him now because I'm standing in the car park."

"That's okay," he said quietly. "He doesn't know I've rung."

Claire felt her anger melt away because this wasn't coming from Greg, it was Scott trying to do the right thing. "Thank you, love, I'll speak to him."

"Thanks, Mum. Enjoy the rest of your weekend."

The call disconnected. Gravel crunched behind her and she turned but couldn't see anyone. Movement caught her eye as she stepped towards the door. She looked towards the road and gasped, involuntarily.

Someone in a grey hoodie was facing her as they stood on the pavement under a street lamp. She tried to breathe but couldn't. Fear buzzed through her veins and her hand hurt from gripping the phone so tightly.

Chapter 11

A sound from the shadows.

Was somebody there?

The hoodie hadn't moved and that reassured her. The car park stretched a good hundred yards to the road which would give her plenty of time to get back inside if they came at her.

More gravel crunched and a quick scream startled her. A cat rushed out of the shadows and crossed the car park.

A cat? A fucking cat?

Claire looked back towards the road. The hoodie had moved out of the pool of light now and she saw something hanging from their right hand. It looked like a loop of rope. Claire took a step towards the bowling alley.

A dog came bounding from behind the trees near the road and ran straight at the hoodie, who knelt down and clipped on a lead.

Claire felt her adrenaline surge die away. A dog walker? She'd been scared by a cat and a bloody dog walker? Christ almighty, she needed to get a grip.

* * *

Claire was halfway up the stairs to the lanes before she realised someone was coming down. She glanced up and groaned inwardly.

"Claire!" said Keith, with an air of forced jollity. "I was wondering if I'd get to see you tonight."

She gripped the banister as he closed the gap between them. He stopped two steps above her.

"Had to nip out to take a call," she said and held up her phone as if for proof.

"I see. Very loud in there, isn't it?"

She made a non-committal noise because she really didn't want to get drawn into a conversation with him.

He didn't seem to mind and smiled broadly. "Are you keeping well?"

"Yes, and how about you?"

"Can't complain," he said. "Well apart from the usual, you know." He gave her a theatrical wink and didn't seem at all put out when she failed to respond. "Enjoying the bowling though."

"Uh-huh." She looked past him, willing someone to come down and distract him.

"I love bowling. I come a lot."

"Do you?"

He looked at her without expression. "Oh yes, I come a great deal."

She heard the innuendo and waited. She'd been mistaken with the dog-walking hoodie and the last thing she wanted now was to accuse someone of saying something out of turn when they hadn't. "I see."

"I bet you handle balls well."

No expression again. Was she really getting this wrong or was he being deliberately obnoxious?

"Not as well as you, I imagine," she said and watched his face. He didn't flinch. "I have to get back."

"That's a shame because I enjoyed speaking to you. Especially after that misunderstanding back in the Sun."

"Of course."

"Enjoy your game."

"You too," she said. "Enjoy your balls."

He looked at her sharply, so she favoured him with what she hoped was a sweet smile, giving him a wide berth as she went up the stairs.

* * *

Amy was talking to Ben when Claire got back to the lane. Eva was absorbed in her phone and Jane was talking animatedly to Mike. Her hands danced with her words and occasionally brushed his arm.

He saw Claire and pursed his lips as he nodded very subtly towards Jane. She got his point immediately and pursed her own lips.

Jane caught his expression and glanced around. "Hello, Claire," she said and rested her hand on Mike's arm. "Having a good evening?"

"She's not happy because I won so decisively," Mike said.

"That's not the case at all," Claire said with a smile. "Did you get those drinks in?"

"No, I..."

"Oh were you going for drinks?" asked Jane. "That's my fault," she told Claire. "Our game finished, and I was checking on everyone else and saw Mike standing here like a spare part."

"Spare part," he repeated and Claire nodded gravely at him.

"Get your drinks, you two. I think my lot are ready to start again anyway."

Jane patted his arm and nodded at Claire before she went back to her own lane.

"So," Claire said.

"So," he said. "Jane's not exactly subtle and I'm crap at reading signs. Is she being friendly or, you know, over-friendly?"

"It looked over-friendly to me."

"Thanks." He looked relieved. "I owe you one."

"Call it even after you helped with Keith on Wednesday."

"Have you seen him this evening?"

"I have. He was as charming as before."

"Did you want me to speak to him?"

"No," she said. "I think I gave as good as I got."

"I'm happy to hear that, I can imagine he wasn't so pleased."

"I don't think so."

They found space at the bar and while Mike gave his order Claire stood with her back to it.

"Ben's being quite chatty tonight," he said when the barmaid went to get the drinks.

"I think Amy could get conversation out of a rock."

"Pity it doesn't work with Eva."

Claire watched her. She was still engrossed in her phone and pulling at strands of her hair. She looked up as if sensing someone was watching her. Claire smiled and Eva returned it.

"You were talking to her okay earlier," Claire said as she turned back to the bar.

"I was talking and she was listening. We've only really just met though, so perhaps she's not as comfortable talking to new people as we are."

"I'm not usually that comfortable," Claire said.

Mike smiled. "Neither am I, usually. But you're very easy to talk to."

"Thanks." Her stomach flip-flopped quickly.

"We ought to go for a coffee or something."

The flip-flop again. Had he just asked her out? "A coffee?"

Something in the way she said it made him look as if he was worried he'd made a mistake. "Yeah, just to talk crap about people."

"Right."

"I didn't mean as anything else."

"Of course not."

She realised she wouldn't have minded if he had meant it as a date. It wasn't what she'd joined the group for but she liked him. He was easy on the eye and there was something about that lopsided smile of his.

"Well that's good then," he said and held her gaze for a moment too long as the waitress put their drinks on a tray.

* * *

Ben edged the second game and tried to do a victory dance but his coordination was off and made him look like he was fighting an invisible man.

The third game was fun and even Eva joined in the banter. It came down to the last frame and Mike and Ben were so far ahead sides were quickly chosen. Amy supported Mike while Eva and Claire got behind Ben.

"And after our nice chat at the bar," Mike said and affected a disappointed air.

Claire gave him a thumbs up and a cheesy grin. "I like to win."

"Yeah, yeah," he said.

Ben won. He threw up his hands in victory and lumbered back up the lane. Eva sat down quickly and Claire realised he was going to hug her moments before he did. He held her almost at arm's length in the kind of hug you see people do on TV when they don't really know the other person.

* * *

The car park was almost empty when they left and the trees moved in a breeze Claire could barely feel. She wanted to talk with Mike and the more she thought about it, the more she liked the idea of having a coffee with him.

Amy kissed everyone on the cheek. Ben and Eva said their goodbyes and walked to their cars.

Mike took his keys from his pocket. "Don't forget our date," he said and smiled.

"Okay." She enjoyed the sensation his words caused and decided to grasp life with both hands. "I'll be outside The Kino on Monday evening at 6 p.m. If you're there you can buy me a drink."

"Seriously?" He looked startled. "But I have plans on Monday evening."

"I'd cancel them," Amy suggested.

"You have a bit of a dilemma then, don't you?" Claire said and with a breezy "goodnight" walked to her car.

Chapter 12

I enjoy watching you, living your life, following your routines. Existing.

I wish you didn't. I watch and imagine you slipping off the kerb and breaking your leg or tripping as you cross the road to fall under a bus that drags your carcass along the tarmac.

I dream of finding myself driving alongside you and nudging your car. You look over in a panic but before you can do anything else, I force you up onto the verge. In those dreams, there's always a steep ditch on the other side and you end up wedged into it, dirty water filling your car as I stand above, listening to your screams.

You beg me for mercy.

I spit in your face and remind you of the past, of what you did. And, more importantly, of what you didn't do.

I made sure you saw me yesterday because I want you to see me watching you, I want you to feel my presence, I want you to be nervous.

I want you to see me so can you never forget the terrible thing you did.

Chapter 13

The alarm woke Claire.

She swiped the sound away and brushed hair out of her face and looked at the lines of sunlight that arced across the ceiling. The house was quiet and all was at peace.

She thought of Mike and the look on his face when she called his bluff and felt a warm stirring in her belly. It had been a while since anyone had asked her out – if you didn't count the twats who'd done so as soon as they discovered her marriage was on the rocks – and it was nice to get that attention from someone she found so charming.

Would he be outside The Kino?

She hoped so.

When the alarm went off again she threw back the duvet and padded to the bathroom.

* * *

Sundays were her days, which, in truth, usually meant catching up on everything she hadn't done during the week. It was once a family day, another thing lost when Greg left. The arrangement that Scott spent the weekend there had knocked Claire's world seriously askew for the first few weeks. Sundays became a yawning abyss. She would while away the minutes before Scott came home but he, having been Greg's sole object of attention all weekend, wanted some peace. She wanted to talk but he just wanted to escape to his room and catch up on FIFA.

She dressed in a T-shirt and shorts and went downstairs, standing by the patio doors and checking her phone while the kettle boiled. She made herself a strong coffee and took it out onto the patio. The sun was low and off to her left and she sat at the bistro table, feeling the soft warmth on her face. She enjoyed the morning smell in the air.

The entry door opened and closed and she heard the brisk patter of claws on concrete. Harry home from a walk. She opened her eyes and squinted into the light and wondered if Roger had mended the gap in the fence. When Harry didn't appear she assumed Roger had done his work and closed her eyes again.

"Lovely morning."

"Morning, Roger." She knew from experience he wouldn't leave without trying to have a chat, so she opened her eyes and shielded them with her hand.

Roger stood on his patio and leaned on the fence watching her.

"You're up early," she said.

"The joy of dog ownership," he said with a rueful grin. "Annie's asleep and Lou's doing something on the computer. Since I was about to go on my run, I drew the short straw for toilet duties."

"Lucky you."

63

"I know." She watched his eyes move to look at her legs. "Have you already been for your run?"

"I never run on Sunday mornings."

"That's a shame," Roger said and looked back at her face. "We should run together."

"Another day perhaps."

"I'd like that." Harry barked at something and Roger glanced at him, annoyed. "No, not that. Oh, you stupid dog." He disappeared behind the fence and she heard Harry bark again. Roger shouted "no" and then made a disgusted sound. "Bollocks." His head reappeared over the fence. "I'll see you later, Claire."

"I'm sure," she said.

* * *

Claire stripped the beds, put the sheets on to wash and blitzed the ironing pile fuelled with coffee and the first two Killers albums. She made lunch and sat under the shade of the umbrella to eat with her legs and feet sticking out into the bright sunshine.

Her mobile rang as she was about to go back into the kitchen to get a drink.

"Hello, Eva, this is a nice surprise. Did you enjoy yourself last night?"

"Yes, apart from Ben trying to chat me up."

Claire wasn't sure she'd heard correctly. "He chatted you up?"

"Yes, it got very annoying."

"I didn't realise. If he made you uncomfortable you should have said something."

"Would you have had a word with him?"

"Absolutely."

"That's nice of you. And how did things go with Keith? I noticed you two talking."

"We exchanged a few words on the stairs."

"Was he horrible again?"

"I think so, but it was like before, innuendo and misdirection all rolled into one." Claire told Eva what was said. "I think I embarrassed him in the end and that's why he gave up."

"I wouldn't have thought to do that. Maybe you could give me some lessons in case Ben tries again."

Ben hadn't struck Claire as that type of bloke, but she barely knew him. "I will but I'm sure everything'll be fine."

"Thanks," said Eva and sounded grateful. "Do you think we could meet up for a chat?"

"I'd like that."

"Perhaps before the friends group? Are you about tomorrow?"

"I'm out tomorrow evening," Claire said. "And I'm at yoga on Tuesday. We could meet up one lunchtime in town and grab a bite to eat?"

"How about Tuesday? Can you suggest anywhere nice? I've been away for a while, as I said, and I'm willing to be guided."

"There's a place called The Kino that does a nice lunchtime menu. We could meet there for half twelve?"

Eva agreed and they said their goodbyes. Claire found herself thinking about Ben. Had Eva misread him completely and, if that was the case, had Claire done the same thing to Keith?

* * *

Claire spent the afternoon making lasagne to freeze for some weekday meals. Roger and Lou waved over the entry gate when they took Harry out for a walk.

A car pulled up at a little after five as Claire debated options for dinner. The entry door clattered and Scott came into the yard a moment or two later. He had his mobile at his ear and a scooter over one shoulder. He nodded at her through the window.

"Dad's outside," he said. "He wants a word."

Why couldn't Greg get the bloody message? She wiped her hands on a tea towel and walked up the entry barefoot. She wasn't in the mood for this – it'd been a nice afternoon, after all – and she didn't want another discussion that ended up talking about them as some golden couple – his words – that had run aground.

Greg leaned on his car, arms folded. His thick dark hair showed plenty of grey at the temples now.

"Hello," he said and let his arms drop.

She thought, for a moment, he was going to try and hug her, but he didn't.

"It's good to see you, Claire."

"What's up?"

He frowned. "What's up? Is that all I get?"

"What else did you want? You made the choice for us that we" – she pointed first at her chest then his – "were over. You can't keep turning up."

"I know."

"So what's with the drunk phone calls and messages? We can be civil if we're discussing Scott but there's no need for us to talk about anything else." She rubbed her arm. "You know how hard it was for me and this, to be honest, feels like you're rubbing my nose in it." She wanted to tell him that it still hurt but didn't want to give him the satisfaction.

"I'm not, I promise you. I just wanted to make sure you're okay." He looked at his dirty Nikes then at a tyre before looking back at her. "I can't get the idea of you being run over out of my head. It scared me. I worry about you."

"But you can't do that." She felt her anger rise and struggled to keep her voice level. She didn't want to argue with him in the street. "Unless it directly affects Scott, you don't have any right to worry about me."

"I still care."

"Why?"

"Because I can't turn that off. We were together for a long time before I was stupid and I can't just deny that history."

"I have," she said, as coldly as she could. There was a small but sour delight at his flinch.

He shook his head. "I don't believe you."

"You don't have to."

"Just tell me you're okay."

"Why?"

"Because I need to know."

"Do you have any idea how selfish you sound, Greg? I'm going in."

"I never meant this to happen, you know."

"Well," she said and opened the entry door. "It did."

* * *

Scott was sitting on the back step with his knees to his chest and from the look on his face he'd heard everything.

"You don't listen to him, do you?" he muttered.

She felt the familiar sinking feeling she got whenever they discussed Greg. "I listen to every word he says," she said carefully.

"He's worried and you just shut him down."

"And if you were listening, I assume you heard my explanation as to why I shut him down?"

His eyes glistened. "I heard but how can you say it?" A stray tear escaped and tracked down his cheek.

"He left me, Scott."

"He left us," he said, pointedly. "But I still see him."

Claire took a deep breath and let it out slowly. One, two, three, she counted. "He's your dad. He hurt me."

"People hurt each other all the time. He's told you he's sorry, why won't you give him a chance?"

Part of the agreement Claire and Greg came to was that they wouldn't apportion blame in front of Scott. He was fourteen at the time and neither felt it necessary for him to know about Matilda, and while it made sense to Claire then it was now something of an albatross. The quickest way to shut the conversation down would be to tell the truth – Greg left because he'd had an affair and the guilt had pushed him to the bottom of a bottle of Jack Daniel's on repeated occasions. She wanted to shout that it was his choice. He chose to fuck someone else and walk out of their lives, nobody else did. It was all on him.

But she couldn't.

"It's not about giving chances, Scott."

"Well that's bollocks."

"Scott!" She could feel herself getting wound up, the blood pumping around her veins.

He stood up defiantly and swiped at the tear track as if embarrassed she'd witnessed it. "Why can't you work it out, eh? Why can't you make things better?"

"Because that's not how it works," she said, more sharply than she'd intended. Her anger towards Greg was acid in her throat. He'd put them in this situation and now she and Scott were falling out over it.

"CBA," he said, shaking his head.

"Well that's a grown-up attitude to take," she said without thinking.

He stalked into the kitchen. "Except I'm apparently not a grown-up because no one pays any bloody attention to what I want."

Claire watched him go and tried to keep her breathing steady. It wasn't his fault, she told herself, or hers. This was all down to Greg.

* * *

Scott had thumped his way upstairs and hidden in his bedroom behind a closed door and loud music. Claire needed some air and decided to go for a walk.

The sun was low and glaring where it wasn't hidden behind buildings and she kept herself in the shade. She walked to the market square and back. As the end of

Shelley Street she had the sensation of being watched and glanced back.

Someone in a grey hoodie stood just this side of the Co-op. The person wasn't looking at a phone or waiting for a dog but seemed to be looking directly at her. Except that was impossible to tell because their face was hidden by the shadow of the hood. From this distance she couldn't make out their height or build. There was nothing untoward to attract attention.

"Hello!" she called and raised a hand.

The hoodie didn't respond and, feeling suddenly brave, Claire walked a few paces.

"Hello!"

Still no response and even if the hoodie wasn't looking at her, being shouted at twice should make them at least pay attention.

Claire kept walking. After the confrontation with Greg, she was done with being frightened. The hoodie tilted their head as if considering their options. Claire began to jog. The hoodie turned and ran back towards the Co-op entrance. Claire picked up her pace and tried to work out her next move. She'd obviously frightened the stranger and wanted to keep that pressure up but what would she do if she caught them – pull off the hood and demand to know what they were doing?

The hoodie disappeared around the corner and Claire ran harder to close the gap. As she passed the Co-op entrance, Ben came around the corner with his head down. She ran into the road to avoid him and he looked up. Startled, he held out his arms as if to ward her off, but she was too close and his left hand slapped her belly and she stumbled.

Claire's momentum died. She stopped and put her hands on her knees and felt the sting in her belly.

"Shit, I'm so sorry," said Ben. "Are you okay? I didn't mean to hit you."

"I'm fine."

"If you're sure." He stood quietly as she got her breath back. "I didn't realise you ran."

"I didn't tell you." She stood up straight and arched her back.

"Of course." He frowned at her jeans. "Are you mid-jog or heading home?"

"Heading home."

"You live in the centre?" he asked, looking back towards the market square.

"No," she said and realised he'd seen her running towards him. "I live back that way."

"But you were..."

"It's a long story."

"I won't ask."

"So do you live around here?"

"No." He looked at his fidgeting fingers. "I needed something from here." He looked at her belly. "Are you sure I didn't hurt you?"

"I'm positive."

He smiled sheepishly and glanced towards the Co-op entrance.

"You can go, you know."

"Okay. See you Wednesday?"

"You will."

He gave a little wave and went into the shop. Claire looked towards the market square but the hoodie was nowhere in sight. She walked home slowly.

Chapter 14

It had been a good day.

The auditors had signed off the accounts and included a note to James saying how impressed they were with Claire. He let her go home early on the strength of it and she went eagerly. The sun was shining and the weekend beckoned. Scott was staying at her parents' because Greg, for an anniversary treat, had splashed out on a hotel in London. She was looking forward to a meal in Covent Garden and a trip to the theatre on Saturday evening.

The street was almost empty of cars when she got home.

The front door was open slightly.

Confused, she got out of the car and pushed the door. It opened gently onto a quiet house. She checked the lock but there was no damage, so she closed it carefully. She put her bag down and listened but couldn't hear anything untoward.

She made a fist around her car keys and went cautiously into the dining room. The windows there and in the lounge were intact and the kitchen door was closed.

Back in the hall she stood by the front door, ready to open it quickly if necessary. Her heart thumped so hard she thought an intruder would be able to hear it. She counted to three then shouted, "I've called the police, they're on their way."

There was movement from upstairs.

"I'm going to lock you in." Further movement but no other sound. "They'll be here in a minute."

She opened the door and was about to step through when someone called her name softly. She froze.

"Claire?"

Greg? My God, had he come home early and been attacked? She rushed upstairs and along the landing to their bedroom.

Greg stood at the window and jumped like a startled rabbit.

He looked fine. There were no marks on his face, but his gaze was unfocussed.

"What the hell's going on?" she demanded. "Where's your car?"

He looked at his feet. "Back in town."

And then she smelled the alcohol. "Seriously, Greg? It's three oh-bloody-clock in the afternoon."

He'd always liked a drink but had kept it under control until a couple of months ago when he was moved to a different team in the hospital. Although he hadn't said much, it seemed more desk-bound than he preferred, with significantly less patient contact. To make matters worse the group had a strong drinking culture and Greg was enthusiastic. Claire tolerated it at first, though early evenings spent watching his dinner congeal in the oven quickly tarnished that, especially when he rang to ask for a lift with increasing frequency.

"I don't know what to say," he said and looked lost.

"Was it a hard day?" she asked sarcastically.

He tried to focus on her eyes. "You could say that."

"Unless somebody died, there's no reason for you to be at home pissed at three in the afternoon." He looked so pained it frightened her and took the edge off her building anger. "Shit. Did somebody die?"

Greg sat on the edge of the bed and put his chin in his hands. "No." He sounded defeated. "But that's not the point."

She bit her lip because screaming and shouting wouldn't help either of them now. "What then?" Her voice was as calm as she could make it. "So what is the point? Did you get sacked?"

He laughed bitterly. "Is that what you think is important?"

She blanched at the sneer in his voice. "I don't know what the fuck to think."

"No," he said firmly. "I didn't get sacked. It was nothing as simple as that, it's just a shit situation."

She held out her hands. "Tell me then."

He breathed deeply. "It's just life." He sounded hopeless. "I haven't told you everything."

"What do you mean?"

"I've been keeping a secret," he said quietly. "I always thought you could see right through me."

"Not anymore apparently." Her mind raced. She felt bewildered and angry and sad and scared. "What is it?"

His eyes filled with tears. "I'm so sorry, Claire, but it wasn't my fault. Things weren't good here…"

The realisation hit her. "Don't do this, you arsehole, don't…"

"And Matilda was there, one thing led to another."

"Bastard," she said through gritted teeth.

"Neither of us intended for it to happen," he said and paused, as if trying to focus. "But it did."

"Where?" He looked at her blankly. "Not here, not in our bed?"

"No," he said and had the gall to look offended. "Never here."

"So where?"

"Out and about. In the car." He grew hesitant. "In the lay-by near the woods. It wasn't for long…"

She couldn't take it all in. Worse, it looked like he wanted to say something else, but she didn't want to hear it. What could top this bombshell? Was he going to confess it was still going on, that those drunken evenings with colleagues she'd picked him up from had actually been assignations with this bloody Matilda? She glared at him and her veins were warmed by hatred.

"I'll go," he said. "What're you going to tell Scott?"

"Not a fucking thing. I'll leave that pleasure to you."

He stood up. "Really?"

"Yes really. I'm not making excuses for you." She stepped away from the door so he could get by.

"Thank you," he said and looked into her eyes.

She looked away. "I'm not trying to help you."

He left the room and she stood still. Her hands clenched into fists as tears rolled down her cheeks. She waited until he closed the door quietly behind himself before allowing the sobs to come.

Chapter 15

The bouquet of flowers was pinned under the nearside windscreen wiper.

Claire saw them as soon as she came out onto the street although it took a moment or two to figure out what the colourful lump was.

They'd clearly been positioned carefully so the stems were held securely and the flowers spread across the glass in a blaze of colour. A card was buried among the heads. She picked it out carefully. On one side, in a small, neat script, it read, 'From a mystery admirer'. The other side was blank.

She looked around but the street was empty. She pulled the flowers free. They were beautiful although the anonymity of their delivery made her a little nervous. She took them into the house and filled a vase, then put them on the windowsill.

She kept a watchful eye for her stalker or the grey hoodie on her run. The weight of the rape alarm in the pocket of her shorts was reassuring. Old Man Stan stood by the butcher's and shouted, "Hello," and waved his hand high in the air. She waved back.

The graffiti on the storm drain had changed. Additional supports had been painted onto the gallows and an empty noose hung from the arm. There were now four dashes lined up underneath.

* * *

Scott was eating cornflakes when Claire came down to the kitchen after her shower.

"Morning," she said brightly, not wanting to drag last night's outburst into a fresh day.

He grunted through a mouthful of cereal.

"Did you sleep okay?"

He grunted again then gestured at the flowers with his spoon.

"Flowers?" she said.

He nodded and finished eating. "Are they from someone at your singles club?"

"It's not a singles club." She sighed. He was clearly still raw from yesterday so it wasn't worth explaining again. "I don't know who they're from or even if they're for me."

"Eh? So where were they?"

"Under the windscreen wipers."

"They're for you then. Was there a message?"

"Uh-huh, but it's not got my name on it. Maybe they're for Lou or someone else and the person got the wrong address."

"Why would Roger put flowers for his wife on your car?" Scott's eyes widened. "Do you think she's having an affair?"

"No, of course not. I'm just saying I don't know if they're for me."

"But you've put them on display in the kitchen?"

"I've put them in a vase to keep them alive," she said with strained patience.

"Yeah, okay, Mum." He spooned the last of the cornflakes into his mouth, rinsed the bowl and put it into the dishwasher. "Oh and I won't want dinner tonight. I'm eating at Charlie's."

"Okay," she said and felt relieved she wouldn't have to tell him about meeting Mike.

* * *

"I wish people randomly left flowers on my car," said Amy.

She'd texted earlier and now they were having a gossipy lunch in a Costa in the town centre. Amy unwrapped her sandwich and removed some tomato with a look of disgust before starting to eat.

"They might not be for me," Claire said as she bit into her own sandwich.

"True. It's likely though, eh?"

"It could be a mistake."

"If they were for you though, I could share your romance vicariously."

Claire laughed as she sipped her coffee. "I'm not in the market for romance."

"Ah," said Amy, eyes shining. "Not even with our Mike?"

Claire felt a small thrill at the mention of his name. "No."

"He seemed keen on Saturday."

"I think we were having a laugh, but I hope he's there tonight."

"He'll be there."

"You sound very sure."

"Why shouldn't I be? You're an attractive woman." Amy finished her first sandwich and drank some coffee. "So what're your first impressions of the group?"

"I like it. Eva and I are meeting for a coffee tomorrow and I saw Ben last night too, going into the Co-op near me."

Amy frowned. "Have you moved then?"

Something about her tone made Claire pause. "Why?"

"He lives on the new estate by the A14 and that's quite a trip to the Co-op."

"Maybe he's got a friend nearby."

"Maybe," said Amy, taking the second half of her sandwich out of the box and searching for the tomato. "Have you spoken to any of the other members?"

"I've had a couple of chats with Keith."

"Ah, Keith. He can sometimes be a bit full-on."

"Full-on?" Claire frowned. "I'd have said creepy."

"Really? What did he do?"

"Nothing particularly but he was a bit overpowering and full of innuendo."

"He made you feel uncomfortable?"

"Yes but I gave as good as I got and he didn't seem to like it."

"We've had a couple of issues with him so I'll let Jane know. The group's supposed to make people feel welcome. If someone's being a creep, it's no good for anyone."

They ate in silence for a while until Amy leaned forward. "You genuinely have no idea who sent you those flowers?" The disbelief was clear in her voice.

"Not one."

"A true mystery admirer, eh? I think that's so romantic."

"You watch too many films."

"Maybe," Amy said. "But who wouldn't want a bit of romance in their life?"

Chapter 16

James wanted Claire to run through some figures with him so the afternoon raced by and it wasn't until she heard people calling, "Goodbye," that she noticed the time.

Outside in the sunshine she felt an excited tingle about whether Mike would be there. It had been a long time since she'd experienced anything like this and she missed it. This is what life was supposed to be about. This thrill was what she should be experiencing.

With time on her side, she walked at a leisurely pace and window-shopped when she felt like it. Closer to The Kino and her thoughts began to turn. What if he didn't turn up? A dejected walk back to her car wouldn't be too bad, but seeing him on Wednesday would.

The Kino bar and restaurant was built into an old theatre and the hippodrome playbills had been preserved on the side of the building. It stood on a small plaza that had been urban-renewed to within an inch of its life and lined with restaurants and fast-food places. The central area was open with steps built high enough that they could be used as seating for people to eat their lunch or pass the time of day.

Mike was standing by the steps and clearly hadn't spotted her. She felt a sudden rush of happiness that he was there, and she couldn't help noticing how good he looked in his suit. In his right hand he held a small bunch of what looked like daisies and that made her smile.

He smiled broadly when he finally saw her. She crossed the plaza and they stood awkwardly in front of one another as if unsure of what to do next.

"Hi," she said.

"You came."

"So did you." She laughed and that seemed to break the ice.

They kissed each other's cheek.

"Before I forget," he said and handed her the daisies.

She took them carefully. He must have been holding them in a specific way because in her hand they quickly flopped. She looked at them. He looked at them and then at her.

He smiled. "Sorry about that."

Could those flowers this morning have been from him? Would that make sense? "They're not as good as the others," she said.

The confused look on his face made it clear he didn't know anything about them. "Eh?"

"Nothing," she said quickly. "Don't worry about it."

"Shall we go in?" He gestured for her to go then followed her up the steps and through the doors.

The main room was long and wide, and the original brickwork and metal joists had been exposed to give the space an air of shabby chic. None of the chairs and tables seemed to match. A staircase led up the right wall to a mezzanine.

"I like it," he said and gazed at the ceiling festooned with large industrial lampshades. "I've never been in here."

"The food's good too."

"Let me get us a drink and then we'll decide if we're eating."

"Well I hope we're eating," she said.

"Thank goodness for that. I'm starving."

She felt butterflies in her stomach.

They went to the bar and after they were served, he toasted her. "To friends."

"To friends," she said and touched glasses.

"Where did you want to sit?"

"Up there," she said and led him up to the mezzanine.

Three floor-to-ceiling windows looked out over the plaza. Claire picked a table by the middle window. He sat in a wash of sunlight that coloured half his face a burnished orange and highlighted a hint of stubble. She saw herself reflected in his glasses. When he took them off to rub the bridge of his nose she decided he had kind eyes.

She realised she liked him.

"Have I got something on me?" he asked.

"Eh?"

"My head. You look like you've found something you don't like and can't figure out how to mention it.

"No, you're fine. I was just admiring your hair."

He touched a hand to the left side of his head as if frightened he'd find a stick of dynamite there. "What's wrong with it?"

"Nothing. I like the way the sunlight catches it."

"Not as good as it would with you."

She laughed and sipped her spritzer. "You're a real charmer, aren't you?"

"I try." He leaned forward, suddenly serious. "Can I tell you a secret?"

She leaned forward too, trying to look equally serious. "I don't know, can you?"

"I'm not charming really. It's all an act."

"That's a very brave thing to say."

"I believe in being honest. And as you can probably tell, I haven't been on a date in a while."

Claire sat back in her chair. "Me either."

"Well, that levels things up a bit." He smiled that lopsided smile. She liked that he used it easily and often. "So where does that leave us?"

He wasn't floundering but she could see he wasn't entirely comfortable and decided to make things easier for both of them. "I think it's time to eat, don't you?"

* * *

Their food came quickly, and the waitress was chatty as she put their plates down. They ate in companionable silence and the mezzanine was busier by the time they'd finished.

"That was lovely," Mike said and wiped the corners of his mouth. He put the napkin on his cleared plate and leaned back. "So what do you do, Claire?"

"I'm a finance manager, which is as exciting as it sounds. How about you?"

"Music teacher. And like you, it's as exciting as it sounds."

"Where do you teach?"

"The Academy in Marham, years seven through nine. The age when most of them are really discovering music and don't want to listen to an old fart like me explain it to them."

"Well that's jobs out of the way," she said with a smile. "How about childhood pets?"

"Is this what they call speed dating?"

"Just answer the question."

"A goldfish called Fred that I won at a fairground. My folks expected him to live for a month but he lasted about a decade. How about you?"

"A cat called Smudge who I adored. I tried to change his name when I discovered Snoopy but he never took to it."

"Were you married?" he asked.

"I was," she said. "But not to Smudge."

"Quite. So how long were you married for?"

"Long enough," she said. "Were you married?"

"I was and for about the same length of time as you."

The obvious next question hung in the air like a dark cloud of past experiences waiting patiently to be pulled down.

"Did you want to talk about the reasons?" she asked.

He pursed his lips and looked out of the window briefly. "Did you?"

Now Claire looked out of the window. "Not really. A bit early in the evening to start bringing stuff down, don't you think?"

"Agreed, but I'm a bit rusty with this kind of thing. Have you been on many dates?"

"In my life or since my marriage ended?"

He smiled. "Since your marriage ended."

"A few. Nothing particularly serious. How about you?"

"A few." He leaned forward, elbows on the table. "A lot of my friends have set me up on blind dates; the 'my wife's best mate is single again too, you'll love her' kind of thing where you go out and sit quietly in a restaurant and realise you have nothing in common."

"That's always fun."

"Isn't it? I sometimes wonder if I'm cut out for dating now."

"Really?"

"Yes. I enjoyed being married and I miss the companionship but sometimes you just need a bit of space, if you know what I mean?"

"Absolutely. I haven't been actively pursuing a relationship." She meant it but there was no denying the almost electric tension she could feel between them.

"Same here."

Their eyes met and she felt that peculiar flip-flop sensation again.

"That's childhood pets and our stance on dating sorted then," she said.

Mike smiled his lopsided smile and took a swig of his drink. "So what's next? Films?"

"Our favourites?" She glanced out the window and saw someone across the plaza looking into a pizza place window with their grey hoodie pulled up over their head.

Mike said something but his words were blips of sound she couldn't quite hear. Claire felt her pulse race as a fine line of sweat gathered on her upper lip. Surely not?

"Claire?"

She took some slow deep breaths. It had to be a coincidence.

Mike touched her hand lightly and the contact startled her. She flicked her gaze to him.

"Is everything okay?"

"Yes." She looked out the window again. The hoodie was still there.

Mike followed her gaze. "Are you looking at something?"

"Uh-huh. There's a person in a grey hoodie standing in front of the pizza place."

"What about them?"

She let her head rock back. "This is going to sound really odd, but I think I'm being followed."

He didn't say anything but a querying expression creased his brow and the bridge of his nose.

"I know what it sounds like, but it's true." She told him about the hoodie on Thursday night and the chase from the night before. Her words felt flimsy and inconsequential without the weight to properly convey the unease she felt.

Mike looked out the window. "And you've never seen who it is?"

"No. They always have their hood up and it's been dark."

"It's not dark now."

"No and I want to see them. It's making me uncomfortable."

"I should think so, it's creepy."

A door opened next to the pizza place. A middle-aged woman wearing jogging bottoms and a sweat-stained red vest came out. Another woman followed her. The hoodie stepped back to give them room.

"Must be a class or something," Mike said.

A third woman came through and zipped up her grey hoodie. The woman behind her wore the same colour hoodie. The original hoodie said something, and they all laughed and walked towards the centre of town.

"Bugger," said Claire, her adrenaline replaced by embarrassment. "You must think I'm mad, getting freaked out over someone waiting for their friends."

Mike watched the women go then looked at her. "Why? There could be loads of people with the same colour coat."

"So you think I'm mistaken?"

"Not at all, because that person ran away from you last night."

"Maybe I scared them?" She was beginning to doubt herself now. It sounded ridiculous talking about it now with the sun shining and Mike sitting across from her.

"Maybe. But why take the risk?"

Was she being paranoid? Had her near miss with the stalker made her so convinced someone was following her she'd seen different people and assumed they were one and the same? "I could be making a mountain out of a molehill."

"Is there a reason why someone would follow you?"

"Nothing springs to mind."

"Do you want me to go and check outside?" His concern was so genuine it was touching. "I'll go and get us a drink and have a look."

"No, but thank you. And anyway, the next round is on me."

* * *

As she waited for the barmaid to get their drinks Claire thought about what Mike had said about the coat. The more she reran the images in her mind, the less like her stalker the hoodie appeared – the man in the Astra was bulkier but the hoodie seemed to be of average height and build.

But why were two different people paying her so much attention?

Claire took the drinks back upstairs and their conversation flowed easily. All too soon it was time to go.

Night had fallen and the plaza was empty except for smokers standing outside the restaurants.

"I'm that way," said Mike and pointed towards the town centre.

"I'm the other way," she said. "I left my car at work."

"Did you want me to walk you back?"

"No, I'll be fine."

They faced one another.

"That's it then," he said.

"Yes."

"I've had a good evening."

"Me too."

He leaned forward and hugged her. She kissed him gently on his left cheek.

"We should do this again," he said when they'd separated.

"I think so too," she said and felt warmth in her chest.

"When?"

"We'll be seeing one another on Wednesday."

"It's for the group so that doesn't count. How about Thursday?"

"That'd be nice," she said. She felt like a schoolgirl being asked to the end-of-term disco.

"I'll google some icebreakers so we're not stuck staring at the wallpaper for inspiration." He said it with a completely straight face but then his lopsided smile appeared and she laughed.

"I'm sorry about my paranoia earlier."

"Don't worry, I'm glad you told me. You take care."

"And you," she said and walked back to her car feeling more positive than she had in a while.

Chapter 17

The house was illuminated. After calling, "I'm home," Claire turned off the lounge and dining rooms lights then went upstairs and turned off the bathroom light. Scott's door was pushed to, and she could hear music and someone talking.

She knocked.

"That you, Mum?"

"Yes." She pushed open the door and stepped into the room.

Scott was sitting on his pillow holding his iPad. He smiled at her.

"How was your day?" she asked as she pulled the curtains closed.

"Not bad." He laid the iPad on his lap. "Yours?"

She saw the display on his tablet showed a gallows with a hanging noose and felt a chill pinch at the back of her neck. "What's that?"

He looked down at the tablet. "This?"

"Yes, the hangman thing, what's that?"

"It's that app I'm designing for the project at school. I told you about it the other day."

Had he? "Did you?" She felt something niggle at the back of her mind. "Is it a game or some sort of craze? I saw one on the house and there's graffiti of it at the bridge near the hospital."

"I haven't noticed."

Reality snapped back in and the sharp edges of paranoia filed themselves away. School kids playing games and teenagers doing projects – none of it was aimed at her. "I'm sorry, I'm…"

"It's not just you. Dad properly freaked out about it over the weekend. He didn't like it at all. I don't understand the problem myself. I'm trying to create an app people'll buy. You'd think he'd be pleased."

"Well you crack on with it then. And how was Charlie?"

"Charlie?"

"You said you were eating at Charlie's."

"Of course I did, it was all good."

Claire could read him like a book. "And what did you eat?"

"Erm," he started. "We, um..."

"Hello, Claire," said a soft and muffled female voice.

"Hello, Annie. Where are you hiding her, Scott?"

Pursing his lips, Scott reached behind him and pulled his phone from under his pillow. He held it up so Claire could see Annie on the screen. The girl next door waved. Claire waved back.

"So where did you two eat tonight?" Claire asked.

"McDonald's," Annie said with a big smile.

Claire pulled a face. Annie laughed and Scott scowled.

"Rather you than me. I'm going to make a drink. See you later, Annie."

"Goodbye, Claire."

"Mum?" Scott called her back as she pulled the door to. "I nearly forgot; you had a call."

Claire went back into the room.

"Some bloke," he said. "He didn't say what his name was but to be honest, I couldn't hear him properly. It was really noisy."

"What did he say?"

"Not much. When I said you weren't in, he said something and put the phone down."

"Probably some scammer. He'll ring back if he wants me." Claire pulled the door to. As she started downstairs, she heard Scott and Annie start talking again.

* * *

The conversation about Scott's hangman app stayed with Claire and as she ran down towards the railway bridge the next morning, she slowed her pace until she was walking.

A concrete wall separated the pavement from the grassy dip that led to the storm drain. The morning traffic was slowly starting to build on the hill behind her.

Claire stepped over the wall onto thick and scruffy grass. The incline ran for about six feet before dropping into the brook, which gurgled as it wound its way under the road. The drain itself was a large hole with a grill cemented into the lower half, holding back a variety of branches and all manner of litter. It stood on a narrow concrete shelf – an easy jump of less than two feet over the water.

The gallows was drawn to the left of the hole. There were now five letter dashes added under the base. She looked for signs of activity to show someone had spent time there – cigarette ends, drink cans or fast-food wrappers – but there was nothing.

Feeling uncomfortable and not entirely sure why, Claire went back to the pavement and ran home steadily.

* * *

The Kino was busy.

Claire ordered a coffee and found a two-seat table under the mezzanine next to a big window overlooking the plaza. A lot of young families were sitting on the steps in the sun, kids whooping and laughing as they played.

Eva appeared suddenly by Claire and startled her. "Afternoon," she said. "I'm sorry, I thought you'd heard me."

"Miles away," said Claire. "Sit down."

Eva sat in the leather chair across the table with a sigh. "I've been on my feet all morning."

"Get comfy and I'll get you a drink. What did you want?"

"Decaf tea if they have one. I'd be buzzing all afternoon if I had coffee at lunch."

By the time Claire got back to the table she noticed her own coffee had a film on the surface. She took a sip and it was still palatable. "So how're things?"

Eva pressed the teabag against the spoon with her thumb. "Underpaid and overworked. You know, the usual." She touched the hairline at her left temple and the action seemed as unconscious as it had been at the bowling alley.

"You have lovely hair," Claire said.

Eva seemed taken aback. "Thanks." She touched just above her right ear with her left hand and angled her body slightly as she did so. The movement brought her face into the sun which sparkled in her grey-green eyes.

"You're welcome. Lovely hair and a pretty face."

"Shut up, you'll embarrass me."

"I'm sorry."

Eva tucked her hair behind her ear. "Don't apologise; it's nice to have someone say it. And your hair's gorgeous too. I've always wanted to be blonde and tried it for a while but it didn't suit my colouring."

"Mine has a bit of help these days but at least the grey doesn't really show up."

Eva laughed. "I've been getting greys since my early thirties. I started plucking them out until my hairdresser went mental at me for doing it."

"I just hit mine with more blonde."

"That's the trouble with dark hair. You see people who dye it and it looks as though a kid has gone at them with a Sharpie."

The laughter felt warm and natural and Claire enjoyed it.

Eva sipped her tea and smiled. "So how come you joined the friends group?"

"The usual. Married with child then husband finds someone else and wanders off. A story as old as time itself."

"Sorry to hear that."

Claire shrugged. "It is what it is."

"I like your attitude."

"It's this or go mad."

"How long ago did he leave?" Eva asked.

"Not quite a year."

"How did your child cope?"

"Teenager," Claire corrected. "He's settled down a bit now in time for his mocks, but it wasn't good."

"Do you think you and your husband will reconcile?"

Claire shook her head. "It's unlikely."

"Wouldn't your son prefer you back together?"

"Of course. When Greg moved out and Scott stayed with him over the weekends, he hated it and couldn't understand why I wasn't letting his dad come home to live."

"That can't have been easy."

"It still isn't. We get on pretty well but sometimes – often when I least expect it – I'm the bad guy."

"Can't win, eh?" Eva finished her tea and carefully settled her cup on its saucer. "That's not fair." She looked up through her eyelashes. "I have a thing about unfairness."

"You and me both," said Claire and leaned back. "So what about you?"

Eva picked some imaginary lint off her sleeve with the long slim fingers of her right hand. "I spend my days, as you know," – she pointed to the badge above her left breast – "working for Abbey Recruitment. I don't do much else."

"And what's your story?"

A cloud passed over Eva's face as she flicked the fluff from her fingers and offered a wan smile. "Not much to tell," she said with a shrug. "My husband left me."

"Was there any warning?"

Something pinched in Eva's face that kinked the skin at the bridge of her nose. "Little hints perhaps. I worked for a big recruitment agency back then, essentially headhunting for multinationals, and often spent time out of the UK – I wasn't away a lot, but I wasn't always about. I missed a flight from Paris and it was apparently the final straw. When I got home the next day he'd gone."

"That's awful."

Eva scratched absently at her left wrist and nodded sadly.

"So what did you do?"

"Not a lot. It just ended." Eva pursed her lips. "How do you recover from that level of abruptness? I went down a rabbit hole that day and it took a long while to climb out."

"I'm so sorry."

Eva shrugged. "I got out of Hadlington for a while and went to stay with a relative in the Fens but that wasn't the best thing for me, so I moved back here."

"And have you seen him since?"

"I know where he is but I haven't seen him, as such." She coughed and tucked some hair behind her ear. "We still talk every now and again."

"And do you find that a positive thing?"

"I suppose so except it's always old news and me doing the running. I should just cut myself off; walk away and start afresh."

"But that's what you're doing here, isn't it? Making a fresh start with the group and new friendships, like us?"

"I hope so." Tears formed on her lower eyelids and Eva blinked them away, wiping her finger carefully underneath. "Sorry. I'll go and get us another drink and pull myself together. Same again?"

* * *

Eva set the cups on the table and sat down. "Better now," she said with a smile. "Sorry about that."

"Don't worry."

"Let's keep off the emotive stuff for a moment. Tell me what else is happening with you?"

"I run and work," Claire said. "I do yoga once a week and then it's the weekend."

"I didn't know you ran."

"Probably too grand a term, it's mostly jogging."

"Do you think you'll keep up with the group?"

"Seems like a decent crowd so far."

"I haven't spoken to anyone other than Amy's newbie table," Eva said. "I'm still not sure about Ben. He seemed okay before, just really lonely."

"He doesn't strike me as being creepy."

"What about Mike?"

Claire felt like a teenager being grilled at school about a boy in her class. "He's alright."

Eva's eyes opened wide as the penny dropped. "Mike? Really? Have you spoken since the bowling?"

"Uh-huh, we met for a drink last night."

"You did not," Eva said incredulously. "As a date? That was quick work."

"Oi." Claire laughed, feigning offence.

"You are serious about moving on from Greg then."

"Of course."

Almost distractedly, Eva said, "That's a shame."

Claire felt a jolt at the comment. "Why? He did the dirty on me."

Eva's smile didn't touch her eyes. "Sorry, ignore me. I was just…" She paused as if searching for the right words. "I don't know; I'm an old romantic."

Something about how she said it struck Claire. "Have you dated much?"

"Not at all." Claire's surprise must have showed in her face. "It hasn't occurred to me," said Eva. "And nobody's asked."

"Is that tied up with your feelings for your ex too?"

Eva took a deep breath. "Undoubtedly," she said, her quick smile sad at the edges. "This is wonderful news for you though. I hope it went well."

"Thank you, we had a laugh." She remembered the hoodie and resisted the urge to look across the plaza to check if they were there. "I was an idiot too."

Eva leaned forward. "What did you do?"

"Nothing exciting. I saw someone across the street who made me jump."

Eva frowned. "Greg?"

"No, someone else I…" Claire paused and worried her bottom lip with her teeth. Did she want to talk about this?

Eva didn't break eye contact, plucking at the hair above her left ear.

"It's weird," Claire said finally and gave Eva a quick rundown of the story.

"That is creepy," Eva said and pulled gently at her hair while she spoke. "I read somewhere that kind of thing's on the rise. Nine times out of ten it's apparently someone you know." She braced herself on the arms of the chair and levered up to see out the window. "Weirdly enough, I saw a bloke standing at the corner looking towards here when I arrived. His hood was up but I thought it might have been Ben because he had the same build and I could see sandy-coloured hair poking out."

"Really?" A chill stroked Claire's shoulders as she looked out the window. "Where?"

Eva got up to stand beside her and pointed. "It looks like he's gone."

"And he was just standing there?"

"Yes, looking over here. I mean it's more than likely nothing but it struck me as odd."

The chill had settled through Claire now and she shivered. "Shit."

"It's probably just a coincidence." Eva looked concerned. "I wish I hadn't said anything."

93

"You didn't see his face at all?"

"No. I didn't pay much attention to him and only saw he had sandy-coloured hair."

"Maybe you're right and it was just a coincidence."

"Yes," said Eva emphatically. "It was a bloke waiting for his mate and now they've gone."

"Of course."

"Of course," Eva repeated firmly and looked at her watch. "Damn, I'd offer to get us another drink, but I've got to head off."

Claire glanced at her own watch. "Me too."

"Did you want me to walk you back?"

The stranger's absence and Eva's earnest offer lifted the chill slightly and Claire smiled at her new friend. "No, but thank you." She touched her rape alarm in her pocket. "I should be okay."

They air-kissed and Eva stepped away from the table. "I'll see you tomorrow evening then."

Claire watched her cross the plaza. She couldn't see anyone wearing a hoodie.

Chapter 18

The evening sky was a hazy orange and Claire drove to the church hall car park with the window open.

The small and boxy Methodist church was set back from the road with a car park to its west side and the hall behind. Claire pulled into her usual spot in the far corner, grabbed her mat from the back seat and locked the car.

Chalked roughly on the tarmac between the lines was a crude gallows. The hanged man's face only containing two Xs marking where the eyes should be. The sight of it jolted her and she checked the empty spaces around her. None had chalked hangmen in them.

Claire's arms crawled with goosebumps. It was a kid's game, that was all, but it was near the spot she always used and now she could add it to the gallows on her house and the hangman game on the storm drain.

She shook her head. Now she was being silly and overthinking herself into a panic. It was a game that she'd noticed and now she was seeing it everywhere.

A thick hedge separated the car park from the hall with a path through the gap. Three of her yoga buddies were walking towards it and she rushed across to catch up with them.

Someone came out of the hall wearing a hoodie.

Claire stopped with a jolt then realised it was the wrong colour coat.

"Hi, Claire, how are you?"

Lou smiled broadly and pulled down the hood of her pale pink hoodie. She wore multicoloured leggings and pink trainers and her curly hair had been subdued by the Pilates session. "Are you alright? You look like you've seen a ghost."

How could she have been so startled? Lou's body shape was much more voluptuous than the hoodie's.

"I'm fine." Claire tried to smile. "I'm sorry, my mind was on work."

"Ha. I'd probably look like I'd seen a ghost if I thought too much about work." Lou rubbed the back of her hand across her forehead. "It's hot in there. Some kid from the playgroup poured his Fruit Shoot into the air conditioning gubbins. Apparently, there was a loud bang and a lot of hot and sweaty mothers and toddlers."

"Marvellous."

"Uh-huh." Lou pinched the neckline of her top and wafted it against her cleavage. "I'm afraid we left it warm for you."

"Ah well, we can sweat out the toxins."

Lou touched Claire's shoulder. "I'll leave you to your downward dog then. I'm going home for a lovely cool shower."

Claire went into the humid church hall annoyed and unsettled in equal measure about how paranoid this man in a grey hoodie had made her.

* * *

Claire was coated with sweat by the time her class finished and a low-level headache knocked at the base of her skull.

She walked out with her friend Steffi whose face was normally rosy by the end of a session but today was almost scarlet. Usually they would grab a coffee but both women were hot, sweaty and uncomfortable so they parted at their cars and Claire drove home with her windows down. She hadn't cooled down by the time she got back to the empty house, so she poured a glass of wine before peeling off her clothes. She ran a cool bath and gratefully lowered herself into it. Leaning her head against the rim, she closed her eyes and let herself drift away.

The house phone woke her.

She opened her eyes with a groan and waited for the answerphone to kick in. There was silence after the beep and she closed her eyes again – if they wanted her, they'd ring back.

She stayed in the bath until the water had cooled too much to be comfortable. She dried off and went down to the lounge in her dressing gown, closed the curtains and sat on the sofa. She checked her mobile and saw a missed call from Greg.

"For the love of God." She put the TV on and sat on the sofa with her feet up. The mobile rang again a moment later.

"Why are you doing this to me Greg?"

"I'm sorry. I just wanted to have a chat. Is Scott there?"

"No but he should be home in a bit."

"I wanted to see..."

"To see him?"

"No." He paused, and she didn't help him, content to watch TV. "I've not had a drink."

"I didn't say you had."

"I wanted to have a word."

Claire sighed. "This is getting boring, Greg. I'm going to put the phone down."

"Please don't. I wanted to make sure you were okay."

"As well as I was when you last rang me."

"Don't be like that." He sounded small and passive. "You still mean a lot to me."

"Help me out here. I mean a lot to you based on before or after Matilda fell on your lap?"

"Low blow, Claire."

"You started it," she said and terminated the call.

Chapter 19

Eric Gnome had been decapitated.

He normally stood on the cut-off tree trunk Greg had been threatening to dig out since they'd first moved in. Now just his head, with its jaunty smile and wink, was there. The body lay on its back in the middle of the lawn.

"Oh no," said Claire. "Poor Eric."

Footprints were vaguely visible in the dewy grass and she assumed it was from the 'garden jumpers' who occasional made forays along Brook Street. She hadn't even heard of the 'sport' until Roger complained one day his rhubarb had been trampled. Her garden had managed to avoid damage before, apart from a couple of smashed fairy lights on the fence. Claire picked up the body and head. The jagged break was clean and she thought it could probably be superglued together. She got the shed keys from the kitchen and stored Eric's parts in there to repair him later.

* * *

Roger was in front of her car when Claire went out for her run.

"Morning," she said brightly and he jumped. "You're in front of the wrong car."

"I know," he said and stepped back.

She walked towards him curious as to why he looked so guilty. Then she saw.

The flowers on her windscreen had been shredded. The stems were held in place by the wiper blade as before, but the petals were all over the screen and bonnet as if the bunches had been shaken violently before being put into place.

Her heart thumped. "What the fuck?"

Roger didn't move. "I know."

She pointed at the mess then looked at him. "What the hell happened?"

"I don't know," he said and his voice rose in protest as the penny dropped. "It wasn't me."

"So why did you jump when I said morning?"

"You took me by surprise." He looked at his watch. "It's quarter past six. I didn't expect anyone else around."

"You know I run at this time."

"I thought you ran earlier."

She looked from her car to his. "How did you even notice this?"

"I looked in my rear-view mirror and…" He paused. "Hey, I didn't have anything to do with this. I saw it and came to have a look and was shocked. You came out and startled me."

He clearly hadn't done anything but there was a hint of embarrassment too, as if he'd been looking for a while.

"I'm sorry," she said. "It's a bit of a shock."

"I can imagine, do you know what it's about?"

"No idea. I found a bunch on my windscreen a couple of days ago, but couldn't figure out who'd left them."

"Even if it's the wrong house, that doesn't explain shredding them."

The violence of the floral devastation unsettled her. She checked the mess for a card but couldn't find one.

Roger leaned in close and his arm brushed her. She jumped and shrugged him away.

"It has to be a mistake," he said.

"That's what I said to Scott." Could the sender be angry because they hadn't had a response to yesterday's gift? It wasn't much of a reassurance. "What time did you come out?"

"About five minutes before you did."

"I might have seen something if it wasn't for the garden jumpers."

"Oh no. What have they broken this time?"

"They snapped Eric Gnome's head off."

He looked taken aback. "Oh that's a shame."

"Listen, can you give me a hand with these before you go?"

He checked his watch. "Sure, but we'll have to be quick."

It didn't take long to dispose of the shredded blooms in Claire's compost bin. The activity made her feel better and she followed Roger back out into the street.

"I have to go," he said.

"Thanks for your help. And I'm sorry I was tetchy before."

He shook his head and got into his car. "I'd be tetchy in the same situation. You take care."

* * *

The endorphins failed to wipe away thoughts of the flowers and even passing the market square without seeing her stalker didn't bring any sense of relief. But she kept going, trying to find a good rhythm and keep her breathing steady.

The traffic was already queuing on the hill towards the railway bridge. The graffiti had changed and there were now six dashes under the scaffold.

There was a fog of fumes under the bridge, so Claire jogged on the spot to wait for it to clear and looked up the hill.

The grey hoodie stood in front of a house on the corner of a side road about a hundred yards away. She felt a charge run through her; her arms and legs going cold. She shielded her eyes from the sun to get a better look. The hoodie moved in front of a postbox as if to make his presence more obvious. Claire breathed deeply, trying to keep her panic in check. She wanted to make sure it was the same man and not just a random commuter waiting for a lift. The stand-off played out with seconds stretching away, measured only by the slow progress of cars passing her. She didn't move and neither did he. Panic rolled in her belly and pinched the skin at the base of her skull.

How could he know she'd be here? She wondered if she could get close enough to see his face without him running away. He'd hardly try anything with all these potential witnesses around.

He didn't move when she took a step, so she took another. Had she somehow angered him enough he wanted a confrontation?

Claire walked faster and the gap quickly closed between them. The hoodie didn't move. She kept going and when she'd closed the gap to fifty yards, he stepped back around the postbox and edged into the side road.

He raised his hand as if to acknowledge her and then sidestepped out of sight.

She ran but he was long gone by the time she reached the corner. The street was deserted apart from an old woman walking a very small white dog. There were several cars and any of them could have been his, but she didn't want to walk along the pavement putting herself at potential risk as she tried to find his hiding place.

Her nervous energy drained and she had to lean forward and take several deep breaths. As much as she wanted to confront him, she was glad he'd gone.

* * *

"What do you mean shredded?" Amy asked.

Claire sat in her office with her feet up on the windowsill as she ate her lunch and looked out over Marlborough Street.

"Exactly what I say."

"Do you think it's related to the flowers from a couple of days ago?"

"Has to be, surely? And to make matters worse, I saw my hoodie again."

"Your hoodie? What does that mean?"

Claire explained and Amy chipped in with an occasional "What?" or "Oh no".

After hearing Eva's description, Amy said, "Do you think it's someone you know?"

"I don't know, I mean my stalker was a shock and the idea I now have someone else following me seems so far-fetched it's like I'm imagining things."

"And you're sure he's not the stalker?"

"The body type doesn't fit and I haven't seen my stalker since the incident."

"Do you think it's worth going to police and talking to them?"

"What could they do?" Claire laughed sourly. "If I tell them I have a stalker I haven't seen for about a week and a person in a particular coat who's following me then I'm just going to sound paranoid."

"It's only paranoia if it's not true. And it's not normal to follow someone around in plain sight like this." Amy sounded exasperated. "I think you should at least get it recorded."

Claire considered for a moment. "You might be right. I'll get in touch if I see either of them once more; how's that?"

* * *

Claire put the lasagne pan into the dishwasher after scraping off as much burnt cheese as she could. Dinner had been quiet with Scott distracted by something she hadn't been able to get him to open up about. He, in turn, hadn't asked anything beyond a vague "How was your day?" when she got in.

She switched on the dishwasher and blew her fringe out of her eyes. There was an hour before the friends group started so she went to sit on the patio and read.

Scott came thundering downstairs and rushed through the kitchen. "Mum! Can you do me a huge favour?"

"If I can."

"You're a star. I need a lift to Currys."

"I can drop you off when I go to my friends group if you want."

He made his eyes big and smiled. "Can we go now?"

She smiled, easily swayed. "Grab my keys off the mantelpiece."

Scott pressed his hands against her shoulders. "This is why I tell everyone you're the best mum in the world."

"Yeah, just get my keys."

* * *

Scott was full of life as they drove.

"I saw the part on their online catalogue after Charlie said something at school and it hit me like – bang, big idea, you know?"

She enjoyed seeing him switched on like this; his face animated and his hands doing as much talking as his mouth. "No, I have no idea."

"You'd understand if you weren't so old, Mum."

"It's scary. Once I hit my forties I forgot how everything electronic works."

He nodded gravely. "It's a common thing. I hope they discover a cure before I get there."

"I wouldn't bet on it."

"Nice. I've not even left school yet and you're writing me off."

"Mum of the Year, you see," she said and he laughed.

"It's for Charlie's band."

He played her the track by The Doom Vapers on his phone. She tried hard not to sound like her own parents and bit back the question of why they had forgotten to include a melody.

"They're doing that talent show at the end of term. It's really lame but they get to play in front of an audience and that's cool. He wants me to design the lighting and I need this connector for my laptop." He took a quick breath. "In fact, do you mind if I stay over there tomorrow night?"

"Have you asked Charlie's mum?"

"She never minds. So can I?"

"As long as you promise to get some sleep–"

"Absolutely," he butted in.

"–and get into school on time Friday. I will check."

"I know."

"Then yes, you can."

"You were right about Mum of the Year," he said.

She drove down the hill and glanced into the side road where the hoodie had been.

"I noticed some odd graffiti here when I was on my run."

"Mum, you think all graffiti is odd."

"No, this is different," she said and pointed at the bridge as the came to it.

"Where?"

"On the storm drain."

"What storm drain? I can't see anything."

She glanced over curiously and realised she couldn't see it either.

Claire checked her mirror and braked hard, steering up onto a dropped kerb. Scott exaggerated his surprise at the manoeuvre and grabbed for the handle above the door.

"Blimey, Mum, what're you doing?"

She glanced over to make sure he was okay. "Nice acting."

"Thanks."

She got out and walked over to the wall. From this angle she could see the storm drain and its graffiti clearly. Scott came up behind her.

"It's hangman," he said. "How is that odd?"

The game was apparently underway as a stick figure was now dangling from the noose.

"I thought it might be people playing as a joke on their way to work," she said, "but you can't see it properly from the road."

"Well someone's playing." He pointed toward the six dashes. An *a* had been written over the third. "It could be glared," he suggested. "Or played. Or 'oh my God, we're standing here and not going to Currys'."

"Very clever," she said.

Chapter 20

Claire and Amy arrived at The Rising Sun car park at the same time and walked around to the entrance of the pub together.

"Anything new from your mystery man?"

"Nothing."

"Could the flowers be from someone you know?"

"Like who? It won't be Greg, and any ex-boyfriends still living here have been exes for twenty-plus years."

"What about the group? I mean, you've made some new friends."

"I've only spoken to three blokes."

"One of whom you went on a date with."

"Well yes, but hopefully he's not got to the stage where I've annoyed him enough to send me shredded flowers."

"Fingers crossed. Which leaves Ben and Keith."

"Keith doesn't strike me as being a flowers kind of bloke," said Claire. Even thinking about him made her shiver. "Nor does Ben."

"Maybe. I was thinking about it, and it could be that the flowers were left overnight. What if someone walked by and felt jealous and wrecked them?"

It hadn't occurred to Claire before but did seem like a sensible solution to the issue. "I hope you're right."

Amy patted her arm. "I'm sure there's nothing to worry about."

* * *

The Scrabble group was in full swing and their raucous laughter filled the pub. Four old men sat together at the bar nursing drinks. Another man sat further along and had his back to them.

"Is that Keith?" asked Amy.

Claire looked but couldn't tell for sure.

The barmaid smiled as they approached. "What'll it be, ladies?"

Amy bought the drinks and chatted with the barmaid. After paying, she handed Claire her glass.

They walked by the man and Amy glanced back. "Hello, Keith."

He looked up and his eyes flicked between Claire and Amy. "Hello."

"Aren't you coming up?"

He looked at the half-drunk pint he was gripping. "In a bit."

"Okay," said Amy brightly. "We'll see you up there."

She was called away as soon as they got into the room. Mike stood by a window chatting with a couple in their early fifties. Eva and Ben were at the newbie table and not speaking.

Claire went to join them but Jane intercepted her on the way.

"It's good to see you again," she said and took Claire's elbow and gently guided her to one of the empty tables against the back wall.

"You too, Jane. Is everything okay?"

"Yes but I just wanted to clear the air. Amy told me the other day you'd had a bit of an issue." Jane leaned closer. "With one of our longer-standing members."

"Ah," Claire said quietly.

"I hate the idea of anyone being intimidated and we've had some issues with Keith in the past. I've let most of them go with a warning because of what happened."

"What do you mean 'what happened'?"

"What led him here was very tragic." Jane shook her head quickly, as if to clear away her thoughts. "But it doesn't excuse his behaviour so I've spoken to him and he's on a final warning, okay? I realise that doesn't make the situation right, but I hope it goes some way towards enabling you to think this can be a safe space."

Claire felt a chill across her shoulders. "You gave him a final warning?"

Jane made a soft hushing sound. "Yes, but that's just between us. If he steps out of line again, tell me and no one else and I will sort it."

"I only mentioned it in passing, I wasn't making a complaint."

"I understand that."

She clearly didn't. "But he'll know it was me who complained." Perhaps this explained why he'd ignored her in the bar. It might also explain more, like the destroyed flowers. "I'm not sure I'm comfortable with that."

"Unfortunately, there's not a lot I can do about that except to say that if he steps out of line again, he's no longer welcome."

Claire thought of the wrecked flowers and Keith ignoring her. Could they be linked? "Sounds reasonable."

"Thank you for being understanding," Jane said with relief. "I'll let you get on as I really must mingle."

She walked over to a table of three men and struck up a conversation with them. Claire glanced at Mike but he didn't look over, so she watched Amy instead as she moved from table to table and chatted with members.

Claire couldn't get Keith off her mind and even, for a moment, wondered if he was the hoodie. It didn't seem likely because his body type was too heavy but there was something about the timing that only now occurred to her. She hadn't seen the hoodie before joining the group but did the very next day. The thought felt like a chilly spike in her chest. Could it really be someone from here?

Amy came over and proved a welcome distraction.

"Do you fancy another drink?"

"That'd be nice," Claire said. "But it's my shout."

"Sounds good to me. I'll come downstairs with you."

* * *

Keith's head hung down and an empty shot glass stood next to his pint.

Keeping her distance, Claire leaned on the bar as she waited for the barmaid. She ordered two spritzers.

"Your friend doesn't seem very happy," said the barmaid, gesturing towards Keith with her head. "Isn't he going upstairs?"

"Maybe he's waiting for someone," Amy suggested.

"Well I hope they turn up soon," said the barmaid. "I doubt he'll be able to stand up given the amount he's put away."

"Really?" asked Amy. "I'm sure he drives here."

She patted Keith gently on his shoulder and he moved his head slightly towards her. "What's up?"

"How are you, Keith?" She moved into his line of vision as he shifted slightly on his stool. "Is everything okay?"

"Why shouldn't it be?"

"No reason," she said, a little too brightly. "Just checking. Are you coming upstairs?"

"Might. Bit later."

"Okay. We're going back up now."

"Don't let me stop you," he muttered.

Amy seemed hurt but smiled at Claire. "Come on, I'll have a word with Jane," she said and led them upstairs.

At the doorway, she left Claire as Mike came through from the balcony and walked over.

"Nice to see you," he said and leaned against the wall next to her. She felt his warmth against her arm. "You didn't speak to me earlier."

"I wanted to delay the moment," she said.

He smiled his wonderful lopsided smile and she felt more warmth spread through her. "Any reason why?"

"I like to tease myself," she said carefully and he responded with a coughing laugh.

"You're a terror," he said with a smile.

"I'm not normally like this, I promise."

"Before we join the other newbies, are you still on for tomorrow?"

"I am indeed."

"Excellent, I'm really looking forward to it. Can I buy you a drink?"

"Already got one," she said and held up her glass.

"I'll be back in a bit," he said.

He went to speak to Eva and Ben then went down the stairs. Ben followed him down and Claire sat across from Eva who was writing a text. Claire waited until she'd finished.

"Evening," Eva said. "Sorry for being rude. I hate it when people are on their phones with others around."

"Don't worry. I have a fifteen-year-old who's often lost in a fog of social media."

Eva laughed. "I sometimes wonder how kids texting in the street don't walk into more things."

"The god of communication is clearly having to work overtime these days to protect them."

Something in the sentence made Eva flinch slightly but the movement was quickly buried. "You're right. Any more sightings of your hoodie?"

"I saw him this morning," Claire said and told Eva what had happened.

"I think you've seen him often enough now that it's not some kind of weird coincidence."

"Amy suggested I report it, to have something on file."

"I wish there was some way I could help," Eva said then clicked her fingers. "Hey, I could keep an eye out for him too and if you spot him, text me and I'll come to you. We could be like Nancy Drew and track him down."

"I don't want to cause you any trouble."

"It's no trouble and I'd at least feel like I was helping in some way."

Claire smiled gratefully at the concern.

"Is there something else?" Eva asked as she looked into Claire's eyes.

The flowers were too odd to try and explain so Claire thought quickly. "It's nothing really but we had some business with poor Eric Gnome."

Eva looked blank. "I don't know who Eric Gnome is."

"He's a garden gnome and got broken last night."

"What do you mean by broken? Is someone creeping around after dark?"

Claire knew that wasn't the case but the thought of the hoodie standing in her back garden chilled her. "It's garden jumpers."

"What the hell are they?"

"It's happened two or three times. A handful of kids decide they're going to walk down a street but do it using the back gardens instead. Most of the time, according to the police, they don't cause damage but every now and again they do."

"And you're sure it's them?"

"Well," Claire said, "I was until I told you."

Eva looked concerned. "Don't mind me, I'm always being told I look on the dark side of things. I'm sure it's your garden thingummies and nothing else."

"What's a garden thingummy?" asked Ben as he sat on the chair next to Claire.

"Jumpers," said Claire.

"You have those little bastards too?" he asked and his lip curled. "They came through my estate a couple of weeks back and from the damage you'd think they were riding a fleet of elephants or something."

Claire laughed at his earnest expression. Eva glanced at him then picked up her phone.

Mike slid a small tray onto the table.

"Could be fun downstairs," he said.

"What's happening?" Ben asked and reached for his pint.

"Keith's having a pop at some ladies playing Scrabble. He said they were being too noisy and let them know."

Eva looked up from her phone. "Really?"

"Yes. A couple of the regulars have already had a word and the barmaid's getting involved."

"Blimey," said Ben. "Should we go down?"

Amy walked by with a face like thunder and Mike caught her attention. "Everything okay?" he asked.

"We'll soon see," she replied and went downstairs.

"We ought to help her," said Claire.

"I was thinking the same thing," Mike replied.

He led the way to the bar. Amy was standing to Keith's left and a couple of regulars were on his right. The

Scrabble ladies were talking loudly but it seemed their game was over and two of them stared at Keith.

"Keith, you need to come upstairs," Amy said, leaning down to look into his face.

"Don't want to," he said, voice gravelly.

"Then you're going to have to leave because you're being a nuisance."

"Who to?"

One of the regulars started to say something but the barmaid raised her finger to quiet him.

Amy mouthed "thank you" to her then looked at Keith. "The people in the bar."

"Who cares?"

"You're out of order, Keith," Mike said. "Amy's trying to help. You need to either go upstairs or leave."

Keith turned to look at him and, in doing so, locked eyes with Claire. His blank expression slowly soured.

"I ought to have guessed you'd be here," he said and glared at her.

Chapter 21

The venom in his voice was so intense Claire knew instantly he'd made the connection with the complaint.

"What the hell did I do?" she asked and felt heat rise in her cheeks. "You were drinking when I got here."

Mike moved into Keith's line of sight. "Claire hasn't done anything," he said. "You're out of order."

"I'm not going upstairs."

"Why not?" asked Amy. "What's wrong?"

Keith made a sound deep in his throat but said nothing.

"You two go back upstairs," Mike said. "I'll see if I can sort it out."

"Are you sure?" asked Amy.

"Yes," Mike said. He smiled at Claire. "Go on, I'll be up in a minute."

"Okay," Claire said and allowed Amy to lead her towards the door. "The bloke's an arse."

"Agreed," said Amy as they started up the stairs. "Jane's really got to review the situation with him."

* * *

The atmosphere upstairs was charged, as news spread of Keith's meltdown. Jane and Amy had a quiet talk in one corner and Claire sat with Ben and Eva and filled them in on what had happened.

"He's a twat," said Ben. "And he drove here."

"So how's he getting home?" asked Eva.

Claire shrugged. "Who cares? The way he's been with me, I'd as soon ignore him."

"What did he do to you?" Ben asked.

Eva jumped in to tell him, which made Claire feel uncomfortable, like an observer of her own life story.

"That's awful," said Ben.

"Let's move on," Claire said. "How about we change the subject?"

"Good idea," said Eva. "Tell us your story, Ben."

"Now?"

Eva nodded emphatically so he cleared his throat.

"I was married to a girl and discovered too late that she was more interested in my money than me. When she realised I didn't have as much as she thought, the rows started. There was a lot of shouting and it got really unpleasant and then our divorce left both of us with pretty much nothing."

"Oh," said Eva.

"And then to top that wretched period off, Dad was taken ill and ended up in hospital."

"Sorry to hear that," said Claire.

"Since there was nothing for me in Birmingham I moved back here to stay with Mum and try to sort stuff with Dad. Then he passed away."

"Oh no," said Claire.

"I'm convinced there was negligence," he said. "But you've got to prove that kind of thing."

"That's awful," said Eva.

Ben looked uncomfortable. "Yeah."

Claire saw Amy and Jane cross the room and head downstairs.

"I'm going to see how things are going," she said and Ben followed her down to the bar.

Mike was standing to one side of Keith who glared at him with an unfocussed gaze.

"Come on," Mike said. "The taxi's out front."

Keith growled and swatted at Mike's hand.

"Why are you behaving like this?" Jane asked. "I thought you enjoyed the group."

Keith squinted at the little group surrounding him. "I did." He jerked his thumb towards Claire and Amy. "But now we've got all these prissy bitches."

"Hey," said Claire angrily.

She felt someone's hand on her arm and Amy said, "It's okay."

Mike held out his hand towards Claire, palm up, as if trying to calm her. "This has nothing to do with anyone but you," he said to Keith, calmly but with force. "There's no need for that kind of language and if I hear you say it to Claire or Amy again I'll chuck you out of the pub myself."

Keith grumbled as Mike and Ben helped him to his feet. He shook them off and swayed for a moment before steadying himself by holding onto the bar.

"Fuck off," he slurred. "I can sort myself out." He looked at Jane. "I'm going."

"I think that's for the best," she said.

"Fucking stupid group anyway."

"I'll ring you tomorrow after you've sobered up."

"Fucking stupid group," he repeated.

Ben reached out to steady him but Keith shrugged his hand off.

"I can do it," he insisted.

"Fine," said Ben.

Keith took a couple of steps forward and looked at Claire. "Fucking prissy bitches," he said and staggered, slopping some of his beer onto her leg.

"Hey!" shouted Mike, grabbing the glass.

"And you're a fucking creep," Claire hissed, wiping the alcohol away.

"He's drunk," said Jane and something cracked in her voice.

Claire looked at her and was surprised to see tears balancing on Jane's lower eyelids. Why the hell was she almost crying over this idiot?

"Get him out of here," said the barmaid, "before I bloody bar him."

Mike held Keith's shoulder and steered him quickly through the pub with Ben's help. Somebody cheered quietly and one of the Scrabble ladies said, "Good riddance." The regulars parted to let the men go.

Claire flexed her fingers, trying to calm herself. Amy rested a hand lightly on her shoulder. Jane crossed her arms tightly and bit her upper lip. None of them spoke.

Mike and Ben came back and, with the action over, the regulars went back to their drinks.

"Thanks," said the barmaid.

"You're welcome," Mike said then looked at Claire and Amy. "You two okay?"

"Yes," said Amy. "Thanks for that."

"My blood pressure is at boiling point right now," said Claire.

"He doesn't mean it," said Jane. She'd composed herself now and dried her eyes. "I know it sounds like I'm making an excuse but I'll speak to him tomorrow when he's sobered up."

"I've never seen him drink like that before," said Amy. "He was horrible."

"He's drunk," said Jane. "We've all been there but it's a real shame you and Claire were his targets."

"That's what tipped me," said Mike. "It's done now though, he's in a taxi and off home to a splitting headache." He put his hand in his pocket. "I also have his car keys."

"I'll take them," said Jane and held out her hand.

Mike gave them to her.

* * *

Keith's actions dampened the atmosphere even if no one acknowledged it and for a while Claire wished she'd gone home straight after he'd been ejected.

Jane didn't speak to her again and Amy spent a lot of time out on the balcony. The newbies talked about trivia with the Keith business an unspoken undercurrent eddying around them. Mike tried to make light of things and even told a few jokes, she assumed they'd come from his pupils as Scott had already told her most of them. She joined in with a few of her own once she'd calmed down sufficiently. Ben followed up her joke but got his words muddled which made them laugh more. Eva was adamant she didn't know any jokes.

People drifted away before the last orders bell rang. Amy left with a couple and mimed "I'll call you".

The newbie table trooped downstairs together with Mike bringing up the rear.

"Are we still on for tomorrow?" he asked her.

Claire smiled, barely turning her head towards him. "Of course."

"Shall I pick you up?"

"Do you know where I live?"

"No."

"I'll text you my address then."

115

They parted at the front door, Eva and Mike walking together towards the Corn Market car park. Ben walked Claire around behind the pub.

"I wonder how safe this car park is?" he asked

"Not sure," she said and looked for cameras.

"I meant for Keith, leaving his car overnight."

"I don't care. He shouldn't have got so drunk he had to leave it here, should he?"

"Perhaps that's what Eva was telling him."

"When?"

"They were talking when I got to the pub. I assumed she was telling him to ease up with his drinking." They reached his car first. "It's been good to see you again, Claire."

"Likewise. I'll see you Saturday."

She was aware of him watching as she walked to her car and got in. When she drove away, he looked up from checking his phone and waved.

* * *

Whether it was paranoia or not, everything rolled together in her mind on the drive home until she felt unwell. By the time she pulled up outside the house she knew what to do.

"Is that you, Mum?" Scott called as she locked the front door.

"Yes." She kicked off her shoes and went upstairs.

White light flickered under his bedroom door. She knocked and went in. He sat on his bed playing *Grand Theft Auto*.

"How was it?" he asked without looking at her.

"Okay." There was no need to tell him the truth. She pulled his curtain back and looked into the dark garden. "Have you been onto the patio?"

"No."

"Eric got injured."

116

"What? No way!" He paused the game and looked at her. "What happened?"

"Got his head knocked off, probably by garden jumpers."

"Gits," he muttered. His attention wandered back to the game.

"It got me thinking about that security camera you were planning to set up."

"Oh yes?" His attention was caught again and he put down his controller. "It's dead easy, we can run a camera through my Pi Drive and record it."

"How quickly could you set it up?"

"An hour or two." He shrugged. "Minutes maybe?"

"Great stuff. How about doing it tomorrow?"

"I will." He picked up his controller. "We'll catch those bloody garden jumpers."

"Uh-huh," she said and wondered just what the camera might find.

* * *

Claire was unloading the dishwasher when the house phone rang. A quick annoyed glance at the clock confirmed it was late – almost eleven – and she stormed into the dining room.

"Yes?"

She'd expected it to be Greg but there was just a peculiar all-encompassing sound of silence.

"Hello?"

There was clearly no one there so she put the handset down. It rang again almost immediately, and she snatched it up.

"What?" The same silence as before. "Go to bed, Greg."

There was a blip in the silence. Had she heard a word?

"This isn't funny, Greg."

117

She jabbed the finish button and dialled 1471. As she'd expected, the BT voice informed her, "The caller withheld their number."

Claire put the handset down and tried to work out if she'd heard a glitch on the line or if someone had really said "hey".

Chapter 22

Time.

It's a funny thing, is time. People say it's supposed to be a great healer, don't they, but they're idiots, each and every last one of them. It's not a great healer, that's rubbish, a shitty little phrase people wheel out when they don't properly know how to respond to someone who's grieving, the hurt where it feels like your heart has been pulled from your chest and some bastard standing in front of you is sadistically twisting the muscle this way and that.

To cause pain.

Like you caused me and I intend to cause you.

It's been a strange week, hasn't it? Lots of odd little things happening and weird developments. You didn't see any of them coming and I like to disorientate you like that. I like to see you unsettled. When I was unsettled you didn't care and didn't see, but I wanted you to, I wanted you to see what it was doing to me, what you'd done to me. Now I can and I'm enjoying it.

Does that make me a bad person? Does it make me terrible to leave you little gifts, to orchestrate things to confuse and confound you?

I hope you think so, I really do, because if you don't, you're not going to enjoy yourself much in the future...

Chapter 23

A horrible sense of trepidation about what she'd find on her car cloaked Claire as she warmed up on the patio.

She opened the entry door tentatively. The street was deserted. A shabby grey cat appeared from between parked cars a few doors down and gave her a disinterested glance before crossing the road. There were no blooms on the pavement.

The windscreen was clear apart from a single A5 sheet of paper held under the driver's wiper blade. She saw the gallows immediately and felt like someone had dropped freezing water down her back. This game had the victim's head and body drawn in. With a deep breath, she pulled the note free. Something had been written on the back.

YOU DESERVE EVERYTHING YOU GET

The words swam and the skin on the back of Claire's neck pulled tight as she read them.

What the hell was going on?

None of this made sense. What could she have possibly done to someone to make them send this to her?

She tilted her head and felt the tendons stretch in her neck.

It couldn't be meant for her, just like the first flowers couldn't have been. Or the shredded ones. This was a horrible case of mistaken identity.

Should she tell the police? What could they do when the only evidence was two bunches of flowers and a note that, if read in a certain way, could actually seem positive?

She folded the paper and slipped it into her pocket under the rape alarm. After doing a few stretches she jogged towards the end of the street.

* * *

Eric Gnome didn't take long to fix.

Claire hadn't intended to do it before showering but decided working on him would keep thoughts of the note at bay. She unlocked the shed and let the door close behind her.

The shed had never been her domain – she loved working with flowers and the soil but left the lawn mowing and tinkering to Greg. During the decluttering after their split she'd been tempted to get rid of the whole thing, but Scott offered to keep it tidy and mow the lawn. He made good his offer and sorted through everything without actually throwing anything away. Since Scott was happy with that, she left it alone.

She wiped around the break at Eric's neck and liberally applied superglue to the wound. She put his head on quickly and pressed down for the count of fifty – a number she'd chosen randomly rather than read in the instructions. When she let go the head stayed where it was which she took for a win. Resisting the urge to prod it, she left Eric to set, locked the shed behind her and went for her shower.

* * *

Amy rang as Claire was caught in a traffic jam.

"Are you okay to talk?"

"Yes," said Claire, "I'm in the car, currently sat outside Matthew's Bakery and the smell is making me hungry."

"Poor you. I wanted to see how you were after last night?"

"As well as can be expected." It felt like another item to be pushed to the back of her mind. Claire seemed to be collecting them.

"I'm not sure what Jane's going to do about it because she's very protective of Keith for some reason, but I've told her she can't let this go."

"Thank you."

"I promise you I'll get it resolved. I feel bad because I was the one who asked you to come to the group."

"It's not your fault, Amy."

"Doesn't stop me feeling guilty. I'll see you later."

* * *

Her phone buzzed mid-morning with a text from Mike.

Hi, I'm supervising on the playground and shouldn't be doing this, but wanted to check we're still on for tonight.

Smiling, she initiated a text conversation:

Claire: I should report you to your headmaster.
Mike: Why would you do that to me ☹
Claire: Why not?
Mike: You're so cruel.
Claire: You have much to learn, Padawan.
There was a pause and she wondered if break was over. Then:
Mike: Very nice Star Wars reference.
Claire: I'm a fan. ☺
Mike: So tonight then. How about I pick you up for 8?
Claire: That's fine. I'm looking forward to it.
Mike: Dress for dinner. And don't forget to send me your address. Bell's just gone, I'll see you soon.

* * *

The few wispy clouds Claire could see as she walked into town at lunchtime looked like candyfloss. The sun was bright and she enjoyed the warmth of it on her skin.

She walked to the deli. It was busy and took almost ten minutes for her to reach the counter. She chatted with the woman making her sandwich before paying and heading back outside.

She sat on a bench and unwrapped her chicken salad sandwich.

"Hello, Claire," said Greg from behind her and she groaned. "Fancy seeing you here."

She turned to look at him. He wore jeans and a sport coat and looked like a gone-to-seed geography teacher.

"What are you doing here?" she asked without bothering to keep the annoyance out of her tone.

He held up a shop-bought sandwich and smiled. "I was in town on a call and thought I'd enjoy my lunch in the sun."

"You don't like the sun."

"That's right," he said and nodded. "But you do."

"Are you following me?" For a brief moment she had the mad idea he might be the hoodie but that didn't make any sense. He wasn't the right build, and she knew how he walked.

"Why would I do that?"

"Because in all the years I've been working here and you've worked at the hospital we have never bumped into each other in town."

"I told you…"

"Yeah, you were on a call and wanted lunch." She turned her back on him. "Don't let me stop you enjoying it."

"We could eat together," he said in the soft voice he always used when he perceived himself hurt. Even when she loved him it had driven her nuts.

"Why would I want to do that?" she asked without turning around.

"Because it'd be nice."

"You couldn't wait to get away from me, Greg. Why would you want to eat with me now?"

He came around to the front of the bench and stood far enough away so he didn't quite invade her personal space.

"I've been wanting to chat for a while."

"And you're not going to give up, are you?" She unwrapped half her sandwich and pressed the slices together before taking a bite. "So what do you want to talk about?" she asked when she'd finished her mouthful.

"Different things."

"That's not how this works. I will sit with you forever and a day to discuss Scott but we're not even friends anymore."

He looked hurt. "Aren't we?"

"Don't make me spell it out."

"Come on, Claire. Please?"

She took another bite and chewed it slowly and deliberately. "Okay. I'll give you acquaintances, but only because of Scott."

He sat on the bench and gave her plenty of space. "Thank you. I can live with that." He opened his sandwich and took it out of the case. It folded in his hand.

"Yours looks a lot better than mine."

"The deli is excellent," she said. "But please don't use it at lunchtimes because that's when I go in."

"Uh-huh." He chewed his sandwich and didn't look like he was enjoying it. "I rang you last night."

"I was out."

"But you answered."

She felt a jolt. "That was you?"

"The battery on my work mobile died and I was on the wards and couldn't remember your number from memory."

"It said you'd withheld the number."

"You know how work phones are."

"Well you scared me, Greg. That's not cool."

"I'm sorry." He took another bite of his sandwich with the enthusiasm of a man eating cardboard.

They ate in silence for a moment and she was content to let time drift.

"Has anything odd happened recently?" he asked finally.

It wasn't what she'd been expecting him to say. "Like what?"

"Like weird stuff?" He looked at her as if trying to find the answer in her eyes or face. When he couldn't, he took another bite of his sandwich and this time didn't bother to hide his disgust as he stuffed the remainder back into the carton. "I want to make sure you and Scott are safe."

"Why wouldn't we be?" Did he know? She hadn't mentioned the hoodie or shredded flowers to Scott so he couldn't have blurted it out to his dad.

Greg looked uncomfortable. "Well you nearly got run over."

"It was an accident and it's not like the bloke's stalking me or anything."

"Stalking? Why did you say that?"

Dammit, she thought, frustrated at making the slip. "Because you said odd and I assumed you meant something unusual or weird like being stalked, but I haven't seen him since." She finished the first half of her sandwich.

"I don't know what I'm trying to say really."

"Then don't," she said curtly. "Scott's fine. He's at Charlie's tonight and you've got him for the weekend so you can speak to him then."

"I will," he said. "Thank you for listening to me."

"I didn't have a lot of choice." She got up and slipped the other half of her sandwich into her bag. "Just don't ambush me like that again."

* * *

It was close to six when she pulled up outside the house to find a silver Mondeo parked in Roger's space. A woman sat behind the wheel writing in a book. As Claire braked, the woman looked up.

Claire got out and the woman did the same. She was slim and her curly chestnut hair was cut into a bob that highlighted her pale-blue eyes. She wore a navy-blue trouser suit and Claire decided she was either a lawyer or a police officer.

"Excuse me," the woman said with a smile. "Are you Claire Heeley by any chance?"

"I am."

"Excellent." The woman reached into her handbag and pulled out a small wallet she opened as she held it up. "I'm Detective Constable Rosie Carter of Hadlington CID. Could I have a quick word?"

Fear thumped at her chest. "Is someone hurt?"

"No. I just want to have a chat."

Claire's heart rate steadied. "What about?"

DC Carter looked around as if checking to see whether their conversation could be overheard. "Would it be possible to do this indoors?"

"Of course," said Claire. "Come through."

She led the way into the yard and opened the back door, gesturing for the policewoman to go in ahead of her. "Take a seat."

DC Carter sat at the table with her back to the patio doors. Claire didn't quite know what to do, so she stood by the dining room door. Her fingers felt twitchy.

"Drink?"

"A cup of tea would be lovely." DC Carter put her handbag on the table and took a slim notebook and pen from it. "Milk, no sugar."

Claire made the drinks in silence then put the cups on the table and sat across from the officer.

"Thank you, Mrs Heeley."

"Call me Claire."

"Thank you, Claire." DC Carter looked towards the window. "Nice flowers."

"Thanks but they're not really mine."

DC Carter smiled and frowned at the same time. "I'm sorry?"

"I found them on my car." Claire waved her hand. "It's a long story and not what you came for."

DC Carter took a careful sip of tea and then licked her lip. "No." She opened her notebook. "I need to talk to you regarding damage sustained on Mr Keith Hasslett's car."

Chapter 24

Lost for words, Claire stared at the policewoman's hair. The sun made the tips of her curls glow.

"Pardon?" Claire ventured eventually.

DC Carter smiled a thin smile that didn't touch her eyes. "Mr Keith Hasslett's car was damaged last night."

"But…" Claire's mind was blank. "I don't understand. What happened?"

DC Carter leaned back in her chair. Her hair seemed much lighter now. "Mr Hasslett was out last night in company that included you. By his own admission he was intoxicated and a taxi took him back to his residence at Hadlington Marina. Today, while retrieving his vehicle from The Rising Sun car park, he discovered it had been damaged."

Claire felt a rush of panic. None of this made sense.

"May I ask you a few questions?"

"Of course."

"Can you tell me where you were last night between 2 a.m. and 3 a.m.?"

"Here at home. In bed." She glanced at the flowers and put both hands around her mug.

"Was anyone else in the house who could verify that?"

"My son. But I imagine he was asleep at that time too."

"Did you use The Rising Sun car park?"

"I did and came out of the pub with my friends."

"Were they all parked in the car park too?"

"Two of us were – myself and Ben Montgomery. We walked to the cars, said our goodbyes and went home."

"And you saw nothing suspicious?"

"Not at all but we'd left by 11:15 or so. To be honest, I wouldn't know Keith's car if I saw it and I wasn't aware he'd parked there."

"Did you leave first or did Ben?"

Realisation began to dawn. "But we were there hours before the times you mentioned. I'm sorry but do you think I had something to do with the damage?"

DC Carter put down her pen. "That has been suggested to us."

Disbelief hit Claire like a slap. "What?"

"His car was vandalised and we need to follow all leads. Your name was put forward."

"That makes no sense," Claire said and suddenly felt hot. "So have you spoken to Ben?"

DC Carter looked at her without speaking.

"No," said Claire after a moment. "Of course you haven't because his name wasn't put forward. Was it?"

"I obviously can't comment on other people."

"Was it Keith who gave you my name?"

"I can't confirm that, Claire."

"Of course not. So what happens now?"

"I need to ask you a few more questions."

"To eliminate me from your enquiries?"

"If you like." DC Carter looked back at her notebook. "I understand there have been cross words between you and Mr Hasslett in the past?"

What should she say? Her only experience of this kind of situation was what she'd seen on television and that probably wasn't going to be any help at all. Could she inadvertently drop herself into the mire by answering a question wrong? What if she said something that sounded, out of context, contradictory? Her pulse raced and she tried to keep her breathing steady in case the policewoman noticed.

"There have," she said while willing her voice to stay steady. "Unfortunately."

"Can you tell me what they were or how they came about?"

"I met him for the first time last Wednesday at a friends group I recently joined. He cornered me on the stairs and made some innuendoes and I didn't respond. The second time we met was on Saturday and he did the same thing, but I stood up for myself and it seemed to annoy him."

"Annoyed him how? Did he say anything?"

"No, he just stomped off."

"And you saw him again last night?"

"Yes," said Claire and told DC Carter what had happened. "When Mike tried to calm the situation, Keith called me and Amy prissy bitches."

DC Carter tapped her notebook absently. "Did you respond?"

Claire looked into her cup at her wavering reflection. "I did. I called him a fucking creep."

DC Carter tapped her notebook again. "One last question, Claire. Do you own a hoodie?"

The word hit her like a punch. "No," she said. DC Carter's eyes were impossible to read. "I can show you the coat rack and my wardrobe if you like."

"How about something that looks like a hoodie?"

"I've got a duffel coat and a rain mac and a runner's jacket. I can show you."

DC Carter held up her hand. "Honestly, it's not necessary."

Claire felt tears in the corners of her eyes but didn't want to cry in front of this woman. "Are you sure?"

"I've been on the force a while now, Claire, and I like to think I can tell when someone's telling the truth."

The relief was almost palpable and Claire felt a weight lift off her chest. "You can?"

"Yes." DC Carter reached into her bag for a card and handed it to Claire. "I can't see anything coming of this but if it does or you need to talk then contact me on the numbers here."

Claire took the card and read the details. "Thank you, Detective Constable…"

"Call me Rosie, please."

"Thank you." Claire took a couple of deep breaths. "Can I ask you a question?"

Rosie nodded and put her notebook in her bag. "I'll answer if I can."

"How was Keith's car vandalised?"

"A phrase was scratched into the bonnet."

"Did it say 'fucking creep' or something similar?"

"I can't confirm that as it's part of the investigation."

"That would explain how Keith made the connection. But why don't you think it was me?"

Rosie leaned back in the chair and looked at the flowers on the windowsill. "It's too obvious. Too many people heard you say it and you're a smart woman."

"So why the specific times?"

"The Rising Sun car park has CCTV and the vandalism was filmed. Unfortunately the culprit hid their identity by wearing a hoodie."

That familiar weight rolled back. "Oh no."

"They seem to know the camera is there but it doesn't bother them and nobody's around at that time of night, so they're not disturbed." She paused and looked concerned. "Are you okay, Claire? You're looking a bit pale."

"This kind of thing doesn't happen to me every day." She thought of Greg and his question about whether anything odd had happened recently. What would he say if she told him about this?

"I understand." Rosie stood up and put her bag over her shoulder. "Give me a call if anything crops up or you want to chat."

"What do you mean 'if anything crops up'?"

"Nothing in particular, and I have no concerns but just be careful with Keith. His bark's worse than his bite but he can be unpleasant."

"You know him?"

"Let's just say he's known to us. He and I have had words in the past." Rosie opened the back door. "Have a good evening, Claire."

Chapter 25

Claire was still sitting at the table when Scott got home.

"Tough day, Mum?"

"You could say that." She gave him a smile that didn't feel adequate. "How was your day?"

"It was good and I have something to show you." He went into the dining room. "Come on."

She followed Scott up to his bedroom. He sat at the desk and pointed to his laptop which showed an image of the garden from the patio doors.

"I put a GoPro on one of the kitchen cupboards and it runs through the Pi into the laptop and takes a picture every second. It'll try and get infrared at night; it should work though I don't know what the quality'll be like and the visual range will be limited."

"How far?"

"Easily to the patio and hopefully halfway down the garden. Certainly to Eric's stump."

"The picture quality looks good."

The time lapse between frames wasn't immediately obvious unless a branch repositioned itself as the breeze took it, or a bird suddenly appeared or disappeared.

"The Pi will store the images and I'll link them as a movie file to fast-forward through. I wish the camera had more range but at least it's something."

"You've done a good job," she said and dropped a kiss on top of his head.

He made an exaggerated noise of disgust and moved away from her reach but turned and smiled.

"Thanks," he said. "Are you alright to drop me at Charlie's?"

She looked at the clock. It was 6:45. "What time do you need to be there?"

"Seven."

* * *

Claire pulled up outside Charlie's house a couple of minutes late and Scott had unclipped his seatbelt before the car stopped.

"Are you going to come in and say hello to his mum?"

"Not tonight." Claire didn't want to get held up and Susan could talk for England.

"Ah," Scott said with a devilish grin. "Got something planned for later?"

"I'm going out."

"With Amy?"

"No."

"With Lou?"

"No."

Scott squinted, a detective on the case. "Anyone I know?"

"I'm going on a date with Mike from the friends group."

"Mike from the singles group, eh?" He raised his eyebrows. "Are you going out or is he coming to ours?"

"He's coming to pick me up."

"Make sure that's all he does," Scott said and waggled his finger at Claire. "I don't want any funny business, young lady."

She looked at him and tried to keep her expression solemn. "Yes, boss."

* * *

She took a detour on the way home and stopped by the railway bridge, parked on the kerb and walked to the wall.

The graffiti had been updated and now the hanged man had arms and legs. His mouth was an upturned U.

There was still only one letter above the dashes – the *a* – but two more – *b* and *t* – had been written underneath and scored through.

The rough artwork was making her feel uneasy. Suddenly thinking she might be being watched, she looked up the hill and across the road. Nobody was standing there but a car sat at the junction waiting to pull out. Was the driver watching her and hiding in plain sight behind the darkened windows? Her pulse quickened. Something appeared at the rear window, it took her a moment to realise it was an arm. The window wound down and a dog's head appeared in the gap. The dog was pulled back and the window wound up.

The car pulled out of the junction and came down the hill. A harassed-looking woman was driving and there were two child seats in the back. The dog sat on the passenger seat and stared out the window.

Claire wasn't being watched; she was being paranoid.

* * *

Claire was sitting on the patio enjoying a glass of wine when Amy rang.

"I have news," Amy said excitedly.

Claire watched a swallow swoop in from somewhere and perform a roll along the length of the garden before flying up into the sky. "What about?"

"Keith and his car. Jane just rang me. She'd gone to make sure he was okay and his car's been vandalised."

"I know. I had a visit from the police about an hour ago."

"Wait... What?"

A door opened and Claire heard Harry bark and race down the yard. Roger said, "Lightning, calm down."

She lowered her voice in case he came onto his own patio. "They came to see me because my name was put forward."

"The bastard dobbed you in?"

Roger appeared at the fence and waved. When he saw Claire was on the phone he covered his mouth with an exaggerated 'whoops' expression and walked down his garden.

"Seems so." Claire gave Amy a quick rundown of what DC Carter had told her. "The unfortunate thing is that I don't have an alibi."

There was an eruption of barking and Claire heard Roger trying to quieten Harry down. "Mate, it's a butterfly..."

"She then asked if I owned a hoodie."

Amy's sharp intake of breath was a hiss. "Surely not a grey one?"

"She didn't say."

"Jane said 'fucking creep' had been scratched so deeply into the paintwork the metal was out of shape in places."

"I didn't know that."

"It's suspicious they wore a hoodie after you've been seeing that person. It's a real shame you don't recognise him."

"I know and Greg made it a bit weirder today. I bumped into him at lunchtime and he asked if anything odd had happened recently."

Amy laughed. "Did you tell him?"

"Not at all. My life has nothing to do with him anymore."

"Well said you. But it's a weird question, though, what with your stalker and the hoodie, the flowers and Keith's car. That's a lot of odd." She paused as if considering the implications of what she'd just said. "It could all be a coincidence, of course, and nothing to worry about."

"I had the same thought. Rosie, the police officer, gave me her card and told me to ring if I needed to."

"Have you seen your stalker again?"

"No." Claire glanced at her watch. "Sorry to cut you off like this but I need to go and have a shower."

"Don't worry. Enjoy your evening and keep me posted."

Roger was at the fence as soon as Claire ended the call. "Evening, neighbour."

Claire smiled what she hoped was a welcoming rather than a let's-have-a-chat smile. "Evening, Roger."

"Just supervising Lightning." The dog barked as if recognising his name. "I should take him for a walk but we're having dinner soon and there isn't time."

"Annie's still holding up her end of the bargain, eh?"

"Indeed. She's at a friend's overnight and didn't have time."

"Smart lady."

"Yeah." Harry barked and Roger looked at him. "No, don't eat that."

He disappeared from sight for a moment and Claire took the chance to push her chair back. Before she could stand up, he was above the fence line again.

"I swear this dog will be the death of me."

"Take him after dinner then you and Lou can have a nice romantic walk."

"Very romantic, especially when we get to argue over who wields the poo bag." He pulled a face. "Have you had any more gifts left?"

"No." She didn't want to have this discussion now. "Whoever left them clearly got the wrong car."

"It seems like it."

She checked her watch and made sure he saw her do it. "Sorry to run but I'm out tonight."

"Anywhere nice?"

"A meal with friends."

"Lucky friends," he said.

Chapter 26

Claire was watching the CCTV feed in Scott's room when the doorbell rang. She checked herself in the mirror, hoped the combination of white blouse and jeans would be smart enough and went downstairs.

Mike held a small bunch of roses against his chest. He was wearing a pale-blue shirt and tan chinos. "Evening," he said and his smile lit up his face.

"Evening, yourself. You look very presentable."

"Well that's better than nothing. You look ravishing."

"I'm wearing jeans and a blouse."

"And both suit you perfectly."

"You're a nut," she said. "Come in."

He came through and waited while she shut the door. She guided him into the dining room and he handed her the flowers.

"I wanted tulips, but the garage didn't have any."

She laughed. "Do you always take dates this seriously?"

"Depends on whether I think there's any chance of getting to a third one," he said.

"A good tactic." She went into the kitchen and took out a vase and half-filled it with water to put the flowers into.

"Seems I'm not your only admirer," he said and nodded towards the windowsill.

"Oh those flowers are a long story."

"I've got all evening."

"If you're sure," she said and told him the story.

"So you do have a mystery admirer then?"

"I really don't think so."

"Why not? You're a very attractive woman. It wouldn't be odd for someone to want to woo you with flowers."

"You haven't heard it all yet," she said and her story of the shredded flowers wiped the smile from his face.

"I think you're right; they're not yours." He shook his head. "I hope my roses make you feel better about receiving flowers."

"They're lovely." She gave him a quick peck on the cheek, and he looked surprised. "I forgot to give you a kiss when you came in."

"Well I'm of European descent," he said and kissed her cheek too. "So any preference for this evening's entertainment?"

"Scott's out overnight at a friend's so we haven't got any worries either way. We can go out and have a drink or something to eat, or we can stay here and listen to music or watch a film and eat."

"I need to eat," he said and patted his stomach for emphasis. "I'm starving."

"So am I. Do you like Indian?"

"I do."

"Good. Let me put my shoes on and we'll go to the Taste Of India."

"Okay," he said and backed into the dining room. "I like decisive women."

* * *

The meal was delicious and Claire enjoyed the company which was good fun and very handsome.

He parked across from her house. She unlocked the front door and stepped out of her shoes.

"I haven't got any beer but there's wine, coffee and tea."

"Coffee," he said and rattled his car keys.

"Fair enough." She went into the kitchen and he leaned against the door frame as she put the kettle on.

"I'd love to have a kitchen with patio doors," he said.

"We had a pantry there when we moved in, but it made the room so dark it was ridiculous. Now one of my favourite things is to sit at the table first thing in the morning and eat breakfast with all this gorgeous golden light everywhere."

"Sounds marvellous."

The kettle clicked and she poured the water. "Do you mind if I have some wine?"

"Nope, you wine away."

The conversation felt a bit slower than it had in the restaurant, as if they were both trying to figure out the situation. Could he be as rusty at this as she was? At the moment she wasn't sure how she felt the evening would go – it might come to him staying overnight or it might not – but she thought wine might take the edge off her nerves.

Claire poured herself a generous glass then took him into the lounge. He sat in the armchair. She sat across from him on the sofa and tucked her legs underneath her.

"Cheers," he said and raised his mug.

"Cheers."

They drank and she stole glances at him, thrilled at the sheer delight of being taken for dinner by an eligible man she found handsome. His eyes glittered when he laughed and his lopsided smile did things to her she hadn't felt in a long time. It was nice to feel that way again.

"How've you found the dating game?" he asked.

"It's different to how I remember it."

"Same here. Sometimes it's as painfully awkward as I remember then at other times it's very brash. I went on a date a few months back and the lady was extremely forward. We went for a meal and snogged in the car when I went to drop her off."

"Your teenaged self would have been very impressed."

"Probably, until we got into the house and her ex-husband was there. He'd run out of booze and let himself in to pinch some of hers. Killed the mood somewhat."

"I can imagine."

"What about you? You're beautiful and intelligent; you must have to ward off potential dates with a big stick."

"You're too kind," she said and raised her glass. He smiled and raised his mug. "My best – or worst – was a friend of a friend through work. I'd seen his photograph – he looked nice – and only knew he was recently divorced. We were going to see a play at The Royal Theatre and he came to pick me up. He complimented me on how I was dressed then suggested I might want to undo a couple of buttons on my blouse. When he asked if we were on for later, I thought I'd misheard him and he said it again, word for word. I reminded him we hadn't even spoken and rather than drive off, he said he wasn't interested in a date unless us getting together was guaranteed."

Mike raised his eyebrows. "What?"

"Weirdly, he looked quite surprised when I got out of the car."

"Did he apologise and take you to the theatre anyway?"

"No, he called me a frigid cow and drove off."

"What a charmer."

"That's not what I called him when he emailed to see if I'd changed my mind."

"He emailed you?"

"Uh-huh."

"Damn. That's where I've been going wrong."

"I seriously doubt you'd ever do anything like that."

"I might do," he said, pretending to be hurt. "I could be a bad boy for all you know."

"Of course you could."

He finished his coffee and put his mug on the shelf next to his chair. "So what brought you to the friends group?"

She drank some wine. "Usual story I suppose. We'd been together for a couple of decades and settled into parenthood and life got a bit samey. He saw an opportunity for a bit of excitement and took it and I found out and everything came crashing down." Claire didn't know if it was the wine or Mike's easy company, but this was the first time she'd told anyone what happened and didn't feel a twist of anger in her chest.

"I'm sorry."

"Not your fault," she said. "But thank you."

"My story is painfully similar."

"You left your wife for a bit of excitement?" she asked with genuine surprise.

"Good God no. Carol, my ex-wife, had always been keen on photography and she was really good at it. When our daughter Monica didn't need us quite so much and we suddenly had spare time, I suggested Carol do something with her skill. She went to night school and got friendly with someone on her course; they went away on a couple of retreats and, as they say, the grass is always greener."

Now Claire felt compelled to say sorry.

"Not your fault," he said.

"It's not fair, is it?"

"Nope, so let's not dwell on it. How about a moratorium on past romantic lives?"

"Agreed. How about some music instead?"

"I like the sound of that." He glanced into the dining room. "I see a stereo. Are you old school?"

"CDs all the way. Scott keeps trying to convince me to go digital and stream but I don't want to have to re-buy my collection."

"Same here."

They went into the dining room and she opened a drawer in a merchant's chest where she kept her CDs.

"So what are you into?" he asked.

"Soul, funk, disco, some rock and pop. And I love 80s music."

"Tonight feels like a soul and funk night to me," he said with a smile.

Feeling flirty she quickly found a CD. "This'll be perfect," she said and held up *Let's Get It On*.

He looked at the cover. "I like it. Have you ever listened to it, like that?"

"Like what?" she asked, her innocent tone at odds with the warm feelings suddenly running through her.

"The way we were told to listen to it as teenagers."

She felt more warming sensations. "I can't say I have."

"Always a first time," he said casually.

His comment took her by surprise, but the laugh didn't kill the building mood. They were standing very close. His eyes were bright behind his glasses and he smiled that wonderful smile and all she wanted to do was... So why didn't she? What was holding her back?

"Are we...?" he said.

"I think so," she said.

He touched her neck, gently and softly and she felt a charge zip through her core.

"I'm a fool," he said quietly. "I can't read signs."

She tried to speak but her voice cracked. She licked her lips. "This is the sign," she said and stood on tiptoe to put her lips against his.

That first kiss lingered and she was content to feel the tingling sensation from the pressure of his mouth against hers. The second kiss was harder. Her heart began to pound. The third kiss was exploratory and her tongue felt his. He pulled her close and she put her hands against his chest and felt his heartbeat.

"Okay?" he asked breathlessly.

"Yes," she said as her lips slid against his cheek. "Yes."

Kissing again, she moved her hands to his back. He cupped her buttocks and lifted her off her feet briefly. She squeaked with surprise and he pulled her tighter to him as their kisses got deeper. She could feel his hardness. Her own heat built.

He set her down and kissed her neck and she tipped her head back. It had been too long since someone had made her feel like this and she wanted his mouth again. She held his face and found his lips. Their tongues met and their breathing grew ever heavier.

"Oh God," he said at one point and she kissed the words away.

He put a hand against her belly and she felt the heat of it through her blouse more so as he cupped her breast. Her breath caught. She touched him and brought a corresponding gasp.

Mike leaned on the merchant's chest. She slipped between his legs and pressed herself to him.

"Do you have anything?" she murmured against his neck.

He nibbled her earlobe. "No, you?"

"Upstairs," she said with barely enough breath to speak.

She kissed him again then rushed upstairs, her heart pounding. She ran into her bedroom, dived across the bed and pulled opened the bedside cabinet drawer. There was the box of condoms. She pulled it out and the date code on top seemed too large.

"Shit, shit, shit, shit."

They were out of date by almost a year.

She heard tentative footsteps on the stairs and checked the date again. It didn't change. She turned to face Mike who stood at the end of the landing.

"I didn't know whether to come up or not," he said. His shirt was untucked but didn't hang low enough to hide his excitement.

Claire sat on the edge of the bed and shook her head. How could this happen? How could she get so close to having the hot sex she really wanted and be prevented by this? Was it worth ignoring the date and hoping for the best? She considered that for less than a second – hoping for the best was as stupid in your forties as it was when you were a teenager. Would he understand?

"I'm sorry," she said and held up the Durex box.

"You're sorry that you've got some?"

"They're out of date."

"Oh."

"Oh," she repeated. "I'm so sorry."

"Hey, it's not your fault."

She stood up and straightened her blouse as she walked along the landing to him. He tucked in his shirt.

"It kind of is," she said and hugged him hard.

"Nah," he said and kissed her quickly on the lips. She made it more and then broke off.

"That was very close and very sexy."

"Yep." He made a show of checking his watch. "Anyway, it's late and it's a school night and…"

She was pleased he was trying to make the situation easier. "I know this doesn't make it better but if I hadn't come upstairs, I wouldn't have stopped."

"Nor would I," he said and kissed her again.

They went downstairs holding hands. He held her tightly and dropped kisses on top of her head. She ran her hand across his chest and down to his beltline.

"Can we do this again?" she asked.

"I'm already planning the next date and I'll make a stop at the chemist on the way."

"Good idea."

He put his shoes on and she opened the front door for him.

"I had a lovely night," she said.

"So did I."

They kissed again, long enough for their breathing to get heavy and she broke off in case she got carried away and pulled him back into the house.

"I'll see you Saturday," he said.

"You will. It's a date, Mr Templeton."

"I like the sound of that very much, Ms Heeley."

She stood in the porch to watch him go. The stone floor was pleasantly cool on her bare feet. He drove slowly away and, as he turned into Ragsdale Street, she noticed his nearside brake light was broken.

Chapter 27

Claire watched the sunlight make the top of the curtains glow. Her alarm wouldn't go off for another ten minutes and she was content to lie quietly.

Memories of last night came to her as shivers of pleasure. Human contact on that intimate and physical level pleased her. She liked caresses and kissing, enjoyed making love and had desperately missed all of that since Greg went. She's missed them before, if she thought back on it, and it wasn't until the split she realised he'd withdrawn from her as he grew closer to Matilda.

Friends told her it should be an exciting time and she should spread her wings but her adventures on Tinder and a couple of dating agencies hadn't exactly been successful.

Holding and touching and making Mike breathe faster was wonderful though. Even better, the way her body had responded to his touch had been just what she'd needed.

She rolled onto her back and ran her hands over her stomach. She would pick some condoms up today even though he'd said he would – better to be safe than sorry.

* * *

Claire put Eric Gnome back in his rightful place on the tree stump. She stuck her thumb up at the patio doors and held the pose long enough for Scott's camera to catch her. Then she did her stretches before walking out to the street.

Claire walked towards the front of her car. There were no flowers but another sheet of A5 paper had been pinned under the wiper blade. A pain throbbed briefly at the base of her skull and flared behind her eyes, making her squint as she pulled the paper free. The hangman image on the back looked like the one on the last note – it looked, she realised as she turned to check it was still there, just like the one chalked onto her house – but the face had been smudged and the two Xs for eyes dragged towards the chin area.

Breathing deeply, she turned the paper over in her hands. The message had been printed in the same cursive, large point font.

HE'S MARRIED

She read it twice and the words began to swim until anger pushed back at the fear. This had to be a case of mistaken identity. She looked at the other cars in the street, trying to guess which owner the note could have been meant for. She knew from bitter experience it was impossible to tell who was having an affair, but she absolutely knew it wasn't her.

Unless Mike wasn't telling her something.

A shiver trailed down her spine. Could he have lied to her? Was he using the group as a pick-up place and his wife had found out and this was her way of warning Claire off?

Except, except… This had to be her paranoia talking. For his wife to have known she must have been at the bowling alley to see Claire and Mike flirting to get angry enough to put the first flowers on the car on Monday. And if it was his wife, did that explain the hangman or was that something completely different? She shook her head. With the stalker and hoodie, to follow this line of conspiracy-theory-level thinking would drive her mad.

She put the note in her pocket and took several deep breaths. Hopefully this morning's run would calm her ever growing feeling of anxiety. One worry she could put to rest quickly by asking Mike outright. He hadn't given off the vibe of telling lies but she'd been wrong about Greg so what did she know?

* * *

The hangman game on the storm drain had progressed. The victim was now attached to the gallows by a single line and a daub of paint made it look as though his tongue poked out the upturned U of his mouth.

An *e* had now been played over the last dash while an *h* was scored through underneath. Something about it nagged at her but she couldn't put her finger on it – annoyed at her inability to make the connection, she ran back up the hill and into town. She passed the Co-op and ran out of Shelley Street.

The hoodie stood at the mouth of an alley across the road. He wore blue disposable gloves, and his hands were crossed over his stomach.

Claire came to a dead stop, her breath harsh and hot in her chest. The hoodie appeared to be looking at her though it was impossible to tell for sure because his face was in shadow. He made no move to get away. She leaned forward and stretched her calves as she watched him and slipped the rape alarm out of her pocket.

Anxious thoughts raced through her – all the times she'd seen him, the way he made her feel, the fact he'd been watching The Kino when Eva arrived. She thought of the flowers and the notes and this twat making her feel threatened.

Her anxiety faded into anger and she felt it build. Then she ran.

Not her normal speed but a sprint. She crossed the road and he looked smaller now both in stature and threat.

Distance had lent him an air of menace but now he seemed slightly shorter than her and heavy in the torso.

He turned into the alley and ran hard but the advantage was hers. She had momentum on her side and pushed herself faster.

The alley mouth was wide and quickly cut sharply left. She ran into it and took the corner tightly. The hoodie was fifty yards ahead and running hard. His breathing echoed against the brick walls and wooden fences that formed the alley. Claire put on a bit more speed and settled into a rhythm that wouldn't drain her energy.

By the time she could see the top of the alley she'd managed to close the gap between them and narrowed it further with every stride.

The hoodie risked a glance over his shoulder and stumbled. He grabbed the wall for support and ripped out the palm of his glove. Clair pushed herself and closed the gap further.

He'd started making a strange grunting sound as if the effort was too much. An overhanging branch from one garden caught the top of his hood and, for a moment, she thought it would rip it away but he grabbed for it to keep his head covered. She ducked under the foliage without pausing.

His pace slowed as his grunting increased. His sleeves looked tight and there were dimples at the elbow as if he was wearing something else underneath. The same with his back, which was bell-shaped with the shoulders falling away.

Twenty yards from the top of the alley. His trainers slapped the concrete, and his breathing was ever more ragged. Claire closed the gap until she could almost reach out and touch him.

She pushed herself and felt the strain in her legs. Her fingers grabbed for him.

The hoodie ducked to his left and ran into the frame of an empty doorway. The sound of the impact and his corresponding "oof" were loud. Claire caught a glimpse of the overgrown garden beyond him as she tried to stop herself. She reached for him and missed. Her left foot skidded on something and her momentum threw her to the ground.

She landed heavily on her side and winded herself. Her left shoulder spiked with pain.

She heard the hoodie run through the garden and the slap of his trainers faded.

Claire rolled onto her back and closed her eyes. The ground felt gritty on her shoulders and arms.

"Fuck!" she shouted.

Her stomach and chest hurt, and she sat up slowly. It took a couple of minutes for her to feel well enough to stand and when she did, she quickly checked herself for injuries. Her arm and hand were grazed. A lump of dog shit had smeared up the side of her trainer.

She limped slowly out of the alley.

Chapter 28

After her shower, Claire sat at the kitchen table in her dressing gown and drank a cup of coffee.

Her mind kept going back to the hoodie and their chase and how dangerous it seemed in retrospect. She'd got away lightly, even counting the extra grazes she'd found on her arm and thigh, but he could have turned dangerous.

Her mobile rang and Mike's name appeared on the screen. She was pleased to see it but remembered the note. If it wasn't a case of mistaken identity, then surely she needed to know?

"Good morning," he said and sounded bright and cheery.

"Morning," she said. In an instant she decided not to tell him about the hoodie. That really needed to be done face to face.

"Finished your run?"

"Yep. Had my shower and now having a coffee."

"Sounds very nice. So, I have a question. Ben's asked me to go for a meal tonight."

"Lucky you."

He laughed. "Yeah, thanks. I'm worried we'll just sit there in silence for an hour or two."

"And you want me to give you conversational pointers?"

"No, I want you to come with me."

"Really?"

"Yes. I thought if you asked Eva and Amy, we could have a newbie table outing. A chance for us all to have a chat about things just in case Keith does come back to the group."

She felt a reaction like a kick in the gut at the mention of his name. "Good point."

"So will you ask them? He's suggested Pizza Shed on Scarborough Place."

"I can try." She sipped her coffee and felt a flurry of nerves but knew if she didn't ask now it would only be harder to do so later. "Can I ask you a question?"

"Seems fair."

How should she phrase this? However she asked was going to be odd so maybe just say it straight and see what happened. "Are you married?"

He started to repeat 'married' but stopped and chuckled. "Sorry. Did you ask if I was married?"

"I did."

"What's brought this on?" he asked. "Yes, I suppose I am technically."

His admission jabbed at her. "Technically?"

"Yes," he said and sounded confused. "My decree absolute hasn't been granted yet."

The sense of relief made her feel light-headed. Of course he wasn't married – the notes really weren't meant for her.

"Are you still married?" he asked.

"Only technically, like you."

"So why ask? Has something happened?"

"Sort of, but I'd prefer to talk about it in person."

"Are you okay?"

"I'm fine."

"If you're sure," he said, without sounding sure. "Ring me when you've spoken to the girls."

"I will." She remembered something from last night. "And by the way, your brake light is broken."

"I'll check it, thanks."

* * *

Claire rang Amy on the way to work.

"Claire! I was going to call you. How did the date go?"

"It went well."

"That good, eh?"

"Not really. We had a condom issue."

"Please don't tell me neither of you had one?"

"I had half a box but they were out of date."

"Oh dear." Amy sounded sympathetic then laughed. "That's awful."

"Your concern is touching. Anyway, I rang to see if you're free tonight."

"I could be."

"You are now. Ben wants us to go for a pizza." She gave the details of when and where.

"That'd be lovely. Have you heard any more from Detective Rosie?"

"No. Do you know if Jane spoke to Keith?"

"I'll see what I can find out before tonight. Oh and, Claire?"

149

"Yes."

"Buy some condoms."

* * *

Claire was at work when Eva rang.

"I realise you're probably in the office, but I wanted to make sure all was well."

"I think so. How about with you?"

Eva made a *pish* sound. "I lead a very boring life, you know that. Any more troubles with your hoodie?"

"No," said Claire. She didn't want to discuss it though her thigh twinged as if on cue. "I wanted to speak to you, actually, to see if you're free tonight."

Eva ummed theatrically. "Fridays usually mean having dinner and catching up on box sets."

"How about coming out for a pizza with the newbie table?"

"I'd like that. Shall I come and get you? That way, you can have a drink if you want."

"If you're sure?" Claire gave Eva her address. "Here for seven thirty?"

"I'll be there."

Claire went back to her spreadsheet. Almost an hour later, her boss came into her office.

"I just got off the phone with Steve at Moore Associates," James said.

She cringed at the memory of her cock-up. "Did it go well?"

"Swimmingly! We've got him. Thanks for all your help with it, Claire, I appreciate it."

It was only after he'd left that Claire realised she'd never found the missing flash drive. That could be a job for Sunday, she decided.

* * *

Mike rang as she walked to the deli.

"Where are you?" he asked.

"In town, where are you?"

"At school but I'd much rather be walking into town to meet you. Did you manage to speak to the ladies?"

"Yes, they're both up for it and Eva's picking me up."

"I'd have happily driven you. Speaking of which, I looked at the brake light and you were right. Some little scrote must have smashed it last night. I know it wasn't there when I left school because I put a tuba in the boot and didn't notice it."

"You mean outside mine?" She felt a pang of guilt. "Shit, I'm so sorry."

"It's not your fault and don't worry. I enjoy spending money on bits of coloured plastic. I've got to go, the headmaster's watching me. I'll see you later."

* * *

As the afternoon wore on, Claire found her mind drifting back to the incident in the alley.

She found Rosie's card in her bag. The detective constable had said to ring if anything cropped up and this was definitely something. While the flowers and notes were probably mistaken identity, the hoodie wasn't and she'd risked her life.

She pushed her office door closed. The phone rang three times.

"DC Carter. Can I help you?"

"Hi Rosie, it's Claire Heeley. We spoke yesterday."

There was a slight pause and Claire heard a conversation in the background.

"Of course, Claire. What can I do for you? Are you and your son okay?"

"We're fine."

"Have you been contacted by Mr Hasslett?"

"No, it's something else altogether but you said if anything cropped up I should call."

"Something's cropped up?"

"I'm not sure how to say this without sounding paranoid but I think someone's following me."

"You've seen them?"

"Actually, it's two people. I saw a stranger in the market square a couple of weeks ago when I was on my morning run and he almost ran me over."

"Ran you over? Were you alright?"

"Just shaken. I haven't seen him since but last week, I noticed a man in a grey hoodie watching me."

"A hoodie?" She heard an upturn of interest in Rosie's voice.

"Yes, like you mentioned from the CCTV. The first couple of times I could have been mistaken but then I was sure."

"How were you sure?"

"Because I saw him when I was running. Today he was standing by the alley on Croft Road."

"What did he do?"

"He stood and watched me so I chased him."

"You chased him?" Rosie's voice rose in surprise.

"I did and I know it was stupid, but I just really wanted to find out who it was and thought I should tell you."

"Talk me through what happened."

Claire did. "I didn't want him to think I was frightened. I know I shouldn't have done it."

"What were you planning to do if you caught him?"

Claire bit her lip and felt like a fool. "I hadn't thought that far ahead. Maybe scream at him."

"That's very dangerous, Claire."

"I see that now. I also had my rape alarm and was fully prepared to use it."

"Even so," Rosie said with a tone in her voice that invited no response. "How many times have you seen this man?"

"Four for definite."

"And could you describe him?"

"I've never seen his face."

"So how do you know it's a man?"

"Because my friend Eva saw him watching The Kino when I met her there for a drink."

"And what did she describe?"

"She didn't look at him too closely and only really saw sandy-coloured hair."

"Okay, Claire, let me process this and I'll see what we come up with. Until I get back to you, I'd suggest you keep your alarm with you at all times. If you see him again then dial 999 and call him a stalker. Do the same for the man on the market square. Until we have more information, or a face, we don't have a lot to go on."

"I understand. I'm glad I told you."

"I'm glad too, Claire. You've done the right thing and hopefully we can catch these toerags and solve two crimes in one go."

"That would be nice."

"Just be aware of where you are and who's around you. I'd love to tell you the hoodie won't try anything because he's really a coward, but I can't guarantee that."

Chapter 29

Claire called into a chemist's shop on the way home and picked up a packet of condoms.

Harry barked excitedly as she got out of her car. His nose pushed under the slats of the gate as she walked down the entry.

"Hello, boy," she said as she opened her own gate.

Harry barked again and Annie told hold him to hush.

"Hi, Claire."

"Hi. He seems very excited."

"I think we've wound him up."

Scott appeared in Claire's line of vision. "Hi, Mum."

Annie unlatched her gate and Harry shot through like a rocket to bounce around Claire's feet.

"Shouldn't you be getting ready, Scott?" Claire asked.

He checked the time on his phone screen. "In a minute."

"It's my fault," said Annie. "I asked him to come over."

Claire smiled at Annie then looked over the girl's shoulder at Scott. He made a pleading expression as if begging for more time and she decided another few minutes wouldn't do any harm.

"You two have fun with Harry," she said. "I'm going to dump my stuff and have a coffee and put my feet up for fifteen minutes."

"Thanks," Scott mouthed at her.

Claire rubbed Harry's head then pushed open her gate. The dog shot between her legs and headed at speed for the lawn.

"Oh no," said Annie. "Sorry." She and Scott ran off in pursuit.

Claire got changed into a pair of shorts and a T-shirt and had just put the kettle on when Greg rang her mobile.

"I'm sorry to drop this on you at the last minute, Claire, but I can't have Scott tonight."

"What do you mean? We're leaving the house in literally ten minutes."

"Something's come up. I'm really sorry."

Frustration pulled at her. "You can't be serious."

"He can come over tomorrow instead."

"Well that's mighty good of you. Has something come up with work?"

He paused long enough to make his "yes" a lie but she decided it wasn't worth the hassle to push him on it.

"It'll have to be fine then, won't it?" she said. "Have you told him yet?"

"No. Would you mind doing it?"

Claire looked at Scott and Annie who were sitting on the patio as Harry ran around their legs. She fought to keep her voice level. "Why can't you do it? We all know you need to be flexible with work, but you could at least do him the honour of telling him yourself."

"I'm asking you to," Greg said. There was an edge to his voice she didn't like. "I'll see him tomorrow."

His tone nudged her frustration towards anger. "I'll tell him not to get his hopes up."

"Claire, that's not—"

"Goodnight, Greg."

She ended the call and opened the patio doors. Harry barked at her.

"Sorry about this, mate," she said and sat opposite Scott, "but your dad can't do tonight so there's no need to rush about."

"Really?" The disappointment was clear in his voice.

"Afraid so, kiddo, but he said sorry, and he'll see you tomorrow."

"He could have told me himself," he muttered.

"I know but it is what it is. How about I make you some tea?"

"What are you having?"

"I'm going out with my friends group."

Scott leaned towards Annie. "That's the dating group I told you about," he stage-whispered and Annie laughed, then looked at Claire and stopped as a guilty expression flooded her face.

"It's not a dating group," Claire said, slowly enunciating each word.

"Can Annie stay for tea?"

"If that's okay with Roger and Lou."

"I'll go check," Annie said, as if eager to get away.

She rushed up the yard with Harry at her heels. Claire watched until they'd gone through the gate.

"I'm sorry, Scott, I did tell him to call you."

"It's not your fault, Mum."

She knew that but often felt as though it was. "That doesn't mean I don't feel bad about it."

"You shouldn't." He leaned forward. "If Annie can have tea here, could she stay on so we can watch a Blu-ray?"

"So long as she asks Lou."

"I'll go and tell her to ask," he said and rushed after Annie.

* * *

Roger and Lou were fine with the plans and even offered to have Scott sleep over but he declined. He and Annie chose a pizza and ordered it from a local place that delivered quickly before going into the garden to play with Harry.

Claire went upstairs to get changed and Amy rang her.

"Glad I've caught you in," she said. "I'm sorry about this, Claire, but I'm going to have to make my excuses for tonight."

"That's a shame."

"Not for me. I got a call from Gayle, my ex-girlfriend, and she wants to meet up for a drink."

"That sounds positive."

"I thought so. Keep me posted on how things go."

* * *

Claire watched Scott and Annie from the kitchen. They sat next to each other on the patio and looked vaguely uncomfortable in that wonderful way she remembered from her own teenaged years; where you clearly liked the person you were with but weren't sure how they'd respond if you said something.

Harry barked and Annie looked at him and Claire saw how Scott watched her. He clearly felt more for her than simple friendship. When he noticed Claire watching him, he smiled shyly as if he'd been caught looking at something he shouldn't.

"What time's the pizza due?"

"About ten minutes. Where are you singles club people meeting?"

"At Pizza Shed. And it's not a singles club."

"Yeah, Scott," said Annie. "Don't be rude." She looked at Claire with a big smile. "I think it's great, Claire, you get back out there."

"Thanks," Claire said, slightly bemused.

"If my mum and dad split up, I reckon it's Mum who'd get herself back on her feet and live her life."

"You don't think Roger would?" Claire said.

His voice drifted over the fence. "Roger wouldn't what?"

Marvellous, Claire thought as he came onto his own patio. His blue dress shirt didn't go at all well with the red shorts he wore.

He winked at Claire. "It's not a big list."

Annie either didn't get or pretended not to hear the innuendo. "If you and Mum split up, I don't think you'd join a singles group."

"What would I do then?"

"Tinder," Annie said.

"Speed dating," suggested Scott.

Claire wanted to say he'd probably sit in his bedsit in his pants lamenting how he'd let Lou go, but kept quiet.

"I like the idea of speed dating," Roger said, "I could go through the ladies like nobody's business."

"Ew gross, Dad," said Annie and pulled a face that made Roger laugh.

"Yeah, that's gross," said Scott and he looked from Roger to Claire. "I mean, no offence, but you two are old."

"Charming," said Claire.

"Yes, charming," said Roger and he disappeared from the patio.

"I don't think you're old," said Annie and looked at Claire as if appraising her. "I think you're very attractive and deserve every happiness."

The doorbell rang and Scott bolted out of his chair. He grabbed the twenty-pound note Claire had left on the kitchen table and ran through the house.

"I think he's hungry," Annie said.

"He often is."

Conversation drifted through from the hallway. The front door closed and Scott trudged into the dining room. Behind him, she could see someone in the hall taking their shoes off.

"It's not the pizza. Your friend Eva's come to pick you up."

Eva came into the dining room, wearing a cotton dress. Her hair had been pulled into a loose ponytail. Her lips were a pale red and there was the lightest touch of make-up around her eyes.

"Hi," Claire said. She went into the dining room and gave her friend a hug. "You look great."

Eva seemed surprised but the sparkle in her eyes showed she appreciated the compliment. "Thanks, it's just simple."

"Like me," Claire said. "I'm not ready yet though."

"Don't worry. I was so looking forward to tonight I left a bit early."

"Can I get you a drink?"

"No. Introduce me to your son and his girlfriend and I'll sit on the patio with them while you get dressed."

Claire led Eva out onto the patio. Scott looked up and smiled.

"Eva, this is my son Scott who you just met. And this is Annie, literally the girl next door."

"Pleased to meet you both," said Eva.

Harry barked and chased his tail.

"And that's my dog Harry," said Annie.

"He's lovely," Eva said.

As if aware he was the subject of the conversation, Harry bounded up onto the patio.

* * *

When the pizzas arrived, Scott and Annie sat with the boxes on their laps and ate with their fingers. Claire finished her coffee in the kitchen.

"Is Amy meeting us there?" Eva asked.

"She can't make it unfortunately. Her ex-girlfriend wanted to meet her for a drink."

"I didn't realise she was gay."

Claire shrugged. "I don't think she's hidden it."

"So it is just the four of us going now then?"

"Yes. It's the newbie table, like I said."

A dark cloud seemed to cross Eva's face and she plucked at the hair above her left ear. "Hold on. I don't want to go on a double date."

"What do you mean? It's not a double date."

Eva pulled at her hair a little harder. "You and Mike clearly like each other and yet you arrange this even though I told you I felt uncomfortable with Ben?"

Eva was clearly getting worked up and Claire decided to nip it in the bud. "I never organised anything, Ben did. I asked you and Amy. I can't help it that Gayle rang out of the blue. Nobody's arranged anything. I promise."

Eva took a deep breath, let it out slowly. After smoothing the hair over her ear, she held out her hands in a calming gesture though Claire couldn't tell which of them it was for.

"I'm sorry, Claire. I just really don't want to go on a date."

"We're not."

"But if you and Mike moon over each other that'll leave me and Ben sitting around like spare parts."

"So don't come." Claire hadn't meant it to sound so cold, but the words hung in front of them and made Eva frown.

"You think I shouldn't go?"

"No, I think you should. I think we'll have a great time and Mike and I won't get all smoochy."

Eva tilted her head down and looked at Claire through her lashes. "You think I'm being selfish."

"I think you misunderstood a situation and panicked."

"You're right." Eva nodded. "I'm sorry."

Claire looked away from her to hopefully ease some of the tension that she could still feel in the air. She noticed an envelope by one of the table legs and picked it up. There was no franking mark, only a slightly skewed first class stamp. She didn't recognise the name, 'Emma Smith', or address.

"What's that?" asked Eva.

"A letter for someone called Emma."

"Oh that's mine," Eva said. "She lives across the hall from me and I picked up her mail by accident this morning and stuffed it in my bag to give to her later. Harry must have knocked it out when he was leaping around."

"He is a lively little thing." Claire gave the letter to Eva who stuffed it into her bag.

"We should be going," Eva said.

Claire finished her coffee. "Yes. Our evening awaits."

Chapter 30

Pizza Shed occupied a corner plot in Scarborough Place, a small retail park just off the main road.

Eva parked close to the front of the building. "Have you been here before?"

"Once or twice. It used to be one of Scott's favourite restaurants but we haven't been in ages."

They went into the restaurant and waited at the service point until a waitress came over.

"Evening, ladies, have you booked a table?"

"Yes," said Claire. "Name of Montgomery."

The woman checked a list, said, "Come with me," and led them between tables. The room was noisy with conversation and laughter while a few kids were larking about at the ice cream dispenser to the left.

Their table was in front of the middle window overlooking the main road.

"Here you go, ladies," said the woman. She put the menus on the table and left.

Mike and Ben had sat across from one another.

"Which side?" Claire asked and Eva nodded towards Mike's side where she took the window seat.

Claire sat next to Ben.

"Evening," Mike said.

She could smell his aftershave and felt a little rise of heat in her stomach.

"Evening, yourself," she said.

"Good to see you," said Ben and looked at her intently. "I'm really pleased you could come." He quickly looked at Eva. "Both of you, it's lovely."

"Thanks for asking. I didn't want you and Mike to have all the fun and leave me and Eva out."

"No Amy tonight?" Ben asked.

"She can't make it," said Eva, looking up from the menu and sounding like she didn't believe it. "Just us four."

"Well that's alright," said Mike. "It'll give us a chance to chat and get to know one another better."

"Absolutely," said Ben. "I hope you ladies are ready to order because I'm starving."

They read the menus and then Mike caught the attention of a waitress.

"Hi," she said brightly. "I'm Gina. Are you ready to order?"

Claire thought Gina looked about as old as Annie. She had badges on her uniform braces and three brightly coloured pens in her left breast pocket.

Gina took their food and drink orders briskly and Mike suggested they should have some garlic bread to share.

* * *

The toilets were at the end of a short corridor and as Claire came out of the ladies, she saw Mike waiting at the restaurant end. Clearly waiting for her, he was watching children squirt ice cream into their bowls and shriek with laughter if any of it spilled. She walked up to him quietly.

"Are you loitering?"

Startled, he stood up straight. "Not at all. I just wanted to say hi because I don't think we'll get much time to talk at the table."

"Eva's worried I've brought her along on a double date."

"Well then it's a good job I decided to wait for you here because I wanted to tell you how great you look in that dress."

"Thanks. As it happens, I thought about you as I was getting ready."

He raised his eyebrows. "Tell me more?"

"Not much to tell, it was just naughty little thoughts. Like whether we'd manage to snatch a quick kiss this evening."

"I like your naughty little thoughts."

"I was even considering playing a bit of footsie with you."

"That's lucky because I'm partial to a pretty foot."

She wanted to kiss him but one of the kids shouted and interrupted the moment. "I'd better get back," she said with reluctance.

"I'd better go to the loo." He kissed her quickly on the lips. "Sorry," he said and looked anything but. "My self-control is flagging."

"So's mine," she said and kissed him quickly back before she went into the restaurant.

Eva stared miserably at the tabletop as Ben talked. She looked up and saw Claire and her expression slipped into a smile.

As Claire got closer, she heard Eva say, "Well I think we'll have to agree to disagree, don't you?"

Ben went to speak but Eva cut him off with a bright "Hi" as Claire sat down.

* * *

Gina brought their drinks and a few moments later, two plates of garlic bread.

"How are you feeling about going back to the group?" Mike asked Claire as he took a piece of bread. "After that business with our loaded Keith."

Claire felt the skin of her shoulders pull tight.

"He's an arsehole," said Ben and gave Claire a subtle nod. "I hope Jane kicks him out."

"I hope so too," said Claire.

"Yes," said Eva with a sympathetic look. "You did seem to catch the brunt of it."

"And," said Ben, leaning forward as if he had something important to share, "that wasn't the end of it."

Mike looked sharply at him. "What do you mean?"

"Didn't you hear?"

Mike looked at Claire with furrowed brows. "Did he say something else to you?"

Claire shook her head.

"Someone had a go at him," Ben said.

"He got beaten up?" Mike looked very confused now. "When did that happen?"

"He didn't get beaten up," Ben said. "His car was vandalised in the Sun car park."

Intrigued, Eva sat forward. "What happened?"

Claire felt like an outsider being told about someone else's life. Her palms were sweaty and her pulse raced. She bit her lip and tried to breathe steadily.

"I'm not entirely sure," he said. "I spoke to Jane today who told me what he'd said to her but whether it's the full picture or not I don't know."

Claire tilted her head to one side and felt her neck creak. Why wouldn't Ben stop talking?

"Someone scratched the word creep into the bonnet hard enough to wreck it apparently."

"Wow," said Mike. "Karma does work then."

Claire looked at him and smiled weakly.

"They don't know who did it," Ben continued, as if enjoying his moment in the spotlight. "But they've got CCTV of the vandal in action."

"Doesn't mean anything," Mike said. "If they can't pull a clear image, they'll never find him. And you know what? Stuff Keith. He was being a creep."

"He was. And didn't you call him that, Claire?" Ben asked.

"I actually called him a fucking creep."

"Well, serves him right," said Eva.

Claire picked up a slice of garlic bread and put it onto her plate. Something clattered under the table.

"Sorry, Claire," Ben said. "I think I just kicked your bag."

Eva leaned down to reach under the table. She held the rape alarm when she straightened up. "What's this?" she asked.

"It's mine," said Claire and held her hand out. Eva put it gently into her palm. "It must have fallen out when Ben knocked my bag."

Ben leaned across the table. "What is it?"

"Ben," said Mike gently. Claire didn't know if he'd figured out what it was or just didn't want her to be embarrassed.

"What?" he said. "I don't know what it is."

Claire sighed. "It's a rape alarm," she said quietly.

"Can I have a look?" Ben sounded curious. "I've never seen one before."

Eva frowned at him then raised her eyebrows at Claire. Claire gave her a what-can-I-do shrug and handed the alarm over.

"They're supposed to be a brilliant deterrent, aren't they?" he said.

"That's the plan," said Claire.

"Oh no," he said, "you haven't…?"

"No, Ben, it's purely a precaution."

"Phew," he said, "I thought for a moment I'd put my foot in it."

"No, you're fine," she said and held out her hand.

It took Ben a moment to realise she wanted it back. He picked the alarm up by its cord and Claire made to grab it but wasn't quick enough. The cord disconnected and the alarm dropped into his palm before bouncing onto the table.

The shrill piercing sound silenced every other noise in the restaurant. Claire managed to grab the alarm as it bounced towards Eva and the edge of the table. She saw Mike pull the cord from Ben's fingers and lean forward. His large warm hand covered hers as she tried to pick up the shrieking unit. She let him take it and he deftly palmed it and slipped the cord connector into place. The alarm stopped instantly.

The restaurant was silent for a moment though Claire could still hear the aural echo of the alarm. She felt her cheeks blaze.

"Sorry about that, folks," Mike said. He sounded too loud. "I knew I shouldn't have played around with it."

There were a few laughs and gradually the noise levels rose as people went back to their dinner and conversations.

"I'm so embarrassed," Claire said. "Thank you."

"No problem. Students sometimes have them go off at school and it always pays to know how to silence noisy objects."

"I'm so sorry," said Ben and looked properly contrite.

"Don't worry about it," Claire said. "You didn't know how it worked."

"That is bloody loud," said Eva and rubbed at her left ear.

"It's just a bit of extra security," said Claire.

"Because of the hoodie business?"

"Hoodie business?" Ben asked.

Eva's eyes widened to protest her innocence. "Sorry. Was I not supposed to say anything?"

"It's okay," Claire said and looked at Ben. "It seems I'm being followed by some bloke wearing a grey hoodie."

"I didn't realise you knew it was a bloke," said Mike.

"Eva saw him on Tuesday when we met at The Kino."

"I didn't pay much attention though, unfortunately," she said.

"When did you realise?" Ben asked Claire.

She gave him the basics but left out the part about chasing him. After how DC Carter had reacted, they would probably only tell her off and she didn't need that now.

"Astonishing," said Ben. "All he does is watch you?"

"That's enough, don't you think?"

"Of course," he said quickly. "And you don't know who he is?"

"Not a clue."

"Wow." Ben rubbed his chin with both hands. "I've only ever seen stuff like this on TV."

"But you must have seen him," Eva said. "Weren't you chasing him that night you saw Ben at the Co-op, Claire?"

"That's right," Claire said. "Did you see anyone in a hoodie before we nearly bumped into one another?"

He frowned and slowly shook his head. "I don't remember."

"What were you doing at the Co-op anyway?" Eva asked, cradling her chin in her hands.

"I was buying something," he said with a look of surprise.

"But you don't live anywhere near Claire."

Ben looked at her as if she'd suggested he was a wanted man. "What's that supposed to mean?"

Eva's eyes opened wide, the picture of innocence. "Nothing. I'm just pointing out you were using a shop halfway across town and happened to bump into Claire when she was chasing this hoodie of hers."

Realisation crossed his face like a dark cloud. "Are you saying I'm in league with this bloke?"

"I don't know," Eva said and glanced at Claire. "Have I caused offence?" She looked at Ben and dipped her head slightly. "I didn't mean to infer anything."

"Good," he said gruffly.

"Does seem odd though," Eva said quietly, and Ben looked ready to react when Gina arrived with two big pizza plates.

She put them in front of Ben and Claire; went off and came back with two more for Eva and Mike.

"Let's try and forget this and enjoy the meal as friends," Mike said.

"Agreed," said Claire and held up her glass of wine. "To friends."

The others joined her in the toast and then Ben held his pint up in front of Eva. With a shy smile, she touched her glass to it. "Friends?" he said.

"Friends," she said.

* * *

The mood of the table was more buoyant by the time they finished their meals. When Gina came to collect the plates, Mike complained he'd eaten so much his belt felt like it was cutting him in half. Gina asked if he wanted any dessert.

"Good idea," he said. "I'll have some strawberry cheesecake."

"You said you were full," said Claire.

"There's always room for cheesecake."

"You're right," said Eva. "I'll have some too."

"I'll head to the salad bar," Claire said. "I can't face anything sweet, but I can't watch you lot eat either." She looked at Mike. "And don't you come complaining to me if you explode."

"I promise."

"Hold up," said Ben. "I'll wander over with you."

They walked to the salad bar together.

"It was a lovely meal," he said.

"I've really enjoyed it. Thanks for suggesting we come."

"I ate here a lot before and when I moved back, I was really pleased to find it still open."

There were a handful of adults and two teenagers at the salad bar and Claire and Ben held back while they made their decisions.

"Did Amy invite you to the group?" he asked.

"Yeah. We've known one another for ages. She's a good friend."

"We need friends, don't we?"

"That's a fact," she said.

"Are we friends?"

"Of course. Why wouldn't we be?"

"It's just that you haven't said anything and I wondered if I'd offended you."

"What, by being at the Co-op?"

"No." He laughed nervously. "I mean the flowers I put on your car."

Chapter 31

His words hit Claire like blows. She felt her stomach roll. Had she heard him correctly? "What?"

"The flowers. Since you haven't said anything, I was worried I'd offended you."

"It was you?" she demanded. Her voice rose and one of the teenagers moved away.

Ben looked very nervous. "Yes."

"Which ones?"

"What do you mean?"

"Which ones did you put on my car?" she said and felt her anger build.

"On Monday." He frowned. "How many do you get? I left a note."

She leaned close and lowered her voice. "What about the shredded ones on Wednesday?"

"Shredded?"

"I had two sets of flowers left on my car and I didn't appreciate either of them. They've caused me nothing but worry."

"I really didn't mean to worry you," he said, and she could see from his expression he meant it. He looked scared now.

"You have no bloody idea."

"I left a note," he said in desperation.

She took a deep breath to calm the anger away. "I'd hardly call 'from a mystery admirer' a note, would you?"

He looked at his feet. "I thought being mysterious would be good."

"You thought wrong, Ben."

"I made a mistake."

"Yes, you bloody did. And what about the rest?"

"The rest of what?"

"The rest of the notes."

"I don't understand," he said, panic in his eyes. "I didn't send any notes and my flowers weren't shredded."

He clearly had no idea what she was talking about. Should she explain or leave it? "Forget it," she said.

"But…"

"I said forget it, Ben," she said slowly.

He looked as if he might press the point until good sense clearly prevailed. "I really didn't mean to worry you."

"That's fine." She took another deep breath.

"Is everything alright?"

"No," she said. She'd reacted badly, that wasn't in doubt but if anything, this cast fresh shadows. "Things have been odd. Let's just get our food."

* * *

After they'd eaten, the group ordered more drinks.

"That was excellent," said Mike and stuck his thumb up at Ben. "Well planned, mate."

"Thanks," Ben said, glancing sidelong at Claire.

She smiled. Her anger with him had faded to annoyance. "Yes, good choice."

"I liked it," said Eva. "And I'm not the biggest fan of pizza."

"But pizza loves you so much," Mike said and Claire laughed, more so at Eva's puzzled expression.

"I don't get it," she said and her puzzled expression made them both laugh more. "It doesn't make sense."

"You must hear some silly jokes at school," Ben said.

"I try hard not to. You wouldn't believe how far off the mark fifteen-year-olds can be when they think they're the next best thing in comedy."

"Tell me about it," grumbled Claire. "When Scott tells a joke I sometimes pretend to laugh and other times I just look at him."

"That's not fair, surely?" said Eva. "You could at least laugh."

"Have you heard their jokes?" Mike asked. "Even we wouldn't have laughed at them when we were fifteen."

"I heard one the other day," said Ben. "It really made me laugh but it's very dark."

"I like dark," said Mike.

"It can't be worse than one of Scott's jokes," Claire said.

"I'm up for it," said Eva.

Ben smiled and settled himself in his chair. "Just don't forget I warned you all."

"We get it," said Mike. "Tell it or shut up forever."

"Fine." Ben held out his hands in a calming gesture. "What's the best kind of pizza?"

"The one I just had," Mike said. "Chorizo, mushrooms, red onion and chilli beef. Bloody lovely."

"You're mad," said Claire. "It's a four seasons, quite clearly."

"You're both wrong," said Eva with a shy smile. "It's a vegetarian."

"Vegetarian?" asked Mike in an exaggerated tone. "Are you serious?"

Ben sat back and folded his arms as they laughed. "If you're not going to take this seriously."

"We're taking it seriously," said Claire. "So what's the best kind of pizza?"

"The emo pizza, of course, because it slices itself."

Nobody said anything. Ben smiled broadly into the silence.

"I have heard it," Mike said. "Even my class reacted badly to it. One pupil said linking emo fans to suicide wasn't cool at all."

"Not good, Ben," Claire said. She watched Eva who was pulling at the hair above her left ear and seemed to be chewing at her lower lip.

"I thought it was funny," Ben said.

Eva made a noise deep in her throat that might have been a cough. She pulled harder at her hair and glared at Ben.

"Are you okay, Eva?" Claire asked.

Eva shook her head but didn't look away from Ben.

"What's wrong?" he asked.

Eva made the noise again.

Mike started to stand up.

Claire glanced at him. "What's going on?"

"I think…" Mike began to say but Eva interrupted him by standing up so quickly her chair skidded backwards.

She stared at Ben but seemed to be looking through him. She yanked at her hair and Claire saw tiny strands drifting onto her shoulder.

Eva grabbed her glass and swept it sideways making Ben splutter as her lemonade sprayed across his face.

"What the fuck?" He pushed his chair back, but it caught against the table leg.

Eva made the weird coughing noise again and reached for Claire's glass.

"Eva," Mike said sharply. He grabbed her left wrist and pulled it towards him. Her body shifted but her gaze didn't.

"Eva," he said again but louder.

She pulled out more hair and threw it at Mike while trying to wrestle her arm free of his grip. He held her tighter and managed to catch her other wrist.

"Eva." His voice was hard but low. "You need to calm down."

She looked at him finally and her lips were tight against her teeth. "Let me go, Mike," she hissed.

Claire flinched at the hate in her eyes. Mike didn't seem to see it.

"No," he said.

"Let me go," she repeated.

"Ben," Mike said without looking away from Eva. "Come round behind me."

Ben managed to free his chair and walked quickly around the table.

"I will scream bloody murder if you don't let me go," Eva said. Spittle had gathered on her lower lip.

"Eva," Claire said. The situation frightened her. "What the hell's going on?"

"It's alright," Mike said without diverting his attention from Eva for even a second. "Are you behind me, Ben?"

"Yes."

"Good. Now piss off out the way, mate, okay? Go and get dried off."

"Right. Are you okay?"

"We're fine," Mike said. "We'd be better if you were out of range for a bit though."

"What's happening?" asked Claire.

As Ben left, Eva turned her attention to Mike.

"We've had a bit of a moment," he said.

Claire looked at Eva's hands. She was struggling against Mike's tight grip.

"Can I do anything?" Claire asked.

"Eva? Can Claire help you at all?"

Eva glared at him. She bit her lip hard. "No."

"That's fine. Now you don't want me to hold your wrists and I don't want to hold them either, but I don't want you to hurt yourself or anyone else. If I let go, will you go outside with Claire?"

Startled, Claire looked at him.

"You'll be fine," he said without looking away from Eva. "You're not the issue. Eva? Will you go outside with Claire and get some air while I deal with Ben?"

"Yes," she said, and her voice cracked as a single tear rolled down her cheek. "Please let me go, you're hurting my wrists."

"I'm sorry."

"Please don't hurt me, Mike."

With a pained look he loosened his grip and Eva shook his hands off. She looked from him to Claire then out the window and tilted her head back until Claire heard tendons creak.

Mike tapped Claire's hand and gestured to the door. Gina was standing in front of it and staring at them.

"Come on, Eva," said Claire and got up slowly.

Eva did the same. Her eyes were downcast as if the very act of moving took everything out of her.

Claire put her arm around Eva's shoulders, which felt rigid with tension. "Are you okay?"

Eva shook her head. "I'm sorry," she said, still looking at the floor. "Are people staring?"

Claire glanced around. Most people were studiously ignoring them. "Not really."

"I'm sorry, Mike. I didn't mean to shout at you or be horrible," Eva said.

"I know."

Claire moved her away from the table and across the restaurant floor. Gina stepped towards the salad bar giving them a clear line to the exit. Claire mouthed "thank you".

"I'm sorry," Eva said so quietly that Claire almost didn't catch it.

"Don't worry about it," Claire said and pushed open the door with her free hand.

The night air was warm as they walked to Eva's car.

"It's been a long time since I felt that angry," said Eva quietly. "I can't believe I made a complete idiot of myself over him. He's a twat and I don't care if he never speaks to me again, but I like Mike and he's annoyed at me and I like you and you're annoyed at me."

"That's not true."

"You're embarrassed then."

Claire put both hands on Eva's shoulders and turned her so they faced each other. "I'm not embarrassed, I'm just surprised at how you acted that's all. We're all of an age that we have baggage and sometimes what sets us off is what others least expect."

"Still no excuse," grumbled Eva.

"Nor is whinging about it. You know where you stand with Ben and I'm sure Mike will be fine with you."

Eva looked at Claire through her eyelashes. "Will you apologise to him for me?"

"Of course."

Eva touched Claire's cheek gently. "Thank you. You have no idea what your kindness means to me."

They hugged and it was quick and hard.

"I've never thrown a glass of lemonade over someone before," said Eva.

"I may have let a few JD-and-Cokes fly in the past during my clubbing days," Claire admitted.

Eva smiled and rubbed Claire's forearm. "I'm going to go."

"Will you be okay?"

"I'm not going to do anything foolish, if that's what you mean."

That was exactly what Claire meant but she thought it better to be gentle. "No, but that anger was fierce. Do you need to speak to someone?"

"I already do, every other Tuesday," Eva admitted. "It's not fun."

"Do you want me to come with you?"

"No. Will you be alright getting a lift?"

"Of course. Go home and have a bath and a good night's sleep. It'll all seem better in the morning."

"A lot of people have said that to me over years," Eva said, "and it's never been true in all that time."

"I know exactly what you mean."

Chapter 32

Mike and Ben had shifted to the next table as Gina cleared their original one. None of them looked particularly happy. Claire noticed her handbag had been put on the chair next to Mike.

"Hi," he said.

"Hey." She sat next to him. "Fun evening."

Ben looked like he was sucking his lips. "I'm so sorry. I didn't realise she'd react like that."

"Nobody did," Mike said.

"I knew she was unhappy," said Claire. "And I'd noticed that when she gets stressed, she pulls at her hair."

"It's called trichotillomania," said Mike. "A girl in one of my classes used to do it and someone was smart enough to notice and get one of my colleagues to speak to her. I wonder if Eva's getting any help."

"She said outside that she was."

Mike nodded. "Well that's reassuring."

"What were you going to say before you grabbed Eva?"

"I had a hunch she might have a history of self-harm," he said. "I didn't see her wrists until she'd thrown her drink." He put his arm on the table underside up and brushed his right index finger over the veins at his wrist. "There were marks there. Not many but a few pale ones."

Claire watched his finger. "I didn't notice."

"It's another school thing. Sometimes behaviour doesn't make sense but then it kind of fits into a routine you recognise when you've seen it enough."

"You think she self-harmed?"

"Almost certainly at some point in her life. I hope whoever she's seeing either knows about them or has seen them."

Claire sat back and looked out the window. Car headlights flared against the glass. "Tonight's been an experience," she said. "But I think I'm going to head off."

"Me too," muttered Ben. "The sooner tonight's over the better."

"It's not your fault, mate," Mike said.

"Maybe not, Mike, but it's me she went for."

"You told the joke," Mike said and stood up. "Let's get the bill. Did you want dropping off, Claire?"

The thought of spending time alone with him was nice but she wanted to get some air and process the evening. "I'll walk. It's not far."

Mike frowned. "What about your hoodie?"

"I have my alarm. Plus, I need to walk off some of this pizza otherwise it's going to lie really heavy."

He smiled his lopsided smile. "You are sure, aren't you?"

"Completely."

They paid and Claire thought Gina looked happy to be rid of them.

They said their goodbyes at the door. Ben moved as if he was going to hug her, so Claire leaned forward and air-kissed his cheek.

"Thank you," Ben said.

"No problem but no more flowers."

"I understand."

Ben shook Mike's hand and walked across the car park.

"What was that about?" Mike asked when Ben was far enough away not to hear.

"Long story. I'll tell you soon."

"Shame you can't tell me now."

"I'm sorry."

"Don't be." He smiled. "To think I invited you and Eva along because I was worried tonight would be boring."

"Funny how things turn out," she said and he laughed.

She hugged him and her stomach tingled as he pulled her tight. She smelled his shower gel and wanted to kiss him.

"You smell lovely," he said.

"So do you."

She pecked his cheek and he returned it a little slower. They looked at one another and his eyes flashed.

"Goodbye then," she said and felt her self-control slipping. "See you tomorrow?"

"Try stopping me. Are you sure I can't give you a lift?"

"Absolutely, get out of here."

She watched Mike walk away and enjoyed the view then walked out of Scarborough Place.

* * *

Even though she wasn't wearing the right shoes for a brisk walk Claire still set a decent pace. The buzz of exercise felt good and settled her food. Traffic was light and she couldn't see any other pedestrians on the well-lit pavements.

She followed the road towards the town centre and planned to head left at the next junction which would take her to the market square.

A hundred yards ahead was a detached townhouse that had been converted into a solicitor's office. She noticed a car parked in the shadowy driveway. Someone sat behind the wheel.

Claire debated crossing but decided not to let paranoia get the better of her. Getting closer she realised it was Eva's car.

Curious, Claire walked onto the driveway meaning to make sure all was well. She heard the low droning sound of someone talking through a speaker. Eva's voice was high and agitated in contrast. Was it an argument? Claire didn't want to scare Eva so turned back toward the pavement, but the movement obviously caught Eva's attention.

She screamed and the droning voice instantly cut off. Eva shoved the door open and got out quickly. Anger distorted her face.

"What the fuck are you doing creeping around like this?" she demanded.

Chapter 33

Claire backed away holding her hands up. "I'm sorry."

Eva looked briefly confused. "Claire?"

"I didn't mean to startle you."

"What the hell are you doing? Were you following me?"

"No, I decided to walk home."

"With everything going on, you decided to walk home on your own? So what, did you see me and think you'd creep around in the dark?"

"No," Claire said. She felt indignant. "Of course not. I wanted to check you were alright."

"Yeah, sure."

The mixture of sarcasm and anger in Eva's tone annoyed Claire and after the performance at Pizza Shed, she'd had enough of it tonight. "I wish I hadn't bothered to check now."

"You shouldn't have. I'm fine."

"I get it," Claire said. She turned on her heel and walked away briskly.

"Hey," Eva called after a few moments. "I'm sorry, Claire."

Claire ignored her and kept moving.

"Please, I didn't mean it."

Claire turned and held up a hand. "Leave it," she said. "It's been a long evening and I just want to go home now."

Eva said something a passing car prevented Claire from hearing, but she couldn't be bothered to ask her to repeat it.

* * *

The walk burned away her annoyance at Eva and Claire wondered how the night's incidents would shift things with the newbie table. Could they go back to how they all were before Pizza Shed? Apart from Mike, she realised it didn't really bother her.

A car slowed behind her but didn't stop. Grit crunched under the tyres and Claire felt a sudden panic. She tried to tell herself it was a taxi, or someone being dropped off but what if it wasn't? What if her stalker had finally decided to come out of hiding? No one knew she was here.

She glanced around but the glare of headlights hid the driver from her view. She walked faster and the car kept pace.

Claire curled her fingers around the cord of the rape alarm and stopped. The car drew level with her.

"Claire?" Eva wound down the window. "I hope I didn't scare you."

Her panic fled, leaving a hollow sensation in her chest that made her pounding heart feel worse. "Well you did," she said, annoyed.

"I'm sorry. I saw someone walking but didn't know if it was you and then – oh well, it doesn't make much sense." She looked flustered. "I wanted to say sorry for before. I massively overreacted but it's been one of those nights and I shouldn't have done it and I'm worried I've pissed you off."

Eva stopped at the kerb and got out. "Honestly. I want to make up for my behaviour."

Claire's heartbeat felt closer to normal now. "Don't worry about it." She'd overreacted too and Eva clearly hadn't meant to scare her. Everything, it seemed, was getting on top of both of them.

"But I do. As Scott's got his friend over, why don't we have a girly night back at mine? I've got wine and chocolates. You can stay over and I'll drop you home in the morning."

The invitation took Claire by surprise and her initial instinct was to say no – she'd seen a different side to Eva this evening and wasn't sure she liked it.

"Please," Eva said as if sensing Claire's worry. "I know I've been a cow, but I really hope I can make things better. I like you a lot and the thought I'd driven you away would be awful."

"You haven't," Claire said, her reserve drifting away.

"And we can't have a heavy session because I'm at work tomorrow."

"I told Scott I'd be back."

Eva glanced at her watch. "You can ring him. It's not too late." Desperation crept into her voice. "I just feel so down after tonight."

Could she turn her back on Eva now? "So long as Scott's alright, I'll come."

Eva's relief was instant, and she smiled widely. "Thank you."

Claire rang Scott and he answered almost straight away.

"Mum! You alright?"

"I'm fine, how's the evening been?"

"Good, the pizza was peng, but the film wasn't so Annie found us another on the Horror Channel. It's very gory, we're loving it."

"Sounds lovely. Eva's asked me to stay over at hers so don't be late to bed, okay?"

"Of course not. How old do you think I am?"

"I trust you, Scott, but you can't fool me because I remember being fifteen. Don't forget Annie needs to go home otherwise Roger and Lou will kill us."

He laughed. "We won't forget, Mum."

"What time are you going to your dad's tomorrow?"

"In the afternoon. I'm seeing Charlie first to do some more for his talent show spot."

"I'll be home about nine or so as Eva's going to drop me when she goes to work."

"See you tomorrow morning then. Now go and enjoy yourself."

"I will. I love you."

"I love you too," he said and ended the call.

Chapter 34

Eva's flat was on the first floor of a new build on the other side of the town centre.

"Nothing glamorous and it faces the car park, but at least I don't get a lot of road noise."

She unlocked the door and led Claire in. "I like things minimalist," she said.

"I like it," Claire said but thought the square room looked cold and barely inhabited. Was this because Eva was on her own? Might Claire's house have looked like this if she didn't have Scott? No, she decided. It wouldn't.

"Thank you." Eva opened a door onto a small kitchen. "Red or white?"

"White would be lovely."

Eva came back into the lounge with a bottle of Prosecco and two large glasses. She sat on the sofa and Claire sat in the armchair as Eva filled their glasses. "To us," she said.

"Cheers."

Conversation was light and safe. They talked about jobs and the weather and what they'd been watching on TV. They also drank steadily until Claire's head buzzed pleasantly.

"Another glass?" Eva looked at her watch. "It's only just gone midnight. We should let ourselves live a little."

"Will you be alright to go to work?"

"Constitution of an ox," Eva said and patted her stomach. She refilled their glasses and leaned back into the cushions. "Ben's joke was out of order, wasn't it?"

"I didn't like it." Claire sipped her wine. "So where did that reaction come from?"

Eva rubbed the corners of her mouth. "I have a bit of history, that's all. It's my way of coping and it all started when I was a teenager. I got it under control but when my husband..." She paused. "Well, it happened again."

"And it's been ongoing?"

Eva looked briefly at the ceiling and her eyes shined with unshed tears. "It comes and goes but I understand it better now."

"Did you go to the doctor?"

Eva barked a sour-sounding laugh. "My doctor would look at me and tell me to stop acting like a silly teenager."

"That's surely not true?"

"It felt like it. What helped me was going to stay with my mother-in-law. As I looked after her, I managed to get my head together."

"I'll have a word with Ben if you want. I'm sure he'll feel awful knowing how much he hurt you."

"I doubt it." Eva pulled her legs up and sat on them. She rested her glass on her knee and rotated it slowly. "He doesn't like me."

"That's not the impression I get."

"He's clever about it. He's pleasant in company but after the flowers he got a bit arsey with me," Eva said.

"What flowers?"

"Didn't I tell you? It must have been a day or two before the bowling night and I opened my door to find a lovely bunch on the mat. There was a card but it just said 'from a mystery admirer'. I thought it was a mistake so didn't say anything but when you and Mike were chatting at the bar Ben told me he'd sent them. I told him I wasn't interested and he got stroppy with me."

"I didn't realise that. When we were in the pizza place he told me he'd put flowers on my car."

"Not the wrecked ones, surely?"

"He only admitted to the first bunch." But did that make sense? Claire's thoughts raced but none of them quite connected. Could Ben perhaps not be the innocent she'd believed him to be? What if she was simply the next in line and once Eva turned him down, he focussed his attention on Claire? "I suppose we'll find out if he's stroppy with me now I've turned him down."

"I hope not. I saw him hanging around on my way home from work a couple of times after the bowling night." She sat forward as if to make her point. "I don't mean he's stalking me or anything, nothing like that but it was odd to see him."

Claire's thoughts began to coalesce. "The evening I saw him was the night before the flowers appeared on my car."

"I saw your hoodie again too after we met at The Kino."

Claire sat forward. "When?"

"On Tuesday. I felt shut in and went out for some fresh air and ended up walking by the old Methodist church."

Claire's skin prickled. "I was up there on Tuesday for my yoga class." She almost told Eva about the graffiti on the parking spot but it would take too long to explain. "What was he doing?"

"Just standing behind some bushes near the car park. I think he was looking out for something at the church hall."

Claire shivered. So he had been there and she was right to feel paranoid.

"When I saw him at The Kino I noticed his hair colour, didn't I?" Eva said. "I know it doesn't make a lot of sense but what if Ben's your hoodie?"

Claire frowned. She'd had too much wine to properly follow the line of thought. "How would that work?"

"Maybe I watch too many TV detective shows," said Eva. "You didn't start seeing the hoodie until you went to the group and the night you chased him Ben got in the way even though he lives across town. I saw the hoodie at The Kino and he had sandy-coloured hair like Ben's. Plus, the whole business with the flowers."

184

Claire could see the logic, but did it make sense? Could it have been Ben she had chased that morning? They had a similar build, but the body shape seemed wrong and she remembered the hoodie jacket looked somehow padded. "But why?" she asked eventually.

"Why not? If he sends flowers with mysterious notes to women he fancies, what's to say he's above hiding his identity so he can watch them undetected?"

There was no answer to that, even though she wanted there to be. "Wouldn't we have realised?"

Eva laughed sourly. "Because he's too nice to do something like this?"

"I don't mean that."

"Well if he's not your hoodie and my theory makes sense; it could be Keith."

"No." Claire shivered at the thought of him watching her even though he was the wrong body shape and surely wouldn't have the speed to outrun her.

"You're right," Eva said. "It's a silly suggestion." She stood up and swayed slightly. "I might need to call it a night soon."

She walked around Claire's chair, caught her foot in the handbag strap and staggered as she dragged it.

"Whoops," she said and looked at the mess she'd made.

Claire got up and her head span.

"I'll tidy it," Eva said and dropped to her knees.

"Don't worry, I'll do it."

"It's my fault." Eva picked up a notepad, a packet of tissues and a small compact. "There you go," she said and handed them to Claire. She seemed to notice something under the chair and reached for it. She'd found the condoms. "'Ribbed for your pleasure'," she read from the box.

Claire smiled. "Why not?"

"So are these for you and Mike? Were you hoping to get lucky tonight?"

"Maybe." Claire laughed at Eva's sudden directness which seemed unlike her. "Better safe than sorry, eh?"

"So it is serious with you two?"

She would have expected the question from Lou or Amy but this wasn't a conversation she'd expected to have with Eva. "I don't know."

"But you'd sleep with him?" Eva's tone – innocent and surprised – wasn't judgemental.

"I don't know. We've known each other for a bit now."

"A week?"

Claire laughed and wasn't sure why she felt guilty. "We're all adults. Anyway, it's not like I've only seen him once in that time."

"I hope you don't think I'm making assumptions about you."

"Of course not."

"Don't you think you'll ever reconcile with your husband then?"

Claire snorted a laugh. "No. And even if I did, I'm single at the moment."

"Have you ever talked about getting back with him?"

The conversation had taken an uncomfortable turn. "He has. I haven't."

"Don't you miss him?"

"Hardly. He walked out on me. It was his choice and not mine."

"So do you think Mike's special?"

"I think he's nice," Claire said. "Have you thought about meeting someone else?"

Eva's eyes opened wide with surprise. "Not at all."

"Why? I spent too long being sad and it feels like I've allowed a year of my life to drift by when I shouldn't have."

"I just couldn't do it."

"Didn't you meet people in the Fens?"

"One or two but most had known the family for years so it wasn't always easy. I did meet a farmer called Felix

186

and he was nice. But he knew my husband from school and my mother-in-law wasn't happy with the situation. She thought I was being unfair."

"But you were caring for her."

"I know. It was hard work."

"That's sad."

"It's real."

"But don't you miss the intimacy? I do. It's not so much the sex but the thought of having someone at home to give you a hug or a kiss. To make that human connection." Claire laughed at herself. "I sound like a self-help book."

"You're right and I do miss it. But what do you do if you think you got the perfect one the first time around before it all fell apart?"

Claire shrugged. "I don't know."

"No, me either," said Eva.

Chapter 35

The grief cycle is a wonderful creation. It makes perfect sense with clearly defined steps and yet when you most need it, when grief is chewing away at your insides and turning your brain to mush, it feels like a mountain you'll never be able to reach the summit of.

I hated it.

I still do but I'm working my way along it and the doctor says I'm doing well but I only go to see him to keep getting the tablets and, honestly, I don't care what he says.

But just in case you're interested, I think I'm at 'Dialogue and bargaining'. That's partly what these notes have been about – the other part is to make sure you realise I'm here, coming after you, and that your life is very shortly going to turn to shit.

I'm "reaching out to you", "struggling to find meaning for what happened" but most of all because I want "to tell my story". My story, my loss, my life now, is all tied up with you and those actions you didn't take back then. Every single last fucking one of them.

Part of telling my story, I think, is making you realise what I went through. What I felt and what I lost.

Imagine it was your son that you lost?

How would that make you feel?

I worry your imagination isn't good enough and won't encompass the way my world was turned inside out, so you're going to live it.

You took away the one thing I really, truly loved.

Welcome to my world…

Chapter 36

A clattering startled Claire awake.

White glare filled her vision and she quickly shut her eyes. Her forehead ached and she groaned as she massaged it.

Her lower back felt numb and she remembered she was on Eva's sofa.

She squinted and sat up slowly. The throb in her forehead slid down to settle behind her eyes.

"Morning," Eva called brightly.

"Morning."

"Ouch. Are you feeling it?"

"Just a bit."

Eva came into the lounge barefoot and clad in her dressing gown. She handed Claire a steamy cup. "I made you a black coffee. It'll make you feel better."

"Thanks." Claire took the cup and had a sip. It was very hot and very strong.

Eva sat in the armchair and crossed her legs. Her wet hair was brushed back from her shiny and make-up-free face. "Would you like some toast? I'd offer you more, but I overslept and haven't done the shopping this week."

The toaster popped and Eva went into the kitchen. "Is your back okay? You should have taken the bed."

"I couldn't do that." She wished she had though — her back really ached.

Eva came back with a plate and two rounds of heavily buttered toast. "Have these and I'll make some for me while I get dressed, then we need to get going."

"Thanks. The coffee and toast should get me going."

Eva went into her bedroom and after eating a slice of toast Claire went into the spartan bathroom. She went to the loo then splashed some water on her face and looked at her reflection. Her hair had skewed to one side, so she damped it down and brushed it with her fingers until it looked respectable enough to go outside.

When she went back into the lounge, Eva was tucking her polo shirt into her trousers. "I hate this uniform," she said.

"It looks alright."

Eva raised her eyebrows in a query.

"You're right, it doesn't," Claire said.

Eva laughed.

Claire finished her coffee as she put on her shoes. "I'm set."

"Great stuff," said Eva and led her down to the car park.

Claire walked around to the passenger side and stopped. Her heart thudded hard. A gallows with a hanged man had been chalked in the empty space next to Eva's car.

"Claire?"

"It's a... There's a hangman drawn on the space."

Eva smiled. "You're surely not scared of hangman?"

"No but I've been seeing them a lot the past week or so."

"Maybe it's a craze with kids at the moment?"

"Could be," said Claire and got into the car.

* * *

Eva dropped Claire outside her house but didn't hang around and sped away with a quick, "Goodbye."

Claire let herself into the house and slipped off her shoes before she went into the dining room and lounge to open the curtains.

Her mobile rang and she dashed back into the kitchen to catch it before the call went to voicemail.

"Morning," said Amy. She sounded very bright and breezy. "How was last night?"

Her tone made Claire think Amy was more interested in talking about her own evening. "Not bad. How was yours?"

Amy squealed. "Fabulous. No, better than fabulous." She laughed. "Can something be better than fabulous?"

"I think so."

"Good because that's how last night was. We had some very good wine. Gayle looked great. We ate and went to Pinkies, and it was like a first date. We danced to our favourite songs and kissed."

Claire smiled. "There was kissing?"

"A lot."

"Are you at hers now?"

"No!" Amy said, feigning offence.

"Is she at yours?"

"She might be having a shower and I might be making us both breakfast and brewing up some expensive coffee."

Claire's smile broadened. "And you're happy?"

"You wouldn't believe it. So did you and Mike manage to enjoy yourselves?"

"Not really," Claire said and gave Amy the bare bones of the evening including Eva's thoughts about Ben.

"I'm really surprised at that," she said. "I'm worried too that Eva thinks he might be the one hiding in the hoodie. That's very icky. So who started it all off with the conversation about the damage to Keith's car?"

"Ben did. He said Jane told him."

"Why would she do that?"

"Who knows?"

"I can always ask," Amy said then she made a breathy noise.

"Are you okay?"

"Yes. Gayle's just come into the kitchen and she's not wearing much."

Claire laughed. "We can have this conversation another time. You go and have fun."

She went upstairs and listened to Scott's gentle snores through his bedroom door before going into her own bedroom to strip off. She put her dressing gown on and padded back towards the bathroom.

"Mum?"

"Yes." She knocked lightly on his door then pushed it open.

The room smelled of Lynx and pizza and she didn't find the combination at all appealing. Scott smiled at her.

"Morning," she said.

"Morning. What time is it?"

"About half nine. I'm going for a shower if you want to use the loo quickly."

"Half nine?" He sat up quickly. "Oh no, I have to be at Charlie's for half ten."

Her head throbbed at the idea of rushing around after him again. "Everything at the last minute, eh? What time did you get to bed?"

"I can't remember. I worked on the hangman app after Annie went home."

"You made sure she got home safely and on time?"

"Of course," he said and offered a shy smile.

"Let me have my shower then I'll drive you, okay?"

"You're the best but I'm going on my bike. We're filming in the park and need to get some tracking shots."

"Well, first you need to get up."

* * *

The hot shower finished the job the coffee had started of reviving her. She took her time and dried slowly. Scott called as she wrapped her hair in a towel.

"Mum! Come quick!"

She pulled open the bathroom door and rushed into his bedroom. He was sitting on his bed with the duvet in a heap beside him. The laptop rested on his thighs and he stared at the screen.

"What's happened?"

He looked up with wide eyes. "The CCTV caught somebody."

"What?" She felt nauseous.

Scott pointed at the screen. "It worked. Come and look."

Claire held up her finger. "One second," she said and rushed into her bedroom for her reading glasses. She ran back into his room and sat on the duvet. "What am I looking at?"

He edged the time marker back. "The Pi recorded from midnight to eight but I've stitched together the shots on this viewer program I, um, picked up…" He coughed. "You can watch it like a film."

She shifted position slightly and leaned against him so she could see the screen more clearly.

"The image isn't great during the night and you can't see much apart from the odd cat wander across the patio. But then this."

He pressed play and Claire watched the garden slowly reveal itself from the darkness as dawn broke.

A person suddenly appeared in the frame and startled her.

"Sorry," said Scott. "I should have said."

"No." She touched his arm to reassure him but couldn't look away from the screen.

With the time delay the person seemed to stutter across the screen.

"Is it a garden jumper?" she asked.

By the time the person was centre screen she could see he was wearing a grey hoodie.

"My God." She shivered and pulled her dressing gown tighter, but the cold was inside her, not in the room.

The hoodie stuttered across the garden to crouch in front of the tree stump. He stayed in that position for a while though his body and the camera angle hid whatever he was doing. When he stood up his hood was too full of shadows to make out his face.

Claire couldn't look away however much she wanted to deny this was happening.

The hoodie turned to the patio doors and stared through them for what felt like an awfully long time.

"What's he doing?" asked Scott.

The hoodie came towards the patio doors in a rush, his movements as jerky as a puppet. Claire made a sound in her throat and Scott looked at her but she kept her eyes on the screen. He stood there for a long time and seemed to be staring directly into the camera.

Then he was gone.

"What the hell was that?" asked Scott.

"I don't know." How could she tell him without scaring him? "Can you email me a copy?"

"Do you think he's a burglar?"

"I don't know but I think I should show this to that policewoman."

"You think this idiot broke Eric Gnome?"

"I don't know but I don't like the idea of him staring into the kitchen. What time was this?"

Scott deftly moved the film back to the point where the hoodie first appeared and the time code in the bottom left of the screen read 5:42 a.m.

"Yuck," he said. "I was asleep."

* * *

Claire got dressed and went to make Scott some toast and another cup of coffee for herself. She glanced at the patio doors and the thought the hoodie had stood there looking into her kitchen made her shudder with revulsion. The bastard.

Knowing he'd been in her garden and watching the house made her feel intimidated and that made her angry. This was just an extension of standing on a street corner and watching her while allowing himself to be seen. He enjoyed the stress and fear he engendered in her. Nobody should be allowed to do that.

The kettle boiled and she made her coffee. What would she do if she found Ben had been behind all this? The first bunch of flowers she could maybe excuse but nothing else.

The toaster popped. She buttered the bread and set it on a plate then called Scott. He came down in his dressing gown with wet hair and they sat at the table together as he quickly demolished both slices. He finished with a hurried, "Thanks, Mum," and raced back upstairs.

Claire put his plate into the dishwasher then stood at the patio doors. She wondered what he'd been doing out of view of the camera. She stood on tiptoe, but the table and chairs blocked her view of the tree stump.

Scott came into the kitchen and bashed the door with his heavily laden rucksack.

"Have you got everything?" she asked.

"Yeah." He dumped the bag by the door. "I don't know how long I'll be at Charlie's because of the filming so I'll take everything with me and go straight to Dad's." He glanced at the patio doors. "Will you be okay?"

"I'll be fine."

He pulled his trainers on. "I should stay."

Touched by his concern – he was of the age when other people didn't really impinge on his thinking too often – she shook her head. "I'll email Rosie the film when you've gone."

"I'm still worried though."

"Don't be. Go and do your stuff." She made shooing gestures.

"You're sure you don't mind me going straight to Dad's?"

"Not at all. Does he know you're going to be late?"

"He does."

Scott put his rucksack on and opened the back door. He pulled Claire into a quick and clumsy embrace. "If you need me then ring. In fact, I'll ring you later."

"Okay and if you need me, ring me."

He kissed the top of her head and went into the garden for his old and battered and much-loved BMX. He pulled open the entry gate and gave her a wave then rode out of sight.

Claire stepped into the yard to shut the gate. The concrete felt warm under her bare feet as she walked around to the patio. She stopped with a gasp when she saw the hoodie's handiwork.

Chapter 37

Eric Gnome had been hanged.

Twine wrapped around his neck and was attached to the top of the tree stump. His feet were a few inches above the grass which had been flattened whilst the hoodie stood there to do his work.

Claire hugged herself as a cold weight settled across her chest. She could almost feel the bastard's presence and just thinking of him standing here made her shiver.

She walked down the lawn to untie the gnome and set him carefully on his feet.

"What the fuck is going on?" she muttered and yanked the twine off the stump.

She heard Lou shout and a door opened. Roger spoke and the door slammed. Claire waited to hear the entry gate open, but it didn't. She sat on the edge of the patio and ran the twine through her fingers.

"You look how I feel," Roger said as he rested against the fence.

"I hope not," she said and gathered the twine in her palm.

"I'm afraid so." His expression suggested he wanted to tell her more.

Claire sat on one of the patio chairs. She didn't want him to tell her anything. She had no desire to hear about their domestic upsets.

"I'm in the doghouse," he said. "Lou's mad at me and so is Annie."

"A full house," she acknowledged.

"I apparently left the gate unlatched but I'll swear until I'm blue in the face I didn't."

"How's that a problem?"

"Because Lightning's got out."

"What?" she asked with genuine concern. "Out in the garden or…"

"He's not in the garden."

"You think he got out into the street?" Had the hoodie left the entry open when he came in?

He shook his head. "The entry was shut."

"You don't sound all that concerned."

"Oh I am because I'm getting it in the neck. He's probably just got through into someone else's garden."

"Did you want to check mine?"

"If he was in there, we'd have heard him."

The back door opened. "Roger! What are you doing?"

He pulled an 'oh shit' expression. "Checking the garden again."

"You know he's not out there. I thought you were going to see the neighbours."

The door slammed shut.

"Bollocks," he said and gave Claire a morose wave as he walked away.

* * *

"Good morning, Claire."

"Hi, Rosie. Is it okay to speak?"

"It's fine. Is everything okay?"

"Not really." Claire tried to order her thoughts so as to cover everything she needed to. "You remember the man in the grey hoodie?"

"Please don't tell me you've chased him again?"

"No it's worse than that." She explained Scott's CCTV feed. "We caught him in our garden," she said and explained how she'd found the gnome.

"I don't suppose you took photographs, did you?"

"No," said Claire and felt stupid for not thinking of it herself. "I didn't think to."

"Don't worry, although I would like to see that CCTV footage."

"I can email it."

"Please do and I'll log it and get you a crime number. Is there any other damage?"

"Not that I can see."

"Do you still have your alarm?"

"Yes."

"Good – keep it close. I'm in the office later and I'll come back to you then. Take care, Claire, and ring me if you need to."

Claire stared at the dark phone screen and her mind raced as she tried to figure out what the hoodie was doing. Standing on corners watching her was one thing but being in her garden and hanging the gnome was something else entirely. Should she have told Rosie her suspicions about Ben?

Her mobile rang and Scott's picture filled the screen. "Hi. Are you okay?"

"Yeah," he said. His voice only just competed with traffic noise.

"You don't sound like you're at Charlie's."

"Not yet. I'm by the railway bridge checking out your hangman game."

Her stomach made a slight rolling movement. "Go on," she said.

"I've been keeping up with it and whoever's playing has made another move. My 'glared' guess was very wrong."

Claire rubbed her temples with thumb and finger. "Why?"

"Well the bloke's had it. He's got Xs for eyes."

"What letters are filled in?"

"Blank, blank, *a*, *i*, blank, *e*," he said. "It's weird though. The wrong letters are either a joke or the other person playing is an idiot."

"What are the wrong letters?"

"They spell out 'bitch'," he said. "Doesn't make sense because *i* is in the word. It's like whoever's guessing doesn't want to win."

'Bitch' clanged in her head like she'd stood too close to a bell being rung. The rolling sensation increased and she suddenly felt nauseous as her mind made a connection. If someone were so inclined – and paranoid enough – the word could be 'Claire'.

"Just thought you'd like to know," he said breezily. A lorry went by with its air brakes hissing loudly. "I'll call you when I get to Dad's."

She hoped the road noise would hide the worry in her voice. "Enjoy your day with Charlie."

"See you later."

"Bye," she said and put the phone on the countertop.

Surely this all had to be a massive coincidence, but it troubled her that she hadn't seen the game until after she'd seen the hoodie. If he'd been watching her and knew her running route, then he would know she'd see the graffiti from the path.

The entry door banged open and slammed shut.

"I don't know," Roger said. He sounded defeated.

"For Christ's sake," said Lou. Her voice was too loud and echoed.

"You never liked Harry from the beginning, Dad." Annie's cheeks shined with tears.

Claire opened her back door and the neighbours looked up expectantly. "Any news?" she asked.

Roger shook his head and opened the gate. Annie knuckled away her tears.

"Nothing," said Lou. "We've been around the block and knocked on doors but nobody's seen or heard anything."

"Can I help?"

Lou offered a tired smile. "That'd be lovely." She frowned. "Are you okay? You look done in."

"Don't worry about me." Claire waved her hand dismissively. "I asked Roger if he wanted to look in my garden."

A quick flash of anger crossed Lou's face and she glared at her husband. "Roger! I told you to ask Claire about her garden."

"I did," he said.

"You looked in it?"

"No, you called me."

Lou looked at Claire and shook her head. "Fuck's sake."

Claire smiled thinly and stepped into the yard to open the gate. "I'm sure he'll be alright."

"I hope so."

They walked to the patio.

"Not many hiding places," said Claire.

There were a couple of small gaps in the fence panels Harry could have got through. The shed stood on a thin strip of earth at the end of the lawn and the patch of dead grass where Scott's trampoline had been.

They looked at each other.

"It's locked," Claire said.

"Could he have got in?" Lou said.

"I doubt it, but I'll get the key."

She went into the kitchen but the shed key with its Pokémon fob wasn't in its usual place. She quickly checked the floor and under the table and under the fridge, but it wasn't there.

"I can't find it," she said as she went into the yard.

"If the door's locked he didn't get in," Lou said.

"We'll check anyway. One of the boards might have come loose."

As she walked down the garden with Lou, she saw the key hanging from the padlock on the door.

"That's odd," she said. "I'm sure I locked it the other day after repairing the gnome."

"I'm not going to ask," said Lou.

"Best not."

The whimpering started as they crossed the dead patch of grass.

"Can you hear that?" asked Lou.

The padlock hung on the hasp keeping the door closed. Claire pulled it out and the whimpering got louder. She opened the door and Lou bent forward.

Nothing moved. Claire edged forward. The whimpering got louder.

"Harry?" Lou said and clicked her fingers. "Come on, boy."

"Have you found him?" called Annie.

Claire turned and stuck up her thumb. "We think so."

Annie ran down the yard and jumped off the patio so fast Claire thought she'd skid into Lou but she pulled up just in time.

"Is he in there?"

"Sounds like it," Lou said.

"Hey, Harry," Annie said. "Come out, boy."

They heard the click of claws on wood.

Annie screamed.

Chapter 38

"What the fuck?" said Lou as Harry walked out of the shed. His ears were flat to his head and his nose and paws were grubby with dust and dirt.

The dog's body had been roughly shaved leaving a few tufts of hair sticking up here and there. 'Bitch' was written across his side with a thick black marker.

Claire gasped. Lou staggered back and grabbed Claire's arm for support. Annie pulled Harry to her chest and she cried as her hands moved over the dog as if the motion could rub the word away.

"Why?" she asked and looked first at Claire and then Lou.

"I don't know," Lou said.

Claire didn't trust herself to speak.

Roger leaned over the fence. "You found him then?" He sounded pleased. "Thank God I'm not in the doghouse anymore." Then he seemed to realise something was wrong. "What is it?"

"This," hissed Annie and turned so the word would be visible to Roger.

"What the hell?" he muttered.

'Bitch' ricocheted around Claire's head and got louder and more taunting. All she could think of was Keith hissing the word at her and Amy.

"I don't know," Lou said with disdain. "Maybe it's something you know about?"

"Eh?" Roger seemed genuinely confused. "What does bitch have to do with me?"

"Well it's not Annie, the dog or Claire, is it?"

Now it was Claire's turn to feel confused. "Am I missing something here?"

"Yes," Lou said. She put her hands on Claire's upper arms. "I'm sorry, Claire, I'll explain another day."

Claire frowned. "Is everything alright?"

"I'm going to call the police," said Roger. He suddenly looked very pale.

"You do that," said Lou. She let go of Claire and put an arm around Annie. "Come on, love, we'll go and get him sorted."

Claire watched them walk up her garden then looked at Roger.

"What's going on?" she asked.

He held up his index finger. "Police please."

"Roger?"

"I'll speak to you later," he said and walked away, talking into the phone.

Claire looked into the shed. White hair was scattered over the floor. The grass was clear of it, so he hadn't been shaved there. Her initial fear this was another message had been disarmed by Lou's reaction. Something was clearly going on there to make Lou believe the word was aimed at her.

Could she be right? It would certainly give credence to her thoughts of mistaken identity with the notes and shredded flowers.

But why put Harry in her shed? And had she really left the key in the padlock on Thursday because that certainly wasn't something she normally did.

She locked the shed up and walked up to the yard spinning the key around her finger. Brushing off her soles, she got her laptop and glasses from the lounge then sat at the kitchen table. She opened her email and clicked the attachment in the message Scott had sent her.

He'd edited the video so only a few seconds of blank screen showed before the hoodie appeared but it still made her jump.

"You fucker," she said and pushed her glasses up onto her forehead. She massaged the bridge of her nose then opened a new email.

> *Hi Rosie*
>
> *As promised, this is the CCTV Scott took this morning, showing my hoodie in the garden. The bit where he crouches down, almost out of view, is when I think he hung the gnome. Unfortunately, even though he gets really close to the patio doors, I can't see anything of his face.*
>
> *Hope to hear from you soon.*

She pressed send and leaned back in her chair. Now what? She didn't want to hang around until Rosie got back to her and a run might clear her head but, with Saturday traffic and pedestrians, it would only increase her stress levels. A walk into town with some window shopping and a nice coffee might take her mind off things. She closed the laptop and went to put on some socks.

* * *

Claire got to the town centre at midday and browsed through a pop-up farmers' market before heading towards the Newborough Shopping Centre.

She stopped at the pedestrian crossing. When the green man appeared, she stepped off the kerb and noticed from the corner of her eye that the nearest car was a black Astra.

The number plate ended HKP.

Chapter 39

Claire felt a spike of fear that made her arms and fingers tingle. With her heart thudding she looked away quickly from the car. Her palms were moist. She didn't want the driver – her stalker – to see her and walked briskly with the other pedestrians crossing, trying to lose herself in the crowd. She focussed on her breathing and only risked a glance back when she reached the other side of the road.

Her stalker apparently hadn't noticed her; he stared ahead at the road and gripped the wheel tightly. For the first time she saw him clearly without his sunglasses. He had small eyes and a scattering of acne scars on his round cheeks, almost hidden in the dark shadow of his stubble.

He peeled away with a little wheelspin when the lights changed. She watched him take the fork in the road towards the shopping centre's multi-storey car park and he braked sharply for the ticket machine.

When the car disappeared into the structure, Claire leaned against a wall. She felt faint and breathed deeply until the sensation faded and her heart rate calmed. She glanced at the car park and tried to figure out what to do. Her anger over the hoodie that morning and seeing her stalker now outweighed her fear. If she was going to stand up to this then she had to start now. If her stalker hadn't seen her – and it didn't seem as if he had – then she had the advantage over him. She could find out what he was doing and tell Rosie.

With her decision made, she felt better. Her head seemed suddenly clear and Claire walked with a confidence she didn't fully feel through the double doors into the Newborough Centre.

The brightly lit foyer had busy coffee shops on either side and a small group of harassed-looking mothers pushed their way out of McDonald's and tried to corral their herd of toddlers.

The centre was split over two floors linked by escalators. The only exits from the car park – two lifts and a stairwell – opened onto both floors to her left. Beyond the escalators was a small area filled with food and if she stood there, she shouldn't miss her stalker when he came into the centre. She walked until she could see both lifts and the stairwell doors clearly and leaned against the window of a fashion store.

The lifts on both floors opened with some regularity but few people seemed to use the stairwell. Nerves chewed at her. The passing minutes didn't make her feel any braver but the thought of turning the tables on him was strangely empowering. She had no plan of what she hoped to achieve and didn't know if she could confront him. But she did know she'd regret not taking this chance to find out more.

The lifts had large numbers above them and Lift One was nearest to the front of the centre. She watched people get on and off the lifts but didn't see the man and after about five minutes she was starting to think she'd made a mistake.

Lift One opened on the first floor. A young couple came out and stood by the barrier looking down towards her. The woman was slim with fine blonde hair held back with a thin Alice band. Her companion was also slim, but he had the shadow of a goatee to go with his shaggy hair. He pointed towards the doughnut stand in front of Claire before they began walking away from the lifts.

She looked back towards the lifts and her stalker was at the barrier. She felt the same spark of fright she'd experienced on the road. Although she was shadowed by the upper floor, Claire felt horribly exposed and pressed herself against the shop window. Her heart thumped wildly. She fought the urge to move and was relieved when the man looked away. He looked much heavier than the hoodie and his black T-shirt strained to cover the extra weight he carried on his belly. His battered brown anorak had seen better days.

He walked away from the lifts and her legs suddenly felt like jelly. Recognising the panic, she leaned forward slightly and moved her neck to relieve the tension.

Her stalker was clearly looking for something. He walked further into the centre craning his neck as he leaned against the barrier. He hadn't seen her – wasn't looking for her – and her curiosity grew. She had to find out what he was doing even if that was dangerous. She looked at the people going about their lives around her – she couldn't guarantee any of them would help if she needed it, but it would be noticed if she made a fuss.

She crossed her bag strap over her chest and, keeping an eye on her stalker as he loitered outside a phone shop, rushed to the escalators. Claire stood by the map on the upper floor and peered around it. Her stalker looked without interest into the window of Zap!, a game shop she knew all too well from the days when she could tell Mario from Luigi and knew one Pokémon from another.

Was he waiting to meet someone?

Lift One opened and half a dozen people got out. Claire used the group for cover and moved closer to the shopfronts. She slowly closed the gap between her and the man.

He turned away from Zap! and ambled towards the barrier with his hands in his pockets. Claire looked into the nearest window and watched his reflection. He took out his phone and studied the screen. After a minute or so he walked away. She counted to three and followed at what she hoped was a safe distance.

Her stalker sat on a bench and she paused by a small island of seats. He undid then retied his shoelace without watching what he was doing; his neck was craned at an odd angle so he could see ahead. He went to the barrier and looked towards the escalators at the far end of the centre. Claire went to the barrier too and followed his gaze. A handful of people were on the escalators and, near to the top and arm in arm, were the young couple she'd seen come out of the lift.

Was that why she hadn't seen him for a while – because having been spotted he'd shifted his attentions to someone else? Claire watched the couple who were clearly enjoying each other's company. They went to the left as they got off the escalator, but her stalker didn't move. He alternated between watching them and the screen of his phone.

She had an idea. If she couldn't confront him then there was nothing to stop her from warning them. And since they were downstairs that gave her enough distance from him to actually do something about it.

Claire headed back the way she'd come and kept close to the barrier so she could follow the couple's progress. Checking to make sure her stalker wasn't watching, Claire held her phone in front of her face as she went down the escalator.

She cut quickly across the food court area and hid from her stalker's view behind a pretzel trolley. The couple were walking towards her holding hands. The man laughed at something the woman said and he kissed her right temple. She looked momentarily startled then hugged him.

Claire waited until the couple were in front of her. "Hey," she said, trying to keep her voice light.

The man looked over and smiled.

"Can I speak to you?" she said.

"I haven't got any change," the man said quickly without changing his expression.

"I don't need change," Claire said, affronted. "I want to speak to you."

The woman looked over. "Who's that, Ted?"

"I don't know."

"My name's Claire Heeley. I need to speak to you."

"Listen, love," said Ted. "I've got a mobile and all the utilities I need. We're fine, honestly." He held the woman's hand tightly and started to walk away.

"I'm not selling you something. I want to ask about the man who's following you."

"What?" asked Ted. He locked eyes with Claire.

The woman glanced around.

"Don't look," Claire said. "Go to that jeweller's window and I'll come over."

Ted guided the woman towards the shop and after a moment or two Claire followed them. She stood a few feet away and looked at a ring display.

"Don't turn around but there's a man on the upper floor who I think is watching you. He's tall and has a paunch and acne scars and a week or two ago he was watching me. He tried to run me over and I haven't seen him again until now."

Claire realised her story sounded odd, yet the woman didn't walk away but touched the window lightly as if pointing out a piece of jewellery she'd like to buy.

"What's he doing now?" she asked.

"Watching you," Claire said. "I haven't looked since I came downstairs."

"How do you know this?" asked Ted.

"I saw him drive into the car park and decided to follow him. I kept a watch on the lift."

"The lift," Ted said as if he remembered something. "Is he wearing a brown anorak?"

"Yes."

"In his forties? I noticed him. He pretended to be on his phone but kept glancing at Elsa."

"Did he?" asked Elsa.

"Yeah. I thought he just fancied you."

"Have you seen him before?" Claire asked.

"No," said Ted. "Not that I remember, anyway."

"Me neither," said Elsa.

"Is there any reason anyone would want to follow you?"

The couple looked at one another.

"It's Luca," said Elsa quietly.

"Shit," said Ted.

"He's Luca?" Claire asked.

"No, that's not him," said Elsa with a sigh. "Luca is my soon-to-be ex-husband. He wouldn't accept I wanted to leave and made life really difficult." Her voice was now so quiet Claire almost didn't catch it. "I met Ted later, but Luca was convinced there was someone else right from the start which was never true."

"So what does that mean?" asked Claire, her confusion mounting. "I don't know you or Luca so why would this man be following me?"

"If Luca hired him," said Ted, "then maybe someone hired him to follow you."

Chapter 40

Claire's breath caught in her throat. He wasn't stalking her; he'd been hired to follow her. But who would want to do that?

She turned away from the window and felt her anger grow. Her stalker hadn't moved but now he glanced at her and it only took a moment for the recognition – and realisation – to spread across his face.

She didn't feel scared that he'd seen her, but he looked worried. He quickly put his phone in his pocket and backed away from the barrier.

"Could he have been filming you two from his phone?"

"I'm not sure," said Ted and Elsa made a disgusted noise.

"I thought he was using it to cover watching you but what if he was taking pictures or video?"

"To gather evidence you mean?" asked Elsa.

"I don't know."

Her stalker was walking briskly towards the lifts.

"Only one way to find out," said Claire and she rushed to the escalator. She watched her stalker as he walked at a brisk pace watching her.

He ignored the crowd waiting for the lift and went through the stairwell door. Claire ran after him but pushed the door open carefully in case he was waiting for her. The landing was empty. She heard his heavy tread and laboured breathing further up the stairs. He was clearly not in the best of shape.

Claire ran after him. The angle of the flight wasn't steep, and she used her left hand to pull at the banister to increase her speed. The landing after the second flight opened onto a floor of the car park. She could still hear her stalker's heavy breathing so kept going and gained on him as she fell into a rhythm.

A door banged and Claire paused; she couldn't hear his ragged breathing anymore. He must have left the stairwell at the next floor. She ran up the flight and stopped by the door which still rocked slightly as it settled in place. She pushed it open slowly – ready for him to jump out – but nothing moved. She peered around and saw a lot of parked cars and several brick pillars and a pay-and-display machine to her right. But he had to be on this floor – he hadn't got that far ahead of her.

Keeping to the middle of the roadway in case he came at her from between the cars or behind a pillar, she walked to the pay-and-display machine. Now she could hear him breathing and whirled around in fright but he wasn't behind her. The low ceiling of the car park had carried the sound and she saw him three rows over against the back wall. He'd reached his Astra.

He seemed scared which gave her a surge of confidence. She cut between cars and took her keys out. She slipped the ignition one between her fingers and gripped the rape alarm in her left hand.

"Hey," she called when she reached the roadway.

Her stalker turned slowly to face her. "You talking to me?"

"Of course I am. I can't see anyone else around here."

"What do you want?"

"I want to know what the hell's going on. Why were you following me a fortnight ago?"

"I wasn't following you. I don't even know you."

"So why did you run?"

Her stalker took a step back. "Wouldn't you if someone came charging after you?"

Claire stepped into the middle of the roadway. "You moved after you saw me talking to that couple. So why run?"

"You startled me."

"How could I if you didn't know me?" she said. He looked annoyed and she couldn't tell if it was with her or because he was tying himself in knots. "You need to be sharper than this, mate. So come on then."

"What?"

She made a frustrated growl deep in her throat. "Why were you following me? I saw you in the market square at least three times and then you tried to run me over."

"No, that was an accident. You took me by surprise and I tried to brake but I wasn't quick enough. I was going to get out and check but saw you move and knew you were okay."

"Bollocks."

"It's true," he said and took another step back towards his car.

"How did I take you by surprise if you were watching me?"

A car came up the ramp onto the parking level and drove towards Claire. She walked forward to get out of its way and her stalker matched her distance. He was now standing almost at the back wall.

Claire waited until the car had passed by. "Are you a pervert?" She took her phone out of her bag. "Maybe I should just call the police and report you for stalking."

"Good luck with that," he said.

"You think I won't?"

"I doubt you'd get a signal in here and I'll be away by the time you do."

"Except I know your number plate and what you look like." Her stalker bit his lip. "So is that it – you're a pervert? Did you leave the shredded flowers and notes on my windscreen?"

"I don't know what you're talking about."

"What about poor little Harry – did you do that too?"

He held out his hands. "You've lost me, love."

"All the crap in my life at the moment started with seeing you."

Her stalker looked around as if searching for a means to escape. He took a deep breath and blew it out quickly. "I was hired to watch you, Claire, okay? To find out about your life and where you lived and your routines."

"What the fuck?" She shuddered with revulsion that felt as though maggots had been dropped on her bare skin.

"I'm a private investigator."

She heard the words and saw his earnest expression but still couldn't make the connection. A private detective? This couldn't be real – this sort of thing didn't happen to people like her. It was something you read about in books or watched on TV. "Are you insane?"

"No." He shook his head. "I'll show you my licence if you let me get my wallet out." He waited for her to nod and took his wallet out of his anorak. "My name's George Gummer. After I'd logged your routines and where you lived my job was finished. Today I'm tailing the woman you spoke to and you just happened to cross my path." He held out his wallet for her. "Take it. Look for yourself."

Claire leaned close enough to grab it then stepped back quickly. The cheap wallet was battered through years of use. It flopped open as she held it up and a photocard was in the plastic window. She squinted but could only make out his picture and the blur of words. She got her glasses from her bag and put them on.

"George Gummer," she read. "Licensed by the SIA as a private investigator."

"See?"

"Anybody could make one of these things. My son got one from Seagrave that said he managed Chelsea."

"Why would I lie?"

"If you're a stalker you would."

"I'm not a stalker," he said. "Have you seen me since the incident with the car? Was I looking for you today?"

"No, but I wasn't looking for you before."

"And yet you saw me."

Claire looked around and took a deep breath. "So if you're who you say you are then who hired you?"

"I don't have a name."

She laughed bitterly. "You did it for charity?"

"Of course not; they paid electronically. I received an email with all the details and never spoke to or met with my client."

"And that's how you conduct your business?"

He shrugged. "It's a living."

"You're a scumbag."

"That's as maybe." Another shrug. "Are we done now?"

"What?"

"Well you've chased me upstairs, blown my cover with Elsa Riccioni and fucked my day up so if we're done, I'll go."

"I haven't even started. What were you hired to find out? Did you go through my rubbish, or hack my phone and laptop?"

He laughed derisively. "I don't go through rubbish and I wouldn't know the first thing about hacking you. I followed you and found out your routine and reported it back."

"And you didn't ask why?"

"Do you ask questions when you do stuff at work?"

She ignored him. "And you never met the person who hired you to spy on me?"

"No."

"I don't believe you."

"I don't care," he said and held out his hand. "Wallet please."

She debated holding onto it and racing back downstairs to call the police but what good would that do? If he was a private investigator he hadn't done anything wrong and if he wasn't, he'd be gone before they got there. Gummer hadn't tried to hurt her and his version of events with the accident made sense too. Except that if she accepted all those as true then it opened up a whole new mystery of who would hire him to find out about her.

Claire threw the wallet and he caught it clumsily. "Crawl back under whatever rock you call home."

He walked around the back of his car. "It pays well," he said as he opened the driver's door.

"Do you tell yourself that so you can sleep at night?"

Gummer looked as if he was going to say something and thought better of it. "I'm sorry about this. It's just business."

"Yeah," she said and watched him until he'd driven away.

Chapter 41

The adrenaline that had kept Claire on her feet disappeared without warning and she staggered back onto a car, then slid to the floor. She rested her head against the bodywork and closed her eyes.

Why would someone hire a private detective to follow her? She couldn't think of anything in her life that would push someone to do that. Then something clicked. If they wanted to disturb her – to stand on corners in a hoodie, perhaps – they'd need to know where she would be so they could be seen. A fresh wave of anger gave her the energy to get up.

An old couple were standing in the roadway looking at her.

"Are you okay, my dear?" asked the man. He was very thin and stooped over.

Claire managed a smile. "I'm okay."

"We saw you tumble," said the woman who was half the man's height.

"Heels," Claire said and remembered too late she wore trainers.

The man looked at her feet and nodded. "You look like you've had a shock," he suggested.

"I'm okay, honestly. But thank you for your concern."

They nodded but kept stealing glances back as they walked away. Claire waited for her balance to settle and walked over to the chest-height exterior wall. She looked over the edge to take in the movement of people and cars far below her. She wanted to escape this terrifying bubble she suddenly seemed to be in.

Claire's friendship circle had been pretty much the same for years but after Matilda and the separation she'd lost a few of them. Everyone she'd seen over the past couple of weeks – Amy, Lou and Roger aside – had all come from the friends group and a thought nagged at her about Gummer. She'd seen him before because she'd told Amy about the incident the morning they met in the cafe, so everything led from him. He'd been hired before she joined the group.

Nothing made any sense and the more she tried to unpick her thoughts, the more complicated they seemed to get. She took out her phone but Gummer had been right about the signal so she went down the stairs.

Ted and Elsa were leaning on the barrier and as she opened the door, they rushed over to see her.

"Hey," he said. "Are you okay?"

"I've been better."

"We were worried," said Elsa. "We should have come after you."

"Don't worry about it. I caught up with him."

"And?"

"He's a private detective who'd been hired to find out my movements. And he's now following Elsa Riccioni."

Elsa looked surprised and Ted looked angry.

"So it was Luca behind it all," he said.

"I've got to go," Claire said and stepped around them. "Take care of yourselves."

"And you," said Ted.

Claire was about to step onto the escalators when Elsa caught up with her.

"We should have followed you," she said, unable to meet Claire's gaze.

"I understand. It was a lot to take in."

"For all of us," Elsa said. "What are you going to do?"

"Ring a friend. How about you?"

Elsa looked at Ted who stood by the stairwell door. "Get my divorce," she said.

"Good luck," said Claire. "I'm sorry but I've really got to go."

"Yes of course."

Claire went down the escalator and walked briskly through the centre keeping an eye out for the hoodie but didn't see him. The centre doors at the far end opened onto a plaza dotted with benches. Claire walked across it and took out her phone. Rosie quickly answered.

"Is everything okay, Claire?"

"No. I just saw my stalker again."

"The man in a black Astra?"

"Yes."

"Where did you see him?"

"At the Newborough Centre."

The slightest pause. "Please tell me you didn't follow him?"

"I had to."

Rosie groaned. "Did you chase him?"

"I didn't have a choice. He saw me and ran."

"I can't stress this enough, Claire. You really shouldn't do this."

"I had my keys in a fist and my rape alarm too."

"And did you catch him?"

"I run almost daily, Rosie, and he looks like he hasn't exercised in years. He had a head start and beat me on the stairs, but I caught him on his parking level."

"You confronted him?" Rosie sighed as if preparing herself to explain once more why this was a bad idea.

"I did and he seemed more scared of me than I was of him."

"A lot of these types are. That's why they're called stalkers, they don't like to be confronted."

"But he's not a stalker. He said he's a private detective." She heard the sound of rapid typing. "He said his name is George Gummer and he was hired to find out my routines."

217

"And I presume he didn't say who by?" Rosie typed quickly as she talked.

"No."

"What did this Gummer look like?"

Claire gave a quick description.

"Hold on a minute," Rosie said and spoke in muffled tones to someone else. A voice responded before she came back on the line. "We know of a Gummer who's private but also ex-job. My colleague worked with him and says he's a good bloke. I have no reason to disagree with that. My colleague can have a chat and see what he can find out."

"He's not the hoodie but I heard something that made a bit of sense." Claire explained Eva's theory about Ben.

"So he admitted the flowers and was also in the car park the night Mr Hasslett's car got vandalised?"

"Yes."

"It might be worth paying Mr Montgomery a visit then. I still have to get the crime number for the business this morning, but I will and my colleague will speak to George Gummer. I'll come back to you but please, for the love of God, don't go chasing after any more suspicious-looking characters."

"I promise."

"I'm serious," insisted Rosie, her voice stark and professional. "You were lucky with Gummer but chase your hoodie again and you might not be."

"Yes," said Claire. "Sorry."

"I'll call you. Stay alert."

"I will. And thank you for taking me seriously."

"Why wouldn't I? I'll speak to you soon."

* * *

The Ratty Coffee House was busy but after asking a man who'd taken over a two-seater table with his laptop and bags to move up a bit, Claire got a seat by the window.

She looked out into the shaded street and plaza and ignored the sidelong glances her tablemate kept giving her.

She was content to be inside and drank her coffee slowly as she tried to make sense of what she knew. Things could potentially start to make sense now she knew who her stalker was, but it made things feel worse about the hoodie. Her stomach rolled afresh at the thought of him in her garden, peering through the window and hanging the gnome.

Her tablemate glanced over again and sighed.

"What?" she asked, exasperated.

The man looked startled. "What?"

Her annoyance with him mixed with her fear about the hoodie and she'd had enough. "You keep looking at me and I really don't appreciate it."

"Sorry," he said and held up his hands. "No offense."

"Plenty taken," she said. "Stop doing it. You weren't using this seat, you'd just spilled into it and it's not even yours."

The man, whose heavy beard and thick glasses seemed to cover most of his face, looked startled. "Do you want me to move?"

"No. Just stop bloody sighing."

"Sure," he said and went back to his laptop.

Claire worried her lip with her teeth. Her hoodie hadn't tried to hurt her even though he could have done quite easily if he'd stopped in that alley. He was doing what this idiot in the coffee shop was – trying to unsettle and bully her. But she wouldn't be cowed. Whether she'd be able to stand up to him remained to be seen but just the act of thinking of this – of refusing to cower to him – made her feel a lot better.

She tried to ring Eva to tell her about Gummer, but the call went straight to voicemail.

"It's Claire." She hated recording a message. "Something odd just happened and I wanted to tell you. Can you give me a ring when you get this?"

*　*　*

Claire tried Eva again when she left the coffee shop, but it went to voicemail. Perhaps she wasn't allowed to answer her phone at work. Claire checked her watch and realised it was close to lunch. Maybe she could drop by the office and grab a couple of minutes.

She typed Abbey Recruitment into Google Maps and found it wasn't far from the deli, as Eva had told her.

The office was a slim unit sandwiched between a bookie's and a cheap card shop. The window was filled with A5-sized tickets advertising jobs and Claire couldn't see much past them. If her presence got Eva in trouble she'd quickly leave.

She opened the door onto a long narrow space decorated in primary colours with job sheets covering pinboards attached to the walls.

Four desks seemed to fill the room. One was empty, two had a staff member and clients sitting at them and a young woman with jet black hair and a very white face sat at the fourth. A badge over her left breast said 'Chloe: Here To Help!' She looked up at Claire and smiled.

"Good afternoon," Chloe said brightly. "Can I help you?"

"I hope so," said Claire as she sat down.

"Have you been here before?"

"No, this is the first time."

"No problem," said Chloe. She slid a keyboard in front of her. "I'll just take your name and details and we can go from there."

"I don't want to join your agency," said Claire. "I'm looking for someone."

Chloe's fingers hung over the keyboard braced for action. "Right," she said but sounded unsure.

"My friend Eva works here and I need to speak to her."

Chloe pursed her lips and shook her head. "Doesn't ring a bell," she said.

"Eva Pelham? I'm sure it was Abbey Recruitment. Your uniform certainly looks like hers."

"Hang on." Chloe called to a colleague across the office. "Kim? Sorry to interrupt but do you know an Eva Pelham?"

"No, can't say I do."

"Thanks." Chloe turned back to Claire. "I'm sorry, you must be mistaken."

"Yes," said Claire feeling embarrassed. "I apologise."

"No worries," said Chloe. "We all make mistakes."

"Thanks for your help," said Claire and left the shop as quickly as she could. She tried Eva's number but got voicemail again.

Had she really got the name wrong? She thought back to how Eva had looked this morning and the embroidered badge over her breast and would've bet money her friend worked for Abbey Recruitment.

Chapter 42

A leaden weight settled in Claire's stomach when she got home and noticed the A5 sheet secured under a wiper blade on her car. The hanged man faced out at her. He was secure in a noose with Xs for eyes and a slash for his mouth.

Claire pulled the paper away from the screen with slightly shaking hands.

DID YOU LIKE HIS HAIRCUT, BITCH?

She gasped and dropped the paper as a wave of queasiness hit her. She leaned against the bonnet until she didn't feel as though she was about to throw up.

The paper had landed writing side up by the nearside tyre. The font was the same as before. Was Harry being shaved her fault?

The entry door opened and Roger came through carrying a bucket. "Afternoon, Claire. Bloody hell, are you okay?"

Claire straightened up as her nausea passed. "Not really."

He glanced at the paper. "Is something wrong?"

"You have no idea."

"Oh," he said. "Well I thought if I washed the car that'd keep me out of trouble. We shouldn't have argued in front of you, sorry about that."

"No problem."

"Are you sure there's nothing wrong?"

"You remember I found those flowers on my car? Well after that I had some notes and I thought someone had made a mistake."

"So what's this one?"

"I don't know what's going on. Some weird things have been happening lately and when we found Harry this morning I thought that might be to do with me too."

His brows furrowed. "How?"

"Because he had 'bitch' written on him."

He clearly wasn't following her and shook his head. She picked up the paper and handed it to him. He frowned at the hangman then turned the paper over. His lips pursed as he read it.

"That's awful." He put his arm around her shoulders and squeezed. It made her feel more uncomfortable. "If you ever want to talk," he said. "I'm always here for you."

"Thanks," she said and carefully shrugged him off. "I'll remember that."

* * *

Claire was sitting on the patio when Rosie rang.

"I have your crime number," she said. "I'll text it as soon as we finish. And my colleague had a chat with George Gummer."

Claire sat forward. "Excellent."

"He couldn't tell my colleague much beyond he'd been hired by email and paid electronically."

"There'll be a name on the bank statement."

"Gummer is going to check and come back to my colleague about it. He's intrigued though and says it's the first job he's had where he got chased by his target in the morning and the police asked him about it in the afternoon." She gave a humourless sounding laugh. "Something will come up from the bank records and when it does we should have some information."

"I was thinking the hoodie and the person who hired Gummer are the same."

"Me too. I understand it must seem like we're running through treacle here, but we are moving. I spoke to my DI about Mr Montgomery and we can't do anything yet. I checked his address and your friends were right that he lives on the other side of town."

"Does that mean anything?"

"Not necessarily. Maybe the Co-op near you sells a product he likes and can't find anywhere else, or it could be that he was in the area hoping to perhaps bump into you."

"Sounds lovely."

"Might be perfectly innocent. I remember doing similar at school when I fancied a lad a couple of years above me but, on the other hand…"

"Yes," said Claire, "on the other hand."

"Just keep a careful eye out. I'll come back to you."

* * *

Claire tried Eva again but didn't leave a message on her voicemail. If she'd made a mistake and Eva didn't work for

Abbey Recruitment then Claire didn't want to look any more of a fool.

Mike rang. "Hey. How are you?"

"I'm okay," she lied. "Where are you?"

"In town, I passed The Kino and thought about you and our date."

Claire smiled in spite of everything and thought of him as they kissed at Pizza Shed. The memory warmed her.

"I was thinking," he continued. "Last night took a couple of weird turns and we said about meeting again. Well as it's Saturday afternoon and I remember you saying Scott was out, how about now?"

Claire looked at the shed and a chill ran up her arms leaving goosebumps in its wake. "I'd love to meet up but..."

"'But' is never a good start."

"I want to see you, but it's been a weird day and I'm feeling a little..." She let the sentence peter out, unsure of how to finish it.

"Is everything okay?"

"I'm not sure."

"I could come over if you're home. Nothing heavy but we could have a cuppa and a chat."

The thought of him being there warmed her further. "That'd be nice."

"I'll see you in a bit."

* * *

Claire opened the door and Mike presented her with a bunch of red roses.

"They're lovely," she said.

"And damp. You might want to put them in a vase."

He followed her through to the kitchen. She found another vase, filled it and put Mike's flowers in there and stood them on the windowsill next to the roses he'd bought her before.

"So how are you?"

She held out her arms and he hugged her tightly. She held him a moment longer then stepped back. "I'm having a rare old day of it."

"Anything you want to share?"

"All of it, though I'm not sure how much'll make sense."

"If you make me that promised cup of tea then I'll do my best to listen and make sense of it."

Claire made the drinks, and they took them out to the patio and sat at the table.

"So this is the situation," she said and told him everything in as chronological an order as she could.

He listened intently and she grew slightly worried all this hassle might dampen his enthusiasm for her.

It didn't. "And all this happened after you joined the group?"

"Except for Gummer who must have been hired by someone I already know." She felt deflated. "I hate the not knowing."

Mike leaned forward. "Let's approach this as a problem."

She glanced sideways at him. "It is a problem."

"I'm trying to apply my skill set," he said. "I'm being a teacher."

She offered a thin smile and a mock salute. "Okay, sir."

"First," he said and counted off on his fingers. "Go back a month and think about your friendship circle then. How long had you known them on average?"

She massaged the back of her neck to ease a kink that had started there. "A long time. If I didn't know them through school or college then it was from the early days of me and Greg."

"With no issues?"

"None I'm aware of."

"Second; we know your stalker is a private detective so it's not him."

"Agreed. Which means I'm left with two lines that don't appear to have a common starting point unless he was hired by someone I know."

Chapter 43

Mike nodded. "Would Greg have an interest? You said he'd mentioned odd things happening."

"It's unlikely because he knows everything about me."

"There is one other option. Maybe whoever hired Gummer used your habits to insinuate themselves into your life."

She felt the same jolt as when Ted suggested her stalker had been hired and it took a moment to catch a breath. "But the only new people in my life are the ones I met at the friends group."

"Why else would anyone want to know your movements?"

They looked at each other.

"I don't know," she said and felt like she was missing something. "Being kidnapped?"

"Do you or Greg have much money?"

"Not especially."

"Perhaps not kidnap then," he said and gave her that lopsided smile.

"It's not funny," she said and tried to sound above it all.

"Don't smile then."

Her smile broadened.

"Claire?" A voice echoed through the entry and felt like a cold hand stroking her neck.

By the time she got to the yard Greg was already halfway down the entry.

"What're you doing here?" she asked.

"I tried the front door but there was no answer."

"I'm sitting on the patio to enjoy the sun."

"Can I come down?"

"It's not really convenient," she said. She didn't want him here occupying her time.

"I need to speak to you."

"Again? Shouldn't you be at home waiting for Scott?"

Greg stopped in front of the gate. "I would be except the tracking app says he's here."

Claire frowned. "He went to Charlie's and was heading to yours after that."

Greg kept his expression neutral but something in his eyes struck Claire as terribly sad. It wasn't a look she saw often in Greg.

"Please let me in. There's something we need to talk about."

"You can't just drop in when you feel like it."

"It's important," he stressed.

"And I have other plans."

"Okay," he said. "You win."

He took a photograph out of his messenger bag and handed it to Claire. She held it at arm's length and squinted. The picture showed Scott walking along the high street with Charlie.

"Why are you showing me this?"

Greg took a deep breath. "Because I didn't take it, Claire."

Cold hands now stroked her arms. "What do you mean?"

He looked at his shoes. "It was sent to me with a letter. Now can we please talk?"

Claire felt a chill settle over her chest. "You'd better come in."

He came into the yard. "Thanks."

She closed the gate and he followed. Mike looked at them intently.

"You've got company," said Greg.

"I know," she said.

She introduced them and Mike stood and held out his hand. Greg appraised it as though worried he'd catch something before shaking.

"So you're the new me then?" he asked.

"I don't know," Mike said cheerily. "Claire hasn't mentioned you."

Claire bit back a smirk as Greg scowled.

"Can we talk in private?" he asked.

"If you want." She looked at Mike. "Do you mind if we go into the kitchen? It's family stuff."

Mike sat and waved his hand. "You go ahead. I'll wait out here."

She guided Greg into the kitchen.

"I know my way," he grumbled. "I helped pay for the bloody place."

"I remember."

She leaned against a worktop and he stood by the sink and looked utterly defeated. The last time he'd been like this was earlier in the year when things came to a head with Matilda and she walked out on him. He'd stood around then, morosely drunk and asked for a chat. Against her better judgement she'd let him in and plied him with strong coffee as she listened to him cover the same ground. When she finally shooed him out, he'd hugged her. She'd allowed that but when he kissed her neck and dragged his stubbly cheek towards her mouth, she'd pushed him away.

Now the tension pulled the muscles in her stomach taut. "What's going on, Greg?" She watched his fingers pluck at his cuffs.

"I don't know where to start."

She knew that pushing him wouldn't work so she tapped on the patio door and gestured to Mike for a drink. He stuck up his thumb.

"I'll make a drink," she said and switched on the kettle. "Black coffee and no sugar?"

"You remembered?"

"Why should I forget?"

He shrugged.

She made their drinks and took Mike's out to him.

"I can leave if you want to," he said.

"I want you to say. Greg wants to tell me something but hasn't figured out how to do it yet."

She went back into the kitchen. "Any closer?"

He took a deep breath and rubbed his palms together briskly as the air hissed out between his teeth.

"I did something terrible, Claire," he said quietly and looked at the floor.

She sat at the table facing him. He didn't look up for several moments.

"There was more to that day." His voice sounded on the verge of breaking. "I just couldn't bring myself to tell you."

"More?" she asked and wondered how that could be? She remembered the pain and sense of betrayal as his words sliced her skin and stabbed her heart. "How could there fucking possibly be more than you admitting you were leaving me for another woman?"

"Not more affairs." A thin film of sweat shone on his forehead and his fringe flopped over his eyes as he bowed his head. "I did something terrible."

Even the memory gave her a bitter taste. "You broke up our family. But why bring it up now?"

"Because it's almost a year."

"You remembered this anniversary then?" she scoffed.

"It's the weekend after next."

She nodded exaggeratedly. "Give him a cigar."

He raised his head slowly and his eyes glistened with tears. She ignored them.

"I did something terrible to someone else."

This was the last straw. She was sick and fed up of events happening around her that didn't make sense. "If you've come here to confess about something that doesn't involve me then please just fuck off. I don't care. I don't have to listen to your shit anymore."

"I've been getting notes. I tried to tell you before. I've been getting them for the last couple of weeks but the last few had pictures with them."

"You've lost me."

He laid his messenger bag on the table and took out a few sheets of folded A5 paper and a handful of 6x4 prints.

"Look," he said and pushed them towards her. "They were hand-delivered. I thought someone had made a mistake at first but when I got the pictures I took it more seriously. They scared me and I drank a bit more than I should have to deal with it. That's why I wanted to make sure you and Scotty were okay."

"The phone calls," she said.

He nodded. "I didn't mean to scare you, but I could hardly come out and say it, could I?"

"Why not?"

She put her glasses on and sorted the photographs. The first showed Scott and Charlie in the high street. Deeply involved in a conversation, they were apparently unaware the picture had been taken.

"Because then I'd have to tell you," he said.

The next picture showed her on the sofa watching TV. She'd seen the image before. There was a mark or doodle in the corner. "Did you draw this?"

"No."

She held the picture closer. "Is that a noose and gibbet?"

Greg didn't look. Claire rechecked the picture of Scott and felt that chill on her shoulders again. The same hand-drawn image was in the corner. Was it possible the hangman imagery was aimed at Greg too?

The next picture showed Scott at the patio table. He had his earbuds in as he concentrated on his phone screen.

"I took this," she said and went back to the picture of her. "And Scott took this. So how the hell did you get them?"

"Did you put them on Facebook?"

"I rarely put pictures of him on there and I wouldn't have put that one of me on."

"So how did they get them?"

"Who? You've skipped a bit, Greg; you haven't told me what the notes are about."

He rubbed his hands over his face. "I did something terrible at work."

"What?"

"I was responsible for someone committing suicide," he said.

Chapter 44

It made no sense. "What did you say?"

Greg looked guilty and scared and embarrassed all at once. "I should have been there and I wasn't."

More evasion she didn't need. "Enough," she said and banged her hand on the table.

Mike looked up and when she glanced at him, he frowned. She gestured for him to open the door.

"Are you okay?" he asked.

"We don't need this," said Greg and jerked his head towards Mike.

Claire glared at him. "You're going around the bloody houses and I'm not in the mood. I've had a shitty day so get on with it."

"Okay," said Greg with the air of a man forced to show his hand. He sat at the chair by the sink. Mike sat next to Claire.

"I had a patient," he said and rubbed his hands together as if dry washing them. "He'd done well enough on the ward to get discharged and was put on a normal seven-day follow-up."

"Which is?" Claire asked.

"Where I'd follow the patient's pathway to keep track of him after discharge. It was arranged as a home visit for day six of the cycle which, in this case, was a Thursday." He sighed. "I got distracted and didn't make it. I'd planned to call in on the Friday but when I got to work that morning, they told me he'd killed himself. Of course, nobody knew why I'd missed the appointment and I didn't say anything so everyone said it was just one of those things."

"Just one of those things?" Claire asked, incredulous.

Greg examined his fingernails. "As I'd planned to go on day seven, we fell within the national guidelines so technically nothing had been done wrong." He paused at Claire's sharp intake of breath but didn't look to see her expression. "People in his situation are unpredictable. What happened was terrible but fairly normal."

"How did you cope?" asked Mike.

Greg studied him for a few moments as if to determine whether Mike was being serious. "I started drinking heavily."

Claire ran a hand through her hair. "Why the hell didn't you tell me all this? It wouldn't have made things better, but it couldn't have made them worse."

"How could I?" Greg asked. "The reason I didn't see him on Thursday was because it was a lunchtime appointment and I spent that lunch hour in a lay-by with Matilda."

His words were a slap that made tears prickle her eyes and heat build behind her nose. "You missed the appointment because you were fucking?" Her chest got hot with anger.

He looked away. "Yes."

"You bastard," she hissed. "You absolute fucking bastard."

Claire's stomach churned with the horror of his revelations. She'd assumed the alcohol abuse came because of the split and his regret at losing his family over an affair but that wasn't the case. She and Scott were an afterthought; the inconvenient bit at the edge of the stage, blind to the drama taking place in front of them.

He pursed his lips. "I don't know what to say, Claire."

She ran a hand over her face. Mike had sympathy in his eyes and she gave him a thin-lipped smile. "But why confess now?" she asked.

"Because of the notes and photographs."

Claire picked up the photo of her on the sofa. The nagging sensation about it was still there but she couldn't quite work out why. "Have you told anybody about these?"

"Just you two. Who else would I tell?"

"You didn't think to tell the police?"

"No, I know it sounds stupid…"

It suddenly hit Claire where she'd seen the picture. "They were on my flash drive."

"That's one mystery solved," he said.

"It's not. My flash drive went missing and I got a bollocking at work for it."

"When?" asked Mike.

"The day after my first friends group meeting. James wanted me to run off a spreadsheet and I didn't have the latest edition."

"When did you start going to this group?" asked Greg.

"Last week."

Greg tapped the pages. "These started about a fortnight ago."

Claire picked up the first note and read it through. The anger of the writer was in every line. "It says here you saw someone. Who was it?"

"I didn't see anyone in particular, just the regular people at the hospital."

She reread the note. "They don't like you, do they?"

"It's not funny, Claire."

"I'm not laughing. So what came next?"

"The picture of you with this one." He handed Claire the second note.

This time the words pulled her shoulders tight with horror. "They know who Scott is?" she demanded. "Why didn't you report it?"

"And say what?"

"It's all tied together, isn't it?" she said after reading the third note. "That's what you're scared of. Whoever's sending these knows the man who died."

Greg nodded.

"And he's going to hurt you like he's been hurt which means me and Scott."

"Shit," said Mike. "Who was the patient?"

"Chris Smith," Greg said.

Claire felt exasperation as another corner seemed to lead to a dead end. "I don't know anyone called Smith."

Greg ran both hands through his hair. "I thought someone was pissing about. I asked and you said everything was okay."

"The photographs didn't persuade you?"

"I'm an idiot," he said and held his hands up in defeat. "But I'm scared now and that's why I came to make sure you were both alright."

"We're fine."

Greg put his mobile on the table. "So why does his phone say he's here?" He selected an app and Claire put her glasses on as he turned the screen towards her.

"What am I looking at?"

"I track Scotty's phone and the map says he's here."

"Why do you track it?"

"Don't you remember last summer when he lost it?"

Claire remembered it clearly – Scott reacted like he was about to lose the use of his legs and arms.

"I'd forgotten all about it until I started getting the notes."

"Maybe he left the phone here," said Mike in an even voice.

"Or maybe he's here."

"He's not here," said Claire. Frustration crackled in her voice. "He took the phone with him. He rang me from town."

"But…" The energy had gone from Greg's argument.

"Ring it," she said and ran upstairs to Scott's room. She stared out the window waiting for the ringtone but nothing happened.

"Is it ringing?" Greg shouted.

"No and it won't because he's not here."

"Shit."

She went down to the kitchen. Greg's eyes were shining.

"It went to voicemail," he said.

"We need to tell the police," she said and rang Rosie.

Rosie answered almost immediately. "Hello, Claire, what's up?"

"Something different from the usual," she said and explained the situation.

"That's not good and it sounds dangerous. Can you send me copies of the notes and photographs?"

"I'll scan and email them to you."

"Do that. I'll get back to you."

Claire put her phone on her lap and her head in her hands. What the hell was going on?

"What did she–" Greg started.

The entry door opened. Claire jumped up and raced out into the yard hoping to see Scott, but a tired-looking Eva greeted her.

"Sorry for calling in," she said, breathing heavily. "But I just got chased by your hoodie."

Chapter 45

Claire's heartbeat quickened. "He chased you?"

Eva held up her finger until her breathing had calmed. "From the plaza behind the Newborough Centre," she said. "He came around by that big fountain and I didn't see him at first."

Claire opened the gate and Eva came into the yard. "What did he do?"

"He didn't see me until after I'd seen him but there's nowhere to go, it's a big open space and he came after me."

Eva looked surprised as Mike came into the yard. "I didn't realise you were here."

"I called around for a coffee."

"So what happened?" Claire asked.

"He tried to cut me off on the plaza. I managed to get into the centre and thought I could lose him, but he followed me through. To be honest, I panicked. I'd parked near the office and didn't want to go back." She laughed sourly. "I didn't want him to know where I worked so I kept cutting up and down side streets to try and lose him."

"Did he catch up with you?"

"No. He kept his distance, like you'd said, as if he just wanted me to be aware he was there."

"Did you see his face?"

"I tried, Claire, I really did but his hood was up and I was too far away. It could have been Ben because it was the right body shape, but I couldn't tell for sure."

"But you managed to lose him?"

Eva nodded. "Uh-huh, but by then I was close to the Co-op so I thought I'd come here."

"You must have been terrified." Claire put her arm around Eva. "Come on, I'll make you a cup of tea."

"Are you sure?" Eva said and looked pointedly at Mike. "I don't want to get in the way of anything."

"You won't," said Claire. "You're shaking."

"I can't help it."

Claire guided her through the back door. Eva stopped and her hands flew to her chest as she gave a little shriek.

"Sorry," Greg said. "I didn't mean to scare you."

Claire moved Eva towards the chair she'd been using. "This is Greg, my ex-husband."

Eva glanced at the table as she sat down, her hands still on her chest. "Took me by surprise," she said, almost to herself.

"I should have warned you," said Claire. She gathered the notes and photographs together then switched on the kettle.

"Could I just have some water instead?" Eva asked.

Greg stood up as Mike came into the kitchen and the two men stood side by side near the back door.

Claire got Eva a glass of water and put it on the table next to her. "Are you okay now?"

"I'm fine," Eva said. "I just need to calm down, that's all."

Mike looked at Claire. "I ought to go," he said.

"Don't be silly," Claire said. "Come and sit down."

He did. Greg stayed by the door and leaned against the worktop with his arms folded.

"Have we met?" Greg asked. "I'm sure I know you from somewhere."

"I don't think so." Eva took several sips of her drink. "I have that kind of face."

Greg smiled. "Maybe."

"I just spoke to Rosie," Claire said.

Eva frowned.

"She's the detective I've been speaking to. Did you want me to ring her back and tell her about you seeing the hoodie?"

"I couldn't really tell her much new." Eva looked around the room slowly. "I'll go," she said. "It's obvious I'm intruding."

"You're really not."

"Well you look frazzled."

The bluntness of the statement stung for a moment but Claire smiled it off. "It's been an odd day."

"Really?" Eva asked with surprise and listened as Claire explained the Gummer situation.

"You really shouldn't chase people like that," Eva scolded. "It could have been dangerous. You had no idea who he was."

"I know. And the day got weirder because I called in to see you at work to pass on the news."

Eva closed her eyes and licked her lips. "Ah," she said after a while.

"They had no idea who you were."

Claire watched Eva's throat work for a few moments. When she opened her eyes, they were brimming with tears.

"Sorry," she said quietly. "I didn't mean to lie but once I had, I couldn't figure out how to stop."

"Why did you lie?"

"Because I didn't want to admit I was out of a job. Or that I had a reason to see you in town." Eva pulled at the hair above her left ear. A single tear rolled down her cheek. "I'm lonely and wanted a friend. I wanted to see you and get in your good books and I couldn't think of any way to do it. But now it sounds like I'm a stalker and I know you had that trouble with the man in the car and the hoodie and I feel like I've just added to it."

Claire felt at a loss, torn between sympathy for Eva and her loneliness and concern she was clearly getting anxious. "No," she said. "You haven't added to it at all."

"I bloody have," Eva said. She had twirled some hair around her finger so tightly the tip was white. "I'm sitting in your kitchen taking up your time and you've got all this company but you're having to deal with me." Her words were full of contrition, but her tone wasn't.

"For what it's worth, Claire," said Mike, "I think you'd be best giving Rosie another ring."

"She's going to hate me by the end of today."

"All the same; you mentioned to her Eva had seen the hoodie and if he's now taken to following her around that might be relevant."

"I don't understand this hoodie business," said Greg. "I thought your stalker was the private detective?"

"Different person," Claire said.

"Well I feel like I'm cluttering the place up," Eva said.

Her tone was again at odds with her words and didn't sound like the woman Claire had got to know. Would her panic or shock explain that?

"Are you sure you're okay?" Claire asked.

"Right as rain," she said, grimacing as she twirled more hair and pulled it hard.

"Shit," said Greg. "Emma?"

Eva looked at him sharply.

"What the hell are you talking about?" demanded Claire.

Greg didn't look away from Eva. "I knew it. You've changed – your hair colour and style, lost some weight and your glasses – but…"

"Greg? Are you out of your mind?"

He looked at Claire. "Not at all."

Eva put her head in her hands and began to cry.

Claire stood up quickly. "You need to go."

"What?" he said.

"You've upset her, Greg. Just bugger off home and wait for Scott."

"You don't understand. This woman isn't called Eva, whatever she's told you. This is Emma Smith."

239

Claire watched the sobs wrack Eva. "Are you drunk? I don't even know..." And then it came to her. The envelope she'd found under the table, the one Eva had said fell out of her handbag. "That's her neighbour. I saw an envelope."

"No," said Greg. "She's Emma Smith. She must be the one who's been sending me the notes and photographs."

Chapter 46

"Are you insane?" Claire rounded on him.

Greg stood his ground. "I don't care what she's said. I swear on Scott's eyes that's Emma Smith."

Claire's temper boiled up and she was torn between letting it go and telling Greg just what she thought of him or clamping it down to help Eva. Mike stood up but she didn't want him to help and turned her back to him. She had to control this and stormed over to Greg. "Enough," she said. "I want you to leave."

"Claire," Greg said. His eyes were wide and pleading. "You have to believe me..."

Eva sobbed.

"Give me the letters," he said.

"Can't you see you're upsetting her?"

"I'm not and can prove it. She's Chris Smith's widow."

Mike stepped around the table. "Greg, seriously, you're making things worse."

Greg glared at him with a flash of anger. "I don't understand what's not making sense. She's Emma Smith. His widow. It's been a year and she's been sending the notes."

Claire slowly became aware of a new sound coming from Eva and couldn't quite believe what she was hearing. "Are you laughing?"

Eva shook her head. Her hands still covered her face.

Claire leaned forward and touched her friend's shoulder. "It's okay."

Eva sat up so quickly it startled Claire. She jumped back and caught her hip on the worktop. Eva's eyes and face were red, but she hadn't been crying. "You told," she snarled and pointed at Greg. "You told and you weren't supposed to!"

"What the hell's going on?" Claire demanded.

"Greg has secrets," Eva said in a very matter-of-fact manner. She turned to Claire with a serene expression on her face but continued to pull at the hair above her ear. "I thought if he kept his secrets then he'd keep mine too."

"I've told her my secret," he said.

"Well you're a naughty boy. You've spoiled my surprise."

"What surprise?" asked Claire.

"This!" said Eva and spread her arms wide. "All of this. I wanted to surprise you."

"But you said…" Claire started and faltered quickly. "The hoodie?"

Eva's laugh was mocking and malicious. "Ah yes, your hoodie. How terrible to be so scared of someone walking around in a coat, don't you think?"

"You didn't see the hoodie today, did you?" asked Mike.

Eva just smiled. Strands of hair littered her shoulder.

"Emma," Greg said. "You have to realise nothing was done deliberately."

"Oh I think it was," she told him with a glare. "You certainly didn't seem happy when my complaining got them to set up the oversight review, did you? And I don't remember anyone at the review mentioning you deciding to fuck your girlfriend rather than go to see my husband, do you?"

"Of course not. It was never raised."

"But I found out about it."

"It wasn't raised because it was irrelevant."

Eva slammed her palm onto the table. "Irrelevant?" she demanded sharply. Spittle had gathered on her lips. "Since nothing was said at the inquiry, it was judged that poor, sweet, beautiful Chris took his own life. Do you know how it feels to have someone be so upset and pained they willingly choose to end it all and leave their loved ones behind?" She banged the table again. "Do you know what it's like to come home to a quiet house and hear that rope creak? Do you?"

"Rope?" Claire felt as though the air in the room had been sucked away and she tried to swallow down the panic threatening to overwhelm her. "What rope? Greg, what is she talking about?"

"Chris was on his own the night I didn't visit and Emma was away," he said. "Things got too much for him."

"Oh God," said Claire.

"You're a liar," hissed Eva. She pulled on a hair hard enough to move her head and held her hand in front of her face. There were several strands in her palm. Some had left blood spots on her skin.

"I missed the appointment and you were away so his two supports were missing when he needed them most."

"You lied in the review and you're lying now."

"I'm not," he said, stepping forward. "Chris needed more than he had. I let him down and I feel the guilt for that. But you weren't there either."

Eva made a guttural sound.

"There was no assessed risk," he said. "There was nothing to say more urgent visits were required. Emma, you have to understand this. There was no sign this would happen."

She banged the table again. "There was every sign."

"Greg," said Mike. "Stop winding her up."

Greg looked at him. "Leave me alone. I know what I'm doing."

Claire watched Eva and realised she'd never seen so much hatred in a glare as was being focussed on Greg. Mike reached for Claire's arm and his warm fingers closed around her wrist. He gently pulled her towards him.

"Chris made a decision, Emma, and we weren't able to change it. It's nobody's fault."

"You dirty fucking liar."

"And now she wants to hurt you, Claire," Greg said. "Because she blames me."

"It was you!" Eva screamed and banged her hand hard on the table again. It caught the edge of her glass which shattered.

Claire screamed.

A shard of broken glass had buried itself in the heel of Eva's hand. She banged the table again which pushed it in further. Blood mixed with the spilled water and pooled on the tabletop.

"You're hurt, Eva," said Claire. "Let me help you."

"She can't feel it," said Mike.

Glancing at her hand as if it was only a mild irritation, Eva seemed confused to find the glass there. She wiped away some of the blood from her palm and watched it drop onto the tabletop then rubbed her fingers on the leg of her trousers.

"Eva," said Claire.

Eva looked at Claire and frowned. She looked back at her hand and touched the end of the glass shard. More blood ran across her palm. "Look," she said, bemused.

Mike moved past Claire and stood in front of Eva. "Can I?" he asked and pointed at her hand.

She glared at him. "You want to touch my hand?"

"I need to check it."

243

"If you touch me," Eva snarled, "I will slash this glass across your face."

"Okay, okay." Mike backed towards the sink with his hands up. "You need to sort that out though."

Eva stood up wearing a strange smile somewhere between pleasure and pain. Claire tensed, not sure what she'd do.

"She self-harms," said Greg, as if remembering something.

Claire thought of the marks Mike saw at Pizza Shed.

"It came out of one of Chris's therapy sessions. It was a coping strategy she developed in reaction to him. I suggested she speak to someone, but she refused."

"And let some uncaring fucker look into my head? It didn't help poor Chris, did it?"

Eva advanced on Greg who backed himself against the door. She held her arm up and the glass caught the light like some exotic form of jewellery. Claire could now see more dull lines running up her forearm from her wrist. Most were widthways, but some ran the length.

"Eva," said Mike. "You need to sort out your hand."

"This?" Without looking away from Greg, she slowly pulled the glass out of her palm and a slight tightening of her lips was the only betrayal of pain. Blood ran into her cupped palm as she held the glass in front of Greg's face.

Claire pulled a tea towel off the oven door and balled it up. She gave it to Eva who took it without comment and pressed it into her palm.

"You don't want to do this, Eva," said Claire.

Eva looked at Claire and smiled sadly. "We could have been friends."

"I thought we were," said Claire.

"You wish."

"Why me? I wasn't responsible for Greg and why he wasn't there for your husband."

Eva turned and her glare was a cold icy light that scared Claire. Even though she wanted to stand her ground she couldn't and had to take a step back.

"I wanted Greg to be scared and experience some of the pain I had."

"Through me?"

Eva tilted her head to one side. "Of course. What better way is there?"

"You bitch," Claire hissed and Eva smiled lazily.

"Greg," called Mike. "Get away from the door."

Eva watched him move then reached for the door handle with her right hand, wincing as blood dripped onto the uPVC panel.

"Please, Eva," said Claire as she opened the door. "Stop this."

"I will," Eva said. Her mouth was a thin hateful line. "I've got someone better now." She slammed the door behind her.

In the deafening silence Claire heard popping sounds and felt faint. She grabbed for the worktop and leaned against it. Mike touched her arm and said something she didn't properly hear. Greg said something forcefully to her. His face was red, but his words were washed out in heavy static.

"Where?" Greg said. She tried to focus on him as the popping sounds decreased. "Is he?" She frowned at him. "Where's Scott?"

"In town," she said.

Greg stared at his phone screen and the colour drained from his face. "It's moving."

"Maybe the GPS is playing up," said Mike.

Claire looked at the door and the thin lines of blood tracking down the panel. Reality seemed to snap back in then and pushed away the popping sounds. Her senses suddenly felt painfully alert. "She must have it."

"Maybe she's got Scott," Greg said.

He moved for the door, but Claire's adrenaline was pumping and she pulled it open before he reached it. She rushed into the yard and with Greg at her heels they raced up the entry.

Claire ran out into the street and looked both ways. She expected to see Eva – even if she'd run, she couldn't possibly have got far yet – but she was nowhere to be seen.

An engine revved behind her and Claire spun round as Eva pulled away from the kerb. Her tyres squealed. The car came close. Eva hunched over the wheel and her teeth were gritted. Claire threw herself out of the way as it sped past.

"I've got my keys," Greg shouted and ran away from the house.

Claire took a last look at Eva's fleeing Citroën then ran to catch Greg. Mike fell into step beside her.

An A5 sheet was fixed under the wiper and Greg pulled it out roughly and read it. His expression grew grim. He shoved the paper into Claire's hands and got into the car. She read the note as she rushed around to the passenger side. On one side was a large circle. It was the hanged man's head and he had two Xs for eyes. On the back was a note.

> YOU KILLED MY LOVE, I KNOW WHO
> YOU LOVE.
> DO YOU KNOW IF THEY'RE SAFE?

Chapter 47

"Go faster, Greg!"

Claire could feel her world collapsing around her and the thought of Scott being in danger churned her stomach. She just wanted to find him. What had happened in her kitchen and what those events meant as part of a bigger picture hadn't sunk in yet. Except for Eva's betrayal which felt like a punch in the gut.

Greg glanced at her then back at the road. "It's a residential street," he said curtly.

"She's already gone," Claire said.

Mike leaned into the gap between the two seats. "Greg's right but we've got her on GPS so we can see where she is."

She knew he was right even though she wanted to snarl at him for saying anything. She checked Greg's phone instead. "Left at the end."

Greg turned out of Brook Street and drove down the hill. The light had started to turn and a warm orange twilight stretched across the sky ahead of them. The sun was low and glaring.

"Right," she said at the next junction.

Greg braked sharply as a Corsa with L-plates stuttered past the junction. "Come on, come on," he said.

The car with a terrified-looking teenager at the wheel seemed to crawl past and Greg sped away as soon as it had gone by.

"We need a plan," said Mike.

"We need to find her," said Greg.

"I know but we need to figure out what we'll do then."

"I'm going to find Scott and make sure he's okay then make it up from there," said Claire. She watched the dot move on the screen. "And if he's not okay then I'm going to kill her."

Mike touched her shoulder. "Ring Rosie. When we do catch Eva we'll need back-up."

"Back-up?" said Greg sarcastically without taking his eyes off the road. "This isn't a TV show."

"I know," said Mike. "But none of us are superheroes either."

Claire nodded at him. "It's a good idea." She handed him Greg's phone and took hers out of her handbag.

Rosie answered straight away.

"Hey, Claire, I was just about to ring you. We had another chat with Mr Gummer and it turns out the payment came from a Mrs E Smith."

For a moment, Claire thought she would throw up. She stared out the window and swallowed back bile.

"Do you know Mrs E Smith?"

Claire's vision swam. "Yes I do now," she said and her voice wavered. "It's been a bad day."

"What? Say that again. You went really faint then."

"It's been a bad day," she repeated and told Rosie everything that had happened in the kitchen and afterwards. As she spoke she listened to Mike feeding Greg directions.

"Good God," said Rosie. "Where are you now?"

Claire glanced out the windscreen. "We're in the town centre."

"Does she live near there?" Rosie asked briskly, her professional mask slipping into place.

"Not really."

"Do you have any idea where else she might be going?"

"No." Claire felt defeated. She wanted to tell Rosie how worried for Scott she was and how terrified the situation made her feel but couldn't find the words. "I don't know that much about her."

"It sounds like you weren't supposed to, Claire." Rosie's voice softened. "Are you okay?"

Greg braked sharply as someone pulled out of a lay-by in front of a fish and chip shop. "Bastard!" he called as he overtook them.

"Not at all," Claire said.

"Keep me on the phone," said Rosie. "When you get to her, I'll get a uniform out and then come over myself."

"Thank you," she said. It made sense but didn't sound like enough.

No one spoke for a while. Claire concentrated on the road as Mike directed Greg along Eva's route until they turned into a road by the college.

"We seem to be heading towards the marina," said Mike.

Claire pressed the phone to her ear. "Did you hear that, Rosie?"

"I did. Keith Hasslett lives at the marina, doesn't he?"

Claire felt a shift in her stomach. "Ben told me he saw Keith and Eva chatting in the pub before Keith had his meltdown."

"That's interesting. How far from the marina are you?"

Claire touched Mike's hand and turned it so she could see the display on Greg's phone. "We're less than a mile," she said. "The dot's stopped now. She's definitely at the marina."

"Okay. Now promise me you're not going to do anything rash. You were lucky before, but we don't know what's going on here so be careful. I'll get a uniform out as quickly as I can."

"Thank you," said Claire and hung up. She looked at Greg. His fingers gripped the steering wheel so tightly his knuckles were white. "Hurry."

"So what did she say?" Greg asked.

"She's going to have a policeman meet us at the marina, but she's told me not to do anything rash."

"So what the hell do we do then?" he demanded, looking at her for the first time. "Just wait?"

"I don't know, Greg," she said. She was frustrated his anger seemed to focus on her and Rosie when it all came down to him in the first place. But now wasn't the time for that; they had to be united. "I've never been in this position before."

"And I have?" he demanded.

"That's not what she meant," said Mike as he leaned between the seats.

"I fucking know." Greg stared at the road and turned left. "There it is."

Hadlington Marina spread out in front of them. A small gatehouse protected a car park bordered on three sides by yellow brick buildings. The largest of them was a small hotel while the other two were labelled 'offices' and 'workshop'.

"In there?" asked Greg.

Claire checked the phone. "No, it's further along."

Greg followed the road which ran parallel to a much larger and almost full car park separated from the pavement by a six-foot-high metal spiked fence. They soon came to another gate, but this didn't have a security box only a barrier. Beyond the car park was the basin where boats were moored.

The dot of Greg's car was now right beside that of Scott's phone. "It's in there," she said.

Greg skidded to a halt and backed up to the gateway. A post next to the barrier had a card slot and a small loudspeaker above it. He parked in front of it. "Now what?"

"Press the buzzer," suggested Mike.

Greg leaned out of his window and pressed the 'Help' button.

"Yes?" said a voice after a few moments.

"Hi," said Greg and turned to Claire with a shrug of his shoulders.

She leaned across him. "Hi," she said, thinking quickly. "My name's Claire Heeley. We've got our boat moored up here, but I've forgotten our pass card."

"Sorry, love," crackled the voice. "Can't do anything about that."

"Oh come on, please help me. We only nipped out for provisions. Our friend gave us a lift and he's got a ticket and everything."

"When are you off?"

"First thing tomorrow morning."

The intercom crackled for a moment. "Okay but just this once. If you need to go out again remember to take your pass card."

"We will. Thank you."

"Yeah," said the voice. The connection went dead and the barrier whirred into action and rose slowly.

Greg drove under it. "Where now?"

The car park was a large rectangle. The office and hotel bordered it to the left and were partly hidden from sight by a thin strip of conifers. A heavier line of trees closed off the right.

"Just park anywhere," Claire told him.

Greg drove around the car park. Closer to the water the spaces were numbered and Claire assumed that related to the moorings. He pulled into the first blank space and Claire was out before the car stopped moving. Mike quickly followed her.

"Where's the dot?" asked Greg as he got out and leaned on the roof.

"The scale's not big enough," she said frustrated. "Both dots are in the same square so it's somewhere close." She slid his phone over the roof and took her own out of her bag. She found Scott's contact and rang him. The phone rang but she couldn't hear his handset.

"So what now?" Greg asked.

"What can we do?" Her frustration grew from knowing they were so close but not quite there. Waiting for the police went against her better judgement because that just delayed things. She wanted to find Scott and Eva even though she knew Rosie was right. Claire had been lucky in the past when she raced into things but now there was too much at stake.

"I can't wait for the police," said Greg. "Not when that bitch has Scott."

"But if we go charging in like a bull in a china shop we might just make things worse. You helped create this mess, surely you don't want to escalate it."

He glared at her. "Low blow, Claire."

She knew it was as soon as the words were out of her mouth, but they were the truth and that was what stopped her automatic apology.

"Let's try a different tack and try to find Keith," said Mike.

"Who's he?"

"Someone from the friends group," said Mike.

Greg raised his eyebrows. "And how the fuck is he going to be able to help?"

"His car was vandalised by the hoodie who's been following me," Claire said.

"What the fuck are you talking about?"

"Long story," she said.

"Eva's come here," said Mike. "We know Keith lives here and Ben saw them talking. It might be nothing, but it might not."

"So let's ask," said Greg.

"We don't know his boat but we could look for his car in one of the numbered bays," Claire suggested.

Mike checked his watch. "Good thinking but we'll need to do it sharpish. If he's meeting up with the group tonight he'll be leaving soon."

"What's his car?" Greg asked. "How will we find it?"

"Look for the damage," said Claire. "It'll have 'creep' scratched into the bonnet."

Chapter 48

Greg found Keith's car.

Claire had taken the right side of the parking area and Mike the left while Greg worked his way through the middle. When he called, "It's here!" Claire ran over to him as fast as she could. Mike arrived just before she did, slightly out of breath.

"Here," Greg said, pointing at a silver Audi.

The level of damage surprised Claire even though she was prepared for it. The bonnet had dents at the edges where it had been stamped on and the words 'fucking creep' were clearly legible even in the poor light, the foot-tall letters gouged deeply into the paintwork.

"Jesus," said Mike. "This is what he blamed you for?"

"Uh-huh," said Claire. She knelt to look under the bumper of the car. The number '48' was stencilled on the tarmac. "Come on."

A narrow strip of well-tended grass dotted with picnic tables separated the basin from the car park. The quayside had four wide wooden gangways reaching out from it like fingers. Narrower metal walkways ran off them like spines with the gap between each making a mooring.

The spines were bunched in blocks of twelve and Claire walked briskly to a large sign that showed the mooring numbers. Keith's was furthest to the right, and she led the way. Most boats they passed were occupied with lights showing in various windows. People sat on the decks of a few and said, "Evening," as they enjoyed a drink.

When she reached the end of the quayside Claire looked out over the dark calm water. "He's not going to answer the door to me." She tried Scott's number again but heard nothing.

"I'll knock," Mike said. "You two stay out of sight."

Keith's well-maintained narrowboat had an array of potted plants on the roof and was moored at the end of the walkway. Claire watched Mike get closer to it and found herself making nervous fists. Mike rapped on the first window he came to.

"Who is it?" Keith called faintly.

"Mike Templeton."

Locks slid on the door by the tiller. It opened and Keith poked his head through. "What do you want?"

Mike took a step closer. "Just to ask you a couple of questions."

"About what? I could ask you some too – like how the hell you know where I live?" Keith looked around and saw Claire and his face fell instantly. "Shit. What is this? I don't have to talk to her."

Claire rushed onto the gangplank with her hands raised in surrender. "I'm not here to cause trouble, Keith."

"Like I'm going to believe that."

"I'm telling you the truth." She stopped by the tiller. "I just need to know where Eva is."

"How the bloody hell should I know that?"

"Because you're friends."

Keith barked out a laugh. "Who told you that?"

"I heard."

"Well you heard wrong." He opened the door slowly and stepped onto the platform. He wore a ratty-looking dressing gown over a pair of black trousers. "We're not friends."

"I thought you were."

Keith's face dropped again and for the briefest of moments he looked vulnerable until the mask slid back into place. "No, I was stupid. She spoke to me after her first session and when she found out about the Lady

Louise here," – he patted the roof gently – "she wanted to see her."

"And you brought her here?" asked Mike.

"Of course. She's a pretty girl, wouldn't you have?" He didn't wait for an answer. "She was very interested in this place and said she'd love to live on a boat and I thought things were good. Then," – he jabbed a finger towards Claire – "you turned up."

"What did I do?"

Keith laughed again but there was no humour in it. "Eva changed and wasn't so interested. The last time I saw her, she arranged to meet me early at the pub and got the first round in. She said you'd explained what happened in the Sun and the bowling alley and said I was a dirty old man." He shook his head. "She said it sickened her to have spent time with me." He rubbed his hand over his cheek and mouth. "She made it quite clear that if it hadn't been for you and Amy being all stuck-up and saying horrible things about me, she might have been interested."

"That's not what happened, Keith…"

"It doesn't matter." He waved a hand dismissively at her. "She rang the next day and said you were pissed off I'd called you a name and that you'd told her you were going to get your revenge."

"The car?" Claire said.

He nodded. "I told the police, but I don't think they paid much attention to me."

Claire bit her lip, feeling her world shift. Eva had been wheedling and chipping away at her life just out of Claire's view right from the very beginning.

"You haven't seen or heard from her since?" Mike asked.

"And I don't want to."

"Thanks," said Claire curtly and turned on her heel. She stalked off the gangway to where Greg was waiting for her.

"And?" he asked.

"He has no idea."

"So where does that fucking leave us? What a waste of time."

"Hey," said Mike.

"No he's right." Claire's stomach churned but she couldn't tell if it was frustration or anger. "Everyone's a liar. Ben said they were friends. Eva lied from the moment I met her. Nothing's what I thought it was. Why is it everyone I've met recently an arsehole?"

"I'm not," said Mike.

"It has to be me. First you," she said and pointed at Greg. "Then Ben and Eva and Gummer and Keith. What the hell did I do wrong?"

Her mobile rang and both Mike and Greg looked at her. She checked the screen and her heart dropped.

"Hi, Rosie."

"I'm so sorry about this, Claire, but I can't get anyone to you straight away. There's an incident in the town centre and no spare bodies unless it's absolutely urgent."

"It is absolutely urgent," Claire said but knew she was grasping at straws.

"I said the same, but my boss wants the fight clamped down. I should be there within half an hour and hopefully uniform will arrive before I do."

Claire rubbed her eyes to try and press back the tears. "I can't just stand around, Rosie."

"I understand that, but you also can't go blundering into anything."

"What if I haven't got time? We've already spoken to Keith and he hasn't seen Eva. It appears she was feeding him duff information about me."

"I'll get there as soon as I can, Claire."

"I hope you're quick enough," she said.

Greg watched as she ended the call. "Quick enough for what?" he asked.

"She's on her way."

"So where's our copper?"

"He's coming," she lied.

"And what're we expected to do in the meantime? Stand here and twiddle our thumbs?"

"Why don't we head back to your car?" asked Mike. "That way we'll see the copper when he arrives."

Lights had come on all over the site in the gathering dusk. Sounds of people enjoying themselves at the hotel filtered through the conifers.

Greg sat on the bonnet of his car and Mike stood to one side looking back at the water. Claire leaned against the passenger door and tried Scott's number again.

She heard a phone ring and felt instantly alert. She pushed herself off the car and focussed on the sound. The call went to voicemail and the ringing stopped before she could pinpoint where it came from.

Excited, her heart racing, she turned to the others. "Listen." She rang Scott again.

"Over there," Mike said and pointed towards the thick line of trees behind them.

"I can't hear anything," said Greg.

"Listen then," Claire whispered at him. She walked towards the trees with Mike beside her. "Can you hear it clearly?" she asked him.

"Clearly enough."

"Do you know what's beyond the trees?"

"Not a clue," he said.

"Are you sure he's in there?" asked Greg as he caught them up.

Claire dialled Scott again and his phone rang twice then stopped.

"It's through there," Mike said.

A narrow gravel bed separated the edge of the car park and tree line and Mike pushed through two of them. He held the branches so Claire could follow. They stood on a strip of bare earth in front of an eight-foot-high chain-link fence covered with ivy. She peered through. The area beyond stretched to the water on her left and too far to see on her right. In between were a lot of boats canted on their sides. Some were holed or missing vital equipment while others looked in good shape. Past them was a line of Portakabins and a large green barn. There were two light stanchions but only one of them worked.

"What is this?" she asked.

"Looks like a boat graveyard where they store all the old stuff and junk," Mike said.

"We need to find a way in," said Claire.

"There must be a road entrance," said Greg. "I'll nip up and check."

He disappeared into the gloom made darker by the trees.

Mike was looking the other way. "There must be access from the water too otherwise they'd never get the boats in."

Greg jogged back. "Two big gates," he said and leaned on the fence as he caught his breath. "They're both padlocked shut."

"We'll try the water way then," said Claire and followed the fence down.

It ended at the quayside and overhung the brickwork slightly.

"That's how we get in," she said.

Chapter 49

It proved more precarious than Claire expected.

A metal brace extended by a foot over the water, forcing them to hold onto the near side then swing an arm and leg around the end and climb back onto the quayside.

Mike went first. The chain-link sagged as he grabbed the other side and Greg pushed on the fence as best he could to make it tauter.

"If I hold the fence up from this end you should be alright," he told Claire.

She looked at the dark water lapping gently against the quay then gripped the fence and swung her legs out past the brace. She grabbed for the links on the other side. Mike reached for her arm, but she didn't need him and he stepped back as she landed on the quayside.

"More graceful than me," he said.

Greg laboured his way around and Mike had to help by grabbing his arm and belt.

A loading ramp ran into the water midway along the quay and steel tracks buried in the concrete led up to the main area. From there, the cabins looked more decrepit than Claire had originally thought. The tall green barn dwarfed them. A crane arm was fixed under the eaves in the pinnacle of the roof and hung over two large doors.

"Must have been a boatyard at some point," said Mike.

A bell clanged from somewhere within the mass of boats and startled them all.

Claire tried Scott's number again, but it went straight to voicemail. "She's switched it off."

"What now?" asked Mike.

"All we can do is work our way through," said Claire.

"I agree," nodded Greg. "I'll take the right, you and Mike go left. If we get to the top of the compound without finding anything, we'll head back through the middle together."

"Be careful," said Claire.

Greg smiled grimly. "You too."

He moved off, skirting along the first line of boats towards the fence. Once he was out of sight, Mike edged to the left. Claire stepped over the tracks on the landing ramp trying to look everywhere at once. There seemed to be so many boats and shadows that Eva could be anywhere. It was like a huge game of hunting for a needle in a haystack and they had no idea where to start. If the police didn't turn up soon there was nothing to stop her making a break for it and heading elsewhere.

Greg was speaking to someone but Claire couldn't make out what he said. More words were exchanged and she walked towards the sound. Perhaps a security guard was challenging him.

She heard a hiss and Greg screamed a moment later. Claire ran over the uneven ground and when she was a dozen or so feet from the fence he staggered out from behind a boat. He groaned loudly and his hands were clutched to his face. He stumbled and fell heavily and was rolling on his back by the time she reached him. Claire knelt beside his head.

"What's wrong?"

She prised his hands away. Her fingers touched thick and tacky liquid and she smelled paint. There was a dark slash across his face covering his eyes and nose.

"She sprayed me," he groaned and tried to scrape the paint away.

"Is it in your eyes?"

"Yes," he cried. "I don't know. I can't see anything."

She pulled the hem of his T-shirt up and he tilted his head forward. He snatched the material from her and wiped at his eyes.

"Hey!" Mike called and Claire turned.

He stood by the quayside. The hoodie ran out from between the boats brandishing a wooden block. Mike didn't have time to react. The hoodie barged into him and brought the block down hard against his neck and shoulder. Mike collapsed with a grunt and the hoodie almost fell over him but managed to stay upright. Mike slowly got to his feet, gripping his shoulder.

The hoodie edged away from the water and Mike, clearly hurt, mirrored his movements. He said something Claire couldn't hear then leapt forward with his arms outstretched. The hoodie stepped back and hit Mike hard on the shoulder again.

"Leave him alone!" Claire called.

The hoodie glanced at her then kicked Mike in the stomach. He curled into a ball on the edge of the quay. The hoodie kicked him over the edge into the water.

"Shit," said Claire.

The hoodie raised a hand in salute to her.

"What's happened?" asked Greg.

"Mike's in the water."

"Is he alright?"

"I don't know. I'm here with you, aren't I?"

"Leave me then and sort Mike. I'm not blind."

She rushed to the quayside. Mike was treading water but only seemed to be moving one arm.

"Are you okay?" she asked.

"Bastard clobbered me."

"Can you get out?"

"I can get to the ramp, I'm fine."

"Good," said Claire and turned. She could just see the fleeing shape of the hoodie as he made his way through the boats. "They must be together," she said. "Playing me off between them."

"No," Mike said and used a sideways stroke to swim towards the ramp. "It's Eva."

The word hit her in the chest like a lead weight and she thought she was going to be sick. Everything, absolutely everything, was a lie. "You saw her face?"

"Yes," he gasped and spat out water.

Of course it was Eva! How could she not have seen through this? It had all been a nasty game to scare her and make her paranoid – wearing padding under the jacket, loitering in plain sight, and drawing hangmen figures everywhere Claire would see them. And now she knew the story she felt sick at the relevance of the hangman itself.

"I have to get her."

"I'm almost out," said Mike. He coughed as he swallowed water. His stroke had slowed with his useless left arm. "Wait for me."

But she couldn't. As much as she knew it was a bad idea she couldn't afford to wait. All the paranoia and fear that had filled her life for the past fortnight came from this bitch she thought of as her friend – Eva couldn't be trusted and the fact she had Scott overrode everything. Greg and Mike could come after her, but she had to do this now – she had to get Eva.

She ran up the incline into a narrow avenue between boats. Mike called her but she didn't look back. She could hear Eva's running footsteps but trying to follow them with the echoes and occasionally ringing bell proved difficult. A door slammed and the footfalls stopped.

Claire stopped, breathing deeply.

She palmed her car keys and checked the rape alarm was still in her pocket. It was, and although it probably wouldn't make much difference here it might give her a few seconds of breathing space. She slowly crept by the next boat and looked left. The green barn was two boats over. One of the large doors had a pedestrian door cut into it which swung slowly open.

Now what?

The smaller door bounced off the bigger one. Darkness lay beyond. She heard splashes from Mike and somewhere beyond the fence an owl hooted. Wood creaked as the boats settled.

Claire crouched low and ran past the two boats onto a pallet walkway that ran down to the water. The pedestrian door was right in front of her. Should she wait for reinforcements or go inside? Everything she knew told her to wait and watch on the door to make sure Eva didn't come out but what if there was a back door or a side one? What if she had the woman cornered now and then allowed her to escape? How could she live with herself, especially if Eva had Scott in the barn?

She made her decision and ran for the door, leaning against the frame and holding her breath to see if she could make out any sounds from within. There was nothing. She switched on the torch app on her phone. Eva already knew she was there so a little light on the subject wouldn't make any difference.

Claire spent a moment psyching herself up then went through the door into a small foyer. Moving in a tight circle she held the phone above her head. She saw some old signs pinned to the wall on either side of a door. The handle turned easily. She pushed it slowly waiting for a flurry of movement from Eva. The hinges squeaked slightly.

The room she went into had once been an office. A doorway stood across the room and its edges glowed with illumination. A grey hoodie hung on it.

Half a dozen 6x4 photographs were pinned to the wall above an old desk with empty space where drawers should have been. Some were copies of what Greg had received, others featured her and Scott from her flash drive. Eva must have stolen it from her that first night in the pub when she asked Claire to go and get her a drink. The thought left a sour taste in her mouth. It frightened Claire how easily she'd accepted this friendship and welcomed Eva into her life and sympathised with a situation that had all been a plot to hurt her and Scott.

Claire walked towards the door. The floor was gritty and she trod on something hard that clattered away. She found the item with her torch and saw it was an aerosol can. Several others were scattered around the desk. She picked up a red can and thought of the hangman on the storm drain. Had Eva spotted the space and thought it an ideal place for a game as she watched Claire on one of her runs? The sheer level of the woman's premeditation made her stomach churn.

The door handle moved easily and Claire licked her lips. Was this it? Was Eva on the other side?

Claire shoved the door and squinted into the bright light. Nothing moved. She put her phone in her pocket and held up the spray can. It wasn't much of a weapon, but it might be useful.

She stepped into a much larger room which appeared to be a workshop. Floor-to-ceiling shelves ran along the left-hand wall while double doors took up most of the wall on the opposite side. A mezzanine floor to her right provided more space for storage.

"Hello, Claire."

Chapter 50

Startled, Claire shrieked. The sound echoed wildly as she staggered to one side and clutched at the wall.

Eva chuckled. "Did I scare you?" She sat under the mezzanine on an office chair with her legs crossed. She smiled. "Didn't mean to."

Claire leaned against the wall trying to catch her breath. She felt her anger building. It burned in her chest like acid.

"You seem all jumpy," said Eva, with a bemused expression.

"Wouldn't you?"

Claire saw a length of rope had been hung over the edge of the mezzanine by the staircase. The end had been fashioned into a noose and a chrome-legged stool stood sentry under it.

She forced her gaze away and looked along the shelves cluttered with nuts, bolts and tools. The sour-sweet scent of oil hung in the air. There didn't seem to be any places to hide.

"So where is he?"
"Safe."

Her nonchalant tone angered Claire and she let it fester, welcoming its heat in her veins. She took a step towards Eva. "Tell me where he is."

"I already did. I told you he's safe."

"If you've hurt him…"

Eva tilted her head to one side. "Yes?"

"I swear to God, Eva…"

"What will you do if he's hurt?"

Claire took another step. "I'll kill you."

"Would you really?"

"Don't push me."

"Or what?" Eva demanded and stood up so quickly her chair scooted back and clattered into the wall. "If I've hurt the person you love then you'd kill me; is that what you're saying?"

"Scott and I did nothing to hurt you or your husband. How is any of this to do with us?"

Eva took a step forward but Claire stood her ground. "Because your husband didn't care and let mine die."

"Greg wasn't there and neither were you."

A cloud crossed Eva's face. "I was in a different country. Greg was in the same town as Chris."

Claire's anger prickled along her shoulders and her head began to ache at the base of her skull. "Scott didn't do anything, you mad cow. He's just a kid, for God's sake."

"He can make a point both to your husband and you. I thought you were innocent before, but now I really want to hurt you too."

Claire flinched. Her words stung like hail. "Why?"

Eva came towards her and Claire realised with horror she was holding a knife by her leg. Claire backed away until she collided with the first shelf unit.

"Because you coped." Eva's voice cracked and she paused. "You had all the chances and every opportunity I wanted and you threw them away."

"What are you talking about?"

"I had a husband I wanted but you walked away from yours without a second thought. You started a new life for yourself on your own terms and I didn't get that opportunity. You had a child to share your life with and I never even got that."

"This is insane, Eva. I didn't hurt you – I didn't even know you."

"But he hurt me," she said and jabbed a finger at her own chest. "He caused all this pain and got to walk away from it scot-free. I went to those review meetings. I sent letters and I complained to everyone I could think of and yet it was all wrapped up in his favour. It's not fucking fair, Claire. I have to make him suffer to avenge my poor Chris. I had to be the one who extracted the pound of flesh."

"And now you're doing the same to me and Scott?"

Eva barked a laugh. "You were the means to an end, you stupid bitch. You pay back the person who took away the one thing in this whole fucking world that you loved by doing the same to them. That's how you make them feel it. Do you have any idea what it's like to find someone who's been hanged? Do you? I can't get the image of him out of my mind. It haunts me every time I close my eyes and Greg is going to know how that feels."

The starkness of Eva's deadly ambition took Claire's breath away and she glanced at the noose.

"You thought all this was about you, didn't you? Poor sweet Claire. Poor silly hard-done-by Claire. You know, the more I found out about you the more I realised I hated you."

Her anger peaked and her blood raced. Claire shoved Eva towards the centre of the room. Caught by surprise, Eva stumbled back. Claire went with her; blinking to try and clear her vision which flickered between hazy and pin-sharp. She'd never experienced a feeling like this before. It was fear and anger and hate all rolled into one as it sluiced through her veins and thudded in her ears.

"Tell me where my son is," she demanded in a voice that didn't sound like hers.

"No. I like seeing you scared."

Claire raised her right fist.

"A key? That's your weapon?" Eva waved the knife. "Are you blind? Hearing you now is like listening to you panic about the hoodie."

Claire held up the spray can and pressed the nozzle. The paint hissed and coated Eva's shoulder. She moved to one side to avoid the cloud and swung her arm up as she did. The knife flashed and vibrated against the can, the impact hard enough to make both women drop their weapons. Claire saw the can hit the shelves and skid away somewhere. Eva spun around almost completely. She stumbled back but kept her balance. Claire let momentum carry her forward and she grabbed Eva's collar and pulled hard. She gave a horrible throaty yelp and her legs gave out from under her. She landed flat. Claire tried to step over her but caught her foot in the crook of Eva's arm and went down as well.

Eva sat up coughing and pulled her T-shirt away from her neck – an angry red line was already showing there. Claire got quickly to her feet and stepped back so she was out of striking range. Her breath was ragged

"Where is he?" she demanded.

She looked around to see if there were any potential hiding places she'd missed before. From here she could see there was a space on the mezzanine and a doorway in the murk over the office.

Eva sounded winded. "He's safe," she said and got to her feet slowly. She coughed hard. "We're all safe. I never told you this, but Chris really wanted a boat. Part of his treatment was that we had to tell each other things – our hopes and fears and that kind of thing. A boat was his thing. Not how close to the edge he felt or how much he loved me, or even how terrifying his mother was in that awful house full of Christ. He really wanted a boat." She rubbed her neck carefully and winced. "I don't know if Chris ever came here but it gives me comfort and makes me feel like it's something we could have done together."

"That's why you and Keith were talking?"

Eva laughed and it sounded horribly brittle. "He came onto me just like he did to you on my first night at the group and told me all about his boat. I came to see it and found this place but he got the wrong idea and thought I was interested in him. I had to put a stop to that."

"In the pub?"

Eva nodded absently and turned in a slow circle looking at the floor. "Ah," she said and walked towards the double doors. She bent down and picked up the knife. "I wondered where that had gone."

Claire watched the blade glint in the light. "Eva, you don't need that."

"You've got your key and tried to spray me in the face."

"We just need to talk."

Eva strode back to the chair. "I've had enough talking. I did enough of it trying to convince nurses, doctors and administrators that Chris shouldn't have died and none of it did either of us any good."

"Eva." Claire tried to keep her voice steady. She wasn't sure why Eva had calmed down but didn't want to push her back into being aggressive. "Tell me where Scott is and this doesn't need to go any further."

"Any further?" Eva laughed. "Seriously? The whole point of this is to make things go further – don't you understand that yet?"

"I do." Claire's rage burned like the worst heartburn in the world and she didn't know how long she'd be able to speak civilly to this woman. "But this isn't the way to do it."

"An eye for an eye, Claire. It's only fair."

Claire felt a tear run down her cheek. "But Scott hasn't done anything wrong."

"Neither did Chris."

"He made his own decision."

"Fuck you." She moved the chair towards the chrome-legged stool. "Come and sit down – let's have a chat."

It was as though they were friends meeting up for the first time in years and Claire was thrown by the shift in tone but tried not to show it. Eva smiled and widened her eyes.

Claire glanced at the noose hanging above the stool. "I don't think so," she said.

Eva jerked the chair so the wheels danced on the concrete. "Come on now, Claire. We've sat and chatted before."

"Maybe so but I didn't know you then. I'm fine here. I'll stand."

Eva's lips went tight. "Come and sit over here."

Claire didn't see she had much of a choice but there was nothing to say she couldn't be prepared. She put her hand in her pocket and her fingers closed around the rape alarm. "Okay."

Eva settled the chair and stepped to one side like a hostess on a tacky game show.

Claire adjusted the alarm in her hand as she walked. Her trainers squeaked on the concrete. From somewhere above she heard a soft thud.

She was three steps away from the chair now. Eva moved behind it and held her arms open. She gripped the knife tightly and smiled. Claire smiled at her.

Two steps.

Eva leaned forward as if reaching for a hug.

Claire pulled the alarm out of her pocket and managed to twist the cord around her fingers. She moved her left hand close to Eva's head as if going in for the embrace.

Eva straightened up at the last moment and sneered. "You really are stupid…"

Claire flicked the cord away and the alarm instantly began its piercing call. Eva shrieked and tried to get away, but Claire pulled her close and clamped the alarm against the woman's ear. The knife swung and whistled harmlessly over Claire's head but grazed the back of her hand on the way back. The pain was white hot and made her cry out but Eva showed no sign of having heard.

Eva twisted in Claire's grip and pulled them both over the chair. It tottered for a moment and almost seemed to balance but then fell. Eva landed heavily and Claire went over her. She rolled towards the office door and the alarm slipped out of her grip and skittered away.

Eva got onto her hands and knees but didn't seem to have the energy to do much else. Claire got unsteadily to her own feet feeling suddenly giddy. She held onto the wall to catch her breath and get her bearings. The wound on the back of her hand ached and she saw blood run out of it.

The piercing alarm echoed off the walls and high ceiling. It disorientated her and each fresh pulse was loud enough that she could feel the thud of it in her bones. She finally spotted the unit almost camouflaged against the grey of the floor, a few feet in front of the shelves. Intending to throw it out the window to draw people's attention to the barn, she grabbed it. The noise this close was so loud it was painful. She swapped hands for her keys and checked for the nearest open window and cocked her arm back.

Eva shrieked and grabbed Claire's elbow halfway through its arc.

The alarm fell onto the floor in front of them and slid away. Eva pushed herself off Claire and stamped hard on the unit.

The alarm squealed. Eva stamped on it again and again until it was silent.

A profound silence seemed to deafen Claire and for a moment it felt like her ears were filled with pressure. She moved her jaw and pinched her nose. Eva did the same as pain twisted her face.

Once Claire's ears had popped she transferred the key to her right hand and closed her fist around it. Eva came at her with arms raised and the knife held high. She swept it around and Claire just had time to arch her back and make her belly concave. The tip of the blade sliced a small gash in her T-shirt. Claire drove her fist into Eva's side and Eva stopped. She looked at her blouse where a small rose of blood blossomed. It seemed to spur her on and she slashed with the knife again. Claire ducked towards the shelves and Eva tracked her moves, sweeping the knife wide as she went.

Claire moved sideways – she didn't want to get trapped against the wall or the shelves. One of Eva's wild swings knocked a small box down and it hit the floor and broke open. Hundreds of cable ties flooded out. Another wild swing clattered a plastic tray of nuts and bolts that rained onto the concrete. Claire glanced around to get her bearings and Eva took advantage. The blade caught Claire over the top of her left forearm and cut deep.

She didn't feel it and couldn't understand why – if she hadn't seen it, she wouldn't have realised. But when Eva drew the blade back the pain came racing up her forearm like fire. Claire cried out. Eva jabbed with the knife this time. There was murder in her eyes now and Claire was truly terrified. This couldn't – and wouldn't – end well.

Eva came at her again and Claire saw an opening. She pushed forward and aimed another punch with her key at the blossoming bloodstain. Eva saw it coming and stepped back but Claire jabbed again. Now on the defensive, Eva threw a wild swing and left herself fully open.

Claire hit Eva hard in the upper chest with both hands and knocked her off balance. Eva windmilled her arms and staggered trying to stay upright. Claire slapped her face hard and Eva's feet got tangled. She fell back and hit her head against the edge of a shelf. The clang of it was audible even over the ringing in Claire's ears.

Claire leaned forward and her mouth filled with saliva. She groaned and waited for the nausea to pass. When it had she straightened up. Eva hadn't moved. Claire checked her pulse then set the chair upright and put her key in her pocket. It took her a while but she managed to heft Eva onto the chair. By the time she'd finished, sweat was running down her back. She fashioned some bindings from a handful of cable ties and looped them around Eva's wrists and tied her to the chair.

Her adrenaline wore off and she fell back. It took a couple of minutes to catch her breath and while she waited the pains in her body started to sing. Her arm burned. She checked for damage and saw the cut was deep. Blood coated her lower arm and wrist and streaked across the back of her hand.

She gingerly stood up and felt dizzy briefly. When that passed she went into the office and pulled the hoodie off the back of the door. A padded gilet hung under it. She went back into the main room and used Eva's knife to cut the left arm off the jacket. She couldn't remember any first aid training and didn't know whether to cover the wound or put on a tourniquet then she decided it didn't matter. She wound the sleeve around her forearm and tied it off. It wasn't brilliant but it would do for now.

Eva groaned.

Chapter 51

"Wake up!"

Eva groaned again and her eyelids fluttered. Her mouth opened slightly and Claire couldn't tell if she was coming to or just playing. Fed up with the woman's deception,

Claire slapped her hard. Eva's head rocked sharply to the left and her eyes sprang open.

"There you are," said Claire.

Eva worked her jaw and her right eye sagged slightly. "Did you hit me?"

"And I'll do again. Where's Scott?"

Eva looked through her eyelashes. "I don't know what you mean."

Claire raised the knife so Eva could see it. "You've lost," she said. "You've got nothing to gain by keeping your mouth shut."

"Oh I do," said Eva and smiled. "Because I can see your face."

Claire looked into Eva's cold grey eyes and searched for a speck of compassion but saw nothing – not even a hint of empathy. "You fucking bitch."

Eva kept smiling. She flexed her arms and tried to see what her restraints were.

"Cable ties," Claire told her. "You won't break them."

Eva went into a frenzy and rocked backwards and forwards on the chair, yanking her arms this way and that. Veins corded in her neck and spittle ran over her chin. A sheen of sweat quickly coated her forehead as she pulled harder. The ferocity made Claire step back in surprise.

Finally, Eva went limp.

"So where is he?"

"Fuck off."

Claire raised the knife. "Where is he?"

Eva looked at her knees. "I told you to fuck off."

Rage burned her veins and Claire struggled to keep control because she needed Eva to tell her. "Eva…"

Eva's right eye was almost closed now and blood had smeared over her front teeth. "Fuck off," she said and smirked.

The smirk tipped Claire over the edge. Her rage was a physical sensation that spiked her skin and screamed in her ears. She slapped Eva hard.

A hand clamped onto her left shoulder. Fingers dug in painfully and yanked her back and around. Startled, Claire staggered towards the wall and found herself staring at a policeman who shouted at her. He gripped a baton in his right hand and his left pointed at her side.

"Put it down and step away," he yelled.

"What?" Why was a policeman here shouting at her? "What do you mean?"

"Put the knife down and step back." His voice got louder and he raised the baton.

"Yes okay," she said and dropped it. "But it's not me you want it's her."

The policeman glanced at Eva who'd now slumped forward then back at Claire.

"Step back further," he shouted.

"Okay!"

Claire did as she was told and he came towards her with the baton still raised. He backheeled the knife towards the shelves and Claire noticed from the corner of her eye that Eva watched it go.

"Against the wall."

She backed into it and raised her hands in submission. "I don't want to cause any trouble."

"Too late for that," he said and reached for his handcuffs. "Hold out your hands."

Panic clouded her like fog for a moment and she looked from him to Eva who met her gaze. She held her hands out. "You don't need to handcuff me."

"You represent a threat to me and this woman, so I have every need to handcuff you. Hold your hands up."

Eva smirked.

With a loud click the bracelet snapped closed over her left wrist and the cold metal bit into her skin. "Ouch, that's tight."

He snapped the other bracelet on even tighter and stepped back.

Claire tried to move her wrists to get the handcuffs comfortable but nothing worked. "Officer," she said and heard the desperation in her own voice. "I'm the one who rang. I spoke to DC Carter."

"What's your name?"

"Claire Heeley."

"Stay there Ms Heeley. I'm going to check on this woman."

"No you don't understand." Claire stepped forward without thinking about it.

The policeman reacted badly. "Get back," he screeched.

"I'm not a threat," she said and there was an edge of hysteria in her voice now.

The policeman edged towards Eva but kept his eye on Claire.

"Miss?" he said.

Eva looked up and let out a sob. Claire stared dumbfounded as tears ran down Eva's cheeks. The ones from her almost closed right eye cut a track through blood.

"Thank God you've come," Eva whimpered.

"You're safe now, miss."

"You've got it wrong," said Claire.

"Shut up," the policeman shouted at her then looked back at Eva. "Where are you hurt?"

Eva sobbed again and Claire was amazed at how convincing she sounded. "She's been punching me a lot. My cheek is really sore and I can't open my eye properly."

The policeman looked her over. "There's blood on your blouse."

Eva nodded. "She stabbed me."

The policeman looked at Claire who shook her head. "Not with the knife," she said quickly.

"She stabbed me and punched me and knocked my head against something. When I woke up, I was tied to this chair."

The policeman edged around and nodded when he saw the cable ties. "And you're Eva Pelham?"

Eva looked at him and her mouth made a perfect 'O'. "Me? No, I'm Emma Smith. I kept telling her she'd got the wrong person but she's a crazy woman – she wouldn't listen."

"That's not true," Claire said. She was so frightened at this turn of events her eyes welled with tears. How could this be happening? "She's lying."

Eva's nose ran. "I'd been at the marina with some girlfriends enjoying a drink in the pub. I was walking back to my car and this woman grabbed me."

"Do you know her?" he asked.

Eva shook her head. "I've never seen her before."

"She's lying," Claire said.

"Ms Heeley, I'm warning you to be quiet. You'll get a chance to speak." He looked back at Eva. "Go on."

"She grabbed me and dragged me here and just started hitting me. She's demented; like some kind of serial killer or something." She looked at him. "I've never been so scared in all my life." She sobbed. "Please help me."

"I will." He looked at Claire. "If you move at all I'll handcuff you to that staircase."

Claire's tears fell. Things were rapidly going from bad to worse and she had no idea how to resolve them properly if the officer wouldn't listen. "I won't move but please don't let her go, she's lying to you."

He scowled and took a multi-tool from one of the pockets on his stab vest then knelt behind Eva and put the baton on the floor.

Eva smiled.

Claire's head felt foggy and heavy and her eyelids fluttered. She tried to shake the sensation away. She heard a thumping sound from above her again but didn't know if it was real or she'd imagined it. Nothing made sense now.

The noise of the policeman snipping the cable ties drew her attention.

"Hurry," said Eva. She didn't take her eyes off Claire. "I'm scared."

"I'm going as fast as I can," he said. He stood up and came around in front of her. "These things are difficult to cut through."

She looked up at him with wide eyes. "Please…"

He glanced at Claire then leaned to Eva's left and began to hack at the cable ties. Claire's fear built. If Eva was freed and managed to convince the policeman she was Emma, would she get away? Worse, how could Claire defend herself if she needed to with these handcuffs digging into her wrists.

"Officer?" she called but he ignored her. "Officer, I know you don't believe me, but she's the person you were told about." He didn't show any sign he'd heard and continued to cut at the cable ties. "She's lying to you."

A loud bang from the office startled Claire and she turned to see Rosie coming through the door. The DC nodded at Claire then looked at the policeman who'd turned around.

"What are you doing, PC Blake?"

"Untying this woman, ma'am. She's been attacked and restrained."

"And why is Ms Heeley restrained?"

"I believe she's the attacker, ma'am."

Rosie moved easily into the room although there was something in her posture that showed she was ready for anything. She scanned the floor and edged around the chair towards Blake's baton.

"There," he said and stood up.

Eva launched at him even though her hands were still fastened behind her back. PC Blake lurched backwards and she collided with him. Her head dipped towards his as they fell and Claire thought at first she was trying to kiss him.

Then he screamed.

He landed on his back and Eva flopped on top of him. Her mouth was bloody. PC Blake shrieked and tried to push her away. Rosie grabbed the ties between Eva's wrists and dragged her off the policeman.

Eva screamed as Rosie pushed her down onto her front and knelt between her shoulders. She quickly snapped handcuffs onto Eva's wrists above the cable ties then rushed over to PC Blake.

"She bit me." He held bloody hands in front of his face as if to confirm it.

"Are you okay?" Rosie asked Claire. "What happened to your arm?"

Claire looked at it and was surprised to see the hoodie sleeve was saturated with blood. "She cut it." She felt more tired than she ever had in her life. "Eva had Scott but wouldn't tell me where he was."

There was more noise from the office and Mike came through holding his left arm close to his body. "Sorry," he said. "I tried to keep up with the detective."

The knocking sound came from above again.

"What is that?" Rosie asked.

"I'll go and see," said Mike.

"Hold on," said Rosie and held out a key. Mike grabbed it. "Release Claire first."

He quickly unlocked the handcuffs and Claire rubbed her wrists. Just being freed lifted some of the fog.

Rosie had her radio out and requested back-up and an ambulance. "I'll go up first," she said.

Mike helped Claire up the mezzanine staircase. By the time they got to the top she noticed he was holding her elbow more firmly and she had to blink away black spots.

"It's coming from there," Rosie said and pointed towards the door over the office. She pulled out her baton. "Keep back."

She opened the door onto a small room that smelled strongly of pepper. Claire saw the room was empty except for a chair which lay on its side. Someone was tied to it. A bag covered their head and they kicked at the floor in a steady beat.

"Scott?" Claire said.

Rosie ran into the room and pulled the hood away.

Scott blinked into the light. His eyes were red-rimmed and his cheeks were slick with tears.

"Mum!" he cried.

Claire rushed into the room and knelt beside his head. "Scott," she said and cradled his head as Rosie untied the ropes. "Are you okay? Did she hurt you?"

"No. Are we safe?"

"Yes, we're safe. Rosie's got Eva."

Scott began to cry. "She told me you were in trouble and needed my help. She said she'd give me a lift then sprayed me in the face with pepper." He sniffed loudly. "It burned, Mum."

"You're safe," she said and rocked him to and fro as darkness crowded her vision. "You're safe now."

Chapter 52

Two weeks later

Claire had been running again for just three days when she saw someone in a grey hoodie watching her.

It had taken a week to get back in her routine and she'd missed it. She needed that touch of normality to give her a taste of the real life she'd had before everything happened.

As she ran along Brook Street and got into a steady rhythm, she adjusted the thin bandage on her arm. She'd lost a lot of blood but the paramedics worked on her as soon as they arrived and dressed it. She'd been kept in hospital overnight and told the wound was deep and advised to rest. She wasn't worried about herself and kept asking after Scott who – aside from irritated eyes for a couple of days – showed no ill effects from Eva's pepper spray. In fact, he seemed to have coped with the ordeal better than she or Greg had, although Rosie said he might react later. All three of them accepted counselling although Claire was adamant she wouldn't share sessions with Greg.

Mike had stayed over last night and she hoped it would become a regular occurrence. It was as good as she could have hoped.

Eva had broken Mike's collarbone in two places. He said he liked the sling because it gave him some street cred at school.

Rosie was keeping her updated about Eva because Claire wanted to know everything but, at the same time, wanted to keep it locked in the past.

She crossed the market square and still found herself looking for George Gummer who'd hidden behind his mirrored sunglasses as he gathered information to allow Eva to insinuate herself into Claire's life.

But Gummer wasn't there.

She crossed the square and glanced towards the butcher's and felt her heart lurch suddenly and hammer in her chest as if it wanted to be free.

The hoodie stood on the corner watching her. He raised a hand to wave and Claire wanted to scream.

Then she saw the shopping bag and Old Man Stan quickly pulled off the hood.

"How do you like my new hoodie?" he called. "I got it special for the summer from the charity shop."

"It looks great," she lied and didn't break her stride.

"Yeah," he called. "I thought so too."

Acknowledgements

To my family – Mum, Sarah, Chris, Lucy, and Milly – who've given me nothing but support, and especially to my dad, Graham West, who unfortunately passed away just before my last novel DON'T GO BACK was published. He was so proud of the book and I know he'd have enjoyed all the hoopla afterwards. I miss him every day.

To Nick Duncan, Julia Roberts, Caroline Lake and Jonathan Litchfield, who make things better; Sue Moorcroft, for everything; Kim Talbot Hoelzli and Katrina Souter; Laura, Barry and Bob Burton; Ian Whates and the whole gang at the NSFWG Writers Group; Ross Warren who led the charge for DON'T GO BACK; Steve Bacon, Wayne Parkin, Peter Mark May and Richard Farren Barber, for support and laughs; Steve Harris, Phil Sloman, James Everington and The Crusty Exterior; Alison Littlewood, Gary McMahon and Gary Fry; and my convention gangs.

David Roberts and Pippa have once again been a tremendous help, with plotting sessions that shaped this book and providing regular sanity checks during our Friday night walks.

Thanks to everyone who supported the last book – buying, rating and reviewing.

Thanks also, of course, to Matthew, my Dude, who listens to my plot ideas on our walks and always tells me straight what he thinks; and Alison, who spent years telling me that my writing was worth pursuing. I'm starting to think that she might be right.

If you enjoyed this book, please let others know by leaving a quick review on Amazon. Also, if you spot anything untoward in the paperback, get in touch. We strive for the best quality and appreciate reader feedback.

editor@thebookfolks.com

www.thebookfolks.com

Also by Mark West

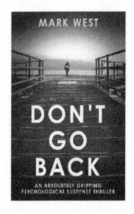

Beth's partner Nick can't quite understand why she acts so strangely when they return to her hometown for the funeral of a once-close friend. But she hasn't told him everything about her past. Memories of one terrible summer will come flooding back to her. And with them, violence and revenge.

FREE with Kindle Unlimited and available in paperback from Amazon.

Made in the USA
Monee, IL
09 June 2022

97737215R00173